ALWAYS
ENOUGH

Without You
Saving You
Holding You
Finding You
Chasing You
Loving You

(Please note: Loving You combines the last books
of both the Broken and Love Wanted in Texas series.)

Broken Series

Broken*
Broken Dreams*
Broken Promises*
Broken Love

The Journey of Love Series*

Unconditional Love
Undeniable Love
Unforgettable Love

With Me Series*

Stay with Me
Only with Me

Speed Series

Ignite
Adrenaline

Boston Love Series*

Searching for Harmony
Fighting for Love

Austin Singles Series*

Seduce Me
Entice Me
Adore Me

Southern Bride Series

Love at First Sight
Delicate Promises
Divided Interests (available early 2020)

YA Novels Written as Ella Bordeaux

Beautiful
Forever Beautiful

Stand-Alone Novels

The Journey Home
*Who We Were**
*The Playbook**
*Made for You**

Cowritten with Kristin Mayer

Predestined Hearts
*Play Me**
Dangerous Temptations

ALWAYS ENOUGH

KELLY ELLIOTT

Published by Montlake, Seattle

www.apub.com

Amazon, the Amazon logo, and Montlake are trademarks of Amazon.com, Inc., or its affiliates.

ISBN-13: 9781542018579
ISBN-10: 1542018579

Cover design by Hang Le

Cover photography by Regina Wamba of MaeIDesign.com

Printed in the United States of America

Dedicated to those who have found themselves lost:
your strength comes from defeating the things you once
believed you couldn't

Everyone is a moon and has a dark side which he
never shows to anybody.

—Mark Twain

Prologue

TY

My dream was taken from me in less than a second. Everyone said it would be the eight seconds that I chased week after week that would end up landing me in the hospital with an injury I wouldn't be able to recover from.

They were wrong.

I'd mastered the eight seconds over years of bull riding. That night had been no different. I'd stood in the middle of the arena and held up the trophy. The winner yet again, on the road to another world championship. My life had been perfect. Everything in my world was exactly how I'd wanted it.

All it took was one second to change it all. One wrong decision made by someone to climb into their car and drive drunk.

"When can I get back up on a bull?" I asked the doctor. My mother held on to my hand tightly as my father stood on the other side of the hospital bed. I was ignoring the throbbing pain in my leg that seemed to grow more intense as the doctor stood there and looked around the room before settling his gaze on me. A feeling of cold tingles rushed through my body, and I already knew the answer before he said it.

My two younger brothers, Brock and Tanner, stood off to the side. Both were in the same business as me. Brock was a professional bull rider and just below me in ranking, and Tanner was ranked in the top five in the Professional Rodeo Cowboys Association standings as a team roper. I took a quick look their way. They both looked exactly like how I felt.

Defeated.

"A bull?" the doctor asked, a bit of shock in his voice.

"Ty," my mother whispered, squeezing my hand. I ignored the sadness in her tone.

"Son, did you even hear a word I just said?" the doctor asked.

I nodded. "Yes, you said my leg was partially crushed in the car accident. I'll need another surgery once I heal from this one, then possibly another after that one, and I'm lucky the leg wasn't severed. I heard you. Now, I'm asking you, when will I be able to get back up on a bull? How long will this injury take to heal?"

The doctor's gaze drifted over to my mother and father, then back to me. He cleared his throat and slowly shook his head. "I'm sorry, Ty. You'll never be able to bull ride again. For one, your leg is so badly injured you'll be lucky if there isn't permanent nerve damage. Putting full weight on it and walking normally will take a great deal of physical therapy. Painful physical therapy, and that's if you're able to regain full use of it. Second, no professional bull-riding association will clear you to ride, not with an injury like this. Ever."

The walls in the room felt like they had begun to close in on me. The doctor's words sounded as if he were talking into a can as each syllable grew more hollow and tinny. The whole room felt like it was disappearing as the only world I'd ever known seemed to be collapsing before me. I closed my eyes and took in a few deep breaths while I let his words sink in. Allowed the reality of my fate to settle around me.

Never bull ride again.

The thought made me sick to my stomach. Bull riding was my life. My dream. The only thing I knew how to do well.

Now it was gone. Taken from me in one alcohol-infused second.

Everyone kept saying I was so damn lucky and that I must have had a guardian angel on my side, because this could've been much, much worse. What the hell did they know? This was the worst thing that could ever happen to me.

When I was finally able to breathe without every inhalation burning my chest, I opened my eyes, looked directly at the doctor, and said, "I will regain full use of my leg again—that I can promise you. That drunk driver won't get to take that away from me too."

My mother leaned down and kissed my forehead.

Despite my declaration, it was in that moment that I felt myself start to slip into a pit of darkness. One so deep there was no way I would be able to see the pain and ultimate addiction that awaited me. With wide-open arms. The feeling of loneliness that would wrap itself around my soul and sink its claws in was smirking at me from a distance.

The knowledge that I'd never be good enough. For anyone. Ever again.

Chapter One

*T*Y

"Junior, are you going to stand there staring off into space, or are you going to pull the damn fence tight?"

I glanced over to my father, who wore a concerned look. I hated that he felt like he still had to worry about me.

I'd been named after him, since I was lucky enough to be born first. My brothers—Brock, Beck, and Tanner—followed after me. Beck died while serving in the marines, something I knew still weighed heavy on my folks' hearts, but my mama never talked about him. I wished she would. I really felt like in some way it would help us all heal from his loss. Mama's knack for avoiding bad or unpleasant situations was one of the reasons I held my own worries and fears inside. Who was I to add any more to their already-full plate of sadness?

Now there was something familiar in my father's eyes as he looked at me. Worry. Fear.

Stella and Ty Shaw Sr. were amazing parents, but when my dad looked at me like he was looking at me right now, the guilt almost crushed me. Heaven knew I'd given them both enough to worry about: both after my accident four years ago and then when I got lost to an addiction to pain pills . . . it had nearly torn my father and mother in two, especially when they'd found out how long I'd been keeping it from everyone.

I knew he worried enough about Brock and Tanner as well. Being the oldest, I also knew I should be the one setting the good example for my siblings, and I'd failed miserably at that so far.

So I looked at him, wanting to quell his unspoken worry. "It's all good, Dad. I've got a lot on my mind, that's all."

He nodded. "Want to talk about it?"

I forced a smile. "Nah, it's nothing, Dad."

His brows pulled in tight, but he nodded again and went back to working on the fence.

"How is the counseling going?" he asked after a minute or two.

"Fine. We've cut it back to meeting every other week," I replied.

"That's good, son."

"Yeah."

I had gone back into therapy last summer, after I was tempted to take a few pain pills that Brock was given after a bull-riding incident left him pretty banged up. He'd left them on the counter in his kitchen, and the temptation to pop them into my mouth scared the living shit out of me. I wasn't sure if it was my own willpower that stopped me or if it was Kaylee Holden walking in and seeing me with that bottle.

Kaylee was the best friend of Lincoln, Brock's wife.

Whatever the reason, I didn't take the pills—but I was left with even more of an unsettled and confused feeling, because Kaylee walked up and kissed me as she took the pills from my hand.

It was the second time she'd kissed me. The first time was only a few weeks after she and Lincoln had moved to Hamilton, Montana, from Atlanta, Georgia. And that first kiss sent me into a tailspin of confusion and fear. It was a fear I'd never experienced before, one that rivaled any anxiety I had felt about a relapse into addiction. One I still couldn't completely understand, or at least refused to understand.

I'd be lying if I said I wasn't attracted to Kaylee from the moment she crawled out of Lincoln's car. She was beautiful. Blonde with the bluest of blue eyes. A smile that made my knees feel a little weak and a laugh that went straight to my dick. She was supposed to be a one-night stand, or maybe a few nights if things really clicked between us. Then she was going to leave and go back to Atlanta, and I would move on to the next woman.

But that kiss, in the back hallway of the Blue Moose bar, fucking shook me to my core.

For the first time in my life, I didn't want a woman purely for sex. And I saw something worth working for when I looked at her. My chest felt tight, my stomach felt like I had stepped onto a roller coaster, and my body longed for something more. Something I never allowed myself to think about.

That night scared the living piss out of me. So I did what I was good at doing. Hid my true feelings and pushed Kaylee Holden directly into the friend zone. She was still a pain in my ass, though. I wasn't sure if it was because I was constantly fighting an erection when I was around her or if she really did just get on my last nerve.

Both were probably true.

I sighed and got to work on the fence. "Brock going to be joining us today?" I asked, looking at the storm clouds that were moving over the valley.

"Ty, he just had a baby. Can we not let him spend time with Morgan and Lincoln?" my father asked, a slight frown creasing his forehead.

Brock had retired from the Professional Bull Riders last November after he'd won the PBR World Championship and was now enjoying life here on the ranch with Lincoln and their two-week-old daughter, Morgan Elizabeth. "I s'pose you're right. I just know that this would go quicker with an extra pair of hands."

Something caught my eye right then, and I stopped working. "What is that over there? Is that smoke?" I asked.

My father turned and gazed in the direction I was looking and laughed. "Yes. Kaylee mentioned she was doing some burning today. She cut down a tree."

I grunted at the mention of her name, then turned to look at my father. "She cut down a tree? By herself?"

"Does that surprise you, son? The woman is spit and fire."

I scoffed. "No. Nothing Kaylee does surprises me."

We went back to working on the fence, but if he didn't think I caught the slight smile on his face, he was wrong. I glanced up again to see the smoke. It was turning darker.

Kaylee. Damn woman.

I slowly shook my head. "Do you think she can handle that?" I asked, wiping my brow. It was hotter than normal for this time of year. March in Hamilton was usually in the thirties, but today it was fifty-eight degrees, and I was working up a sweat.

"Ty, did you really just ask that?" my father asked with a chuckle.

I rolled my eyes. If you looked up the words *independent woman* in the dictionary, you'd see a picture of Kaylee Holden. Not that I thought there was anything wrong with that. I admired her for making the move from Georgia to Montana and taking on the old farmhouse that Lincoln had originally bought from Brock. My brother's first wife, Kaci, passed away while giving birth to their son, Blayze, and Brock decided to sell the house last year, since he hadn't stepped back inside since Kaci died. Lincoln, being an interior designer with a love of old houses, bought it without even looking at it in person.

Brock built another house on the family ranch not long after Kaci died. It was a much bigger, grander house. So when Lincoln found out she was pregnant with Morgan, she ended up moving in with Brock and Blayze.

Once Kaylee decided to make Hamilton her permanent home, she moved into the old house and took over the remodeling of it. The girl had no idea what the difference was between a screwdriver and a hammer. I swore, every time I turned around she was changing or trying to build something.

"Dad, it was just last week that she nearly cut off her hand while trying to cut that sheet metal for the raised beds in her garden. Remember? Not that that made her change her mind. Lord knows what the woman is capable of with a chain saw."

He rubbed his chin as he thought about it. "Maybe you should go see if she needs help."

I swallowed hard, not wanting to risk the raging hard-on I'd suffer being in her presence. "Or Tanner could go."

My baby brother Tanner was home for a few days. He was a world-champion team roper with his friend and team partner, Chance Miller. They had been ranked number two at the time of Tanner's latest injury. Chance decided not to team up with anyone else and was giving his body a rest while Tanner was recovering from a broken ankle. He got hurt while jumping off his horse. It was a stupid injury, and one that shouldn't have happened, but he landed wrong, and the damn thing snapped in two places like a dried-up twig. The only good thing that came out of it was our mama was damn happy to finally have all her boys home.

"Tanner can hardly walk on his ankle, and you want him to go help Kaylee cut down a tree?"

With a half shrug, I replied, "I rode a bull with a broken rib countless times. He just has a broken ankle. It's sort of a sissified injury, if you think about it."

My father wore a tight smile, not wanting to chuckle, but then he allowed the sadness to seep back into his eyes.

My chest ached for a moment, and I fought to push my own pain away. Pain and sadness over a life I no longer had. One I still missed but normally refused to think about.

Bull riding was once my entire life. The only dream I'd chased after. I didn't want to settle down and have kids, didn't want to work on the family ranch, at least not until I was in my midthirties. I loved my life. Bull riding, alcohol, and women. Not necessarily in that order, but more like those three things tied for first place in my own rankings. Those were the three things I lived for. I loved the ranch as well, but I thought I'd have a bit more time to follow my dreams before I helped run the ranch.

I didn't get a say in any of that, though. Four long years ago, my dream was taken from me. Crushed in the blink of an eye. Doctors told me I most likely wouldn't regain full use of my leg. I proved them wrong, but it came at a cost. The pain I endured while in physical therapy was what had me popping the pain pills left and right. Before I knew it, I was getting my hands on stronger pills and taking more than I should. I hid it from my family for a while until eventually I started changing. I got moody and mean, drank a lot.

My mother noticed first, and of course I lied for as long as I could. Told everyone I was fine. Until I wasn't fine. My addiction and depression nearly cost me my life—not that I told anyone how bad it was. After my parents stepped in and intervened, I admitted myself to a rehab clinic and got my shit together.

The demons were still there, though, lurking deep inside me, and I knew if I didn't keep my guard up, they'd reappear. It was a fear I lived with daily. An internal battle that sometimes kept me awake at night.

"Smoke's getting blacker," my father said.

With a mumbled curse, I pulled off my work gloves. "Let me call Brock, see if he can come help you with this fence."

"It's almost done. You go on and see what that girl is burning to turn the sky so black."

"Lord only knows," I said.

I cleaned up the tools I'd used and then headed over to my truck. My father had met me here in the ranch truck, so I was able to just hop in to go see what the little pain in the ass was doing now.

As I climbed into the driver's seat, I called out, "Text me or call if you need any help, Dad."

"Will do!" he said, lifting his hand and giving me a smile.

Turning on the truck, I said a quick prayer for God to give me patience when I got to Kaylee's. It was something I found I lacked when it came to her. Never mind that she drove my body crazy just being near her, but that snarky little mouth of hers only made me want to kiss her to shut her up. And that wasn't going to happen. Kaylee Holden was dangerous, and the last thing I could allow myself to do was give in to that temptation.

One addiction was bad enough to battle. I sure as shit didn't need two.

Chapter Two

KAYLEE

I stood and watched the smoke from the burn pile turn to pitch black. It raced up into the air and covered the picture-perfect blue sky. I couldn't even see the snow-covered mountains on the other side of the burn pile anymore. That wasn't a good sign.

"Oh shit," I whispered as I looked at the old tractor tire I had thrown into the fire. "That might not have been the best idea."

The sound of a truck pulling up had me waving my hand in the air to clear out the smoke. Hopefully it wasn't the fire department again. The last time they were here, I had set fire to a pan filled with grease in my sink. Who would have known how easily grease fires started?

Walking toward the gravel drive, I felt my heartbeat pick up. God help me. It was worse than the fire department . . . it was Ty.

"Perfect, as if this day couldn't possibly get any worse."

I was covered in dirt, smoke, and Lord only knows what else, and Ty Shaw was walking toward me, looking as handsome as ever, which made my heart race a little bit more. The man was too good looking for his own good, and what made him even more attractive was he didn't act like he knew it.

"What is it with you and fires, Kaylee?" Ty asked, a sexy-as-sin smirk on his face as he walked over to me.

Lord, that smile. Dark-brown hair and eyes the color of the Montana sky. Not to mention the smoking-hot body.

I chuckled to myself at the irony of the "smoking-hot" reference, with my huge fire going behind me.

With a half shrug and a wink, I replied, "What can I say, I have weird fetishes."

Ty's eyes darkened with a sexual look that left my lower stomach pulling with desire. We constantly danced around the fact that we were sexually attracted to each other. Or maybe I just secretly wanted him to want me, because truth be told, I wanted this man like no other. My poor overworked vibrator could back up that claim.

"Is that so? Fire?"

"Don't worry," I egged him on. "I keep it out of the bedroom."

Ty stared at me for the longest time before he turned to the fire. "What in the hell did you put in there? It looks like you're burning rubber. Smells like it too."

I cleared my throat. "Um, well. There were these old tractor tires, and I rolled one into the fire and—"

Ty spun around and gaped at me. "You burned tires? Kaylee, it's against the law to burn tires."

My eyes widened, and my heart raced like a hummingbird's wings. "What? No one told me that!"

"Why in the hell would anyone have to tell you that? We need to get away from this fire."

Ty grabbed my hand, making my breath catch in my throat simply from his touch; then he dragged me away from the fire.

"Why?"

"The toxins from the rubber are dangerous."

I looked back over my shoulder at the puffs of black smoke. "Good thing I only put one tire in, I guess, right?" Then I laughed, because what else was I supposed to do?

Ty shot me a look that said he was either going to smack me or kiss me. The man was very confusing with the mixed signals he'd been sending since the first day I'd met him.

"Honestly, I think it's going to be fine, Ty."

But even in my lust-filled mind, I knew it wasn't going to be fine, because I heard sirens in the distance.

Closing my eyes, I pulled in a deep breath—then started coughing. The smoke was bad. Really bad.

When I opened my eyes, Ty was looking at me. A slight smile on his face and a hint of something in those baby blues. What exactly it was, I had no idea, but it made my lady parts tingle. No one had made me feel like this since John, and even this feeling was different. More intense. Or maybe I just secretly wanted him to want me.

A part of me felt guilty because I was ready to move on from John; another part of me hated that I was hung up on this guy standing in front of me who had no interest in me. He had made that clear after our first kiss.

I smiled while trying to contain another coughing spell, which caused him to smile even bigger; then that morphed into a sarcastic roll of his eyes. "You're going to be the first person I know who gets kicked out of Hamilton, Kaylee."

When he took my hand again, I tried really hard to ignore the butterflies in my stomach. Really, really hard. "Maybe, but history only remembers those who broke the rules, right?"

Before he could admonish me again, and just as the trucks—yes, I said trucks—pulled up, Ty let go of my hand. The zap of disappointment surprised me. Why, I wasn't sure.

At first, I'd thought all I wanted was a good romp in the sack. It had been a long time since I'd been with a man, after all, and one good night of sex was a cure for anyone's ills. But after we'd kissed that first night in the Blue Moose, Ty immediately changed. It was as if a switch had flipped, and the simple sight of me left him uneasy.

For the longest time, I'd thought his reaction was due to the natural-deodorant phase I was going through. Maybe I smelled bad? But it wasn't that. Ty had simply pushed me away.

I got over it quickly, or at least I told myself that every time I saw him and he took my breath away. It was painfully obvious, though, that Ty didn't share those feelings. Sure, every now and then he would do something that made me think he might want something more than friendship, but then he would distance himself all over again. It drove me mad. So instead I focused on the chaos in front of me right now.

The fire trucks came to a stop, and I prepared for the worst. Channing Harrell was the first out of the truck. He looked my way and smiled, a knowing smile that spoke volumes. Like a what-the-hell-did-I-get-myself-into-again kind of smile. I couldn't help but grin back at him. He was handsome. Dark-blond hair with stunning hazel eyes. I'd run into him a few times since the grease-fire incident.

"Kaylee, if you want to see us, just invite us over for a cookout or something. After all, it's not necessary to call out the big guns to see us whenever you want," Channing said.

I laughed. Ty, on the other hand, folded his arms over his chest and looked at me as he would a two-year-old who just got caught doing something naughty.

"She threw a tractor tire into the fire," he said, as if I'd committed a crime. Well, I guess in a way I had.

Channing simply tsked my way and moved closer to me. "That is a punishable crime."

The way he was staring at me, with a heated look in his eyes, left me feeling slightly lightheaded. It was nice to have a man give me attention like that. I hadn't really realized how lonely I'd truly been until I saw the fire in Channing's eyes, and it wasn't a reflection of the blaze burning behind me.

Lifting my brow, I replied, "Is that so? What is the punishment for such an offense?"

"Are we really doing this right now?" Ty snapped.

Channing and I both ignored him. Channing, because he was too busy letting his gaze look my body over from top to bottom—thanks to the slightly warmer weather, I had on a pair of yoga pants that show-cased my ass nicely and a sweater that accented my curves in all the right ways—and me, because I knew it annoyed Ty when I ignored him completely.

"Dinner. Tonight." Channing was so confident in his request that I seriously thought about it.

I dug my teeth into my bottom lip and quickly looked at Ty. He huffed and headed over to the other firemen, who were busy getting their hoses and making their way to my toxic burn pile.

Jerking my eyes back to Channing, I sighed. "I wish I could, but I promised Lincoln some girl time tonight. She's been knee deep in diapers and breastfeeding for two weeks."

With a laugh that I found myself really liking, Channing nodded. "I get it. My sister had a baby a few months ago, and getting that little bit of time away every now and then is a lifesaver."

I looked over toward the fire. "So, am I really going to get into trouble for this?"

He winked and shook his head. "I'll take care of it. How about a rain check on that dinner date, though?"

"Yes! For sure."

I was saying yes mainly because the guy was letting me off the hook with yet another task I'd taken on gone bad. I needed to really be more careful with fire in the future. Maybe I needed to avoid it altogether.

"Friday night? I'm off."

A part of me panicked. Why was I so scared to go out on a date? It wasn't like I didn't want to meet someone. I was tired of being alone. Tired of endless nights of crawling into bed by myself.

I took another glance in Ty's direction. A rush of sadness washed over me, and I tried to ignore it. Why wasn't it Ty who was looking at me the way Channing was? Why wasn't it Ty asking me out? It wasn't like I didn't like Channing. I did. It was that my body and my mind liked Ty more. A whole lot more.

"Can I get back to you? I have a book I'm trying to finish up for a client, and honestly, this fire has put me behind. I thought it would be a quick burn; apparently I was wrong."

We both looked toward the burn pile. Channing chuckled again, then turned to face me. "I'll wait to hear back from you. I better go give the guys a hand."

"Thanks, Channing."

He turned and walked backward, a sexy smile spreading over his face. God, he looked hot in his firefighter uniform. What harm would it do to have dinner with the guy? It wasn't like I'd be scraping the bottom of the barrel if I went out with him, after all.

"Anytime, Kaylee."

Jesus, sex just dripped off my name as it passed between his lips. I bet the man was good in bed. Damn good, if I let my mind wander in that direction. He was sexy as all get out. The only problem was, he wasn't as sexy as the cowboy walking toward me, the one who had a scowl on his face. That wasn't anything new for Ty, though. It seemed just being around me made him unhappy.

I started to say something to Ty as he approached, but he spoke first as he walked slowly past me, lowering his voice only enough for me to hear. "Could you eye fuck him any harder, Kaylee? The man has a job to do, after all."

My mouth opened, and for a moment I was devoid of words. So not like me. Not like me one damn bit. No matter what this man threw at me, I had always held my own. But his words felt like a brick landing in the pit of my stomach. Why did he have to be such a dick? What in the hell had I ever done to him?

My moment of speechlessness didn't last long.

Glancing over my shoulder, I called back, "Yes, I could, but I was too busy fantasizing about the punishment he's going to give me Friday night. Multiple punishments, from what I understand."

Ty stopped walking and turned to face me. He looked like he wanted to say something, then shook his head and scoffed. "Watch out, Kaylee. The last thing you want in this town is a reputation as someone who's easy."

Anger pulsed through my veins. How dare he say something like that to me? He knew damn well I hadn't dated a single person since I'd moved here last spring. Hell, I couldn't even remember the last time I'd had sex!

I said the first thing that popped into my head, and the moment the words slipped out, I regretted them. I had let myself stoop to his level, but worse, I saw the hurt in his eyes.

"You would know, wouldn't you, Ty?"

Chapter Three

KAYLEE

"He drives me insane. I don't know if I want to stab him or run him over with my car. Maybe tossing him off one of these mountains is what I need to do . . . after I stab him and run him over."

Lincoln rocked slowly as she held Morgan in her arms, as if nothing I was saying was out of the ordinary. It wasn't really, when it came to me and Ty. We constantly bickered. At times it was fun; other times, not so much.

There were only two times in the past year when we hadn't tried to kill each other and had actually gotten along. One was when we'd found out Lincoln was pregnant with Morgan. Which even Lincoln didn't know at the time.

The second was in Brock's kitchen when we'd shared the second kiss. My heart had broken in two because I could see the torment on Ty's face as he looked at the bottle of pills. I walked over, took the pills from him, and did the only thing I could think of doing. I kissed him. He had kissed me back, and for one moment my world felt whole again. That small empty feeling inside me was fulfilled, if only for the shortest amount of time.

When I pulled back from him and saw nothing in his eyes, I turned and walked away.

Ty Shaw wasn't interested in me, and I needed to let that sink in.

"What did he do now?" Lincoln asked, smiling down at Morgan, then looking my way.

"He called me a slut."

Lincoln's eyes went wide and she stopped rocking. "Brock will kill him."

"Well, he didn't actually call me that."

She frowned. "Then what did he actually call you?"

I shrugged. "He made it sound like people in town would think I was easy, all because I was doing some innocent flirting with Channing."

Lincoln's brow rose. "You were flirting with Channing? The fire chief?"

I shrugged. "Maybe. A little."

"Do tell," Lincoln said with a giggle and a naughty smile.

"Well, I needed a bit of harmless flirting. And the idea of going out with a guy who actually wants to spend time with me is tempting. I'm tired of being alone. Crawling into bed every night without a warm body to snuggle up to is messing with my head." I closed my eyes and sighed. "I just want to stop thinking about him."

Lincoln stood, and that caused me to open my eyes and look her way. She walked over to put Morgan in her bassinet, then leaned down and kissed her daughter before she faced me.

"Let's go for a walk. I'll let Brock know."

Oh, great. My comments now had Lincoln's radar up and running, and her need to protect me was pushed to DEFCON 5.

After grabbing my coat, I slipped it on and stepped outside onto Brock and Lincoln's large wraparound porch. The view of the mountains nearly stole my breath. Almost a year of living here and I still got lost to the mountains. Half the time they looked fake, and I felt like I was staring at a picture. Today they were covered in snow, the sun shining off their peaks and making them look like a million sparkling diamonds. I couldn't help but smile. This was home now, and I would never get tired of this massive blue sky and beautiful country.

"One of these days I'm going to hike you," I said to myself and to no particular mountain.

"Okay, Brock is on duty . . . let's walk for a bit."

Lincoln wrapped her arm around mine and guided us down the steps and to the trail that led down to the small gazebo Brock had built Lincoln for Christmas.

"Do you want to talk about John?"

My head snapped around to look at her. "John?" I asked with a surprised voice. Instant guilt swept over my body. Lincoln had thought I'd meant John, when in reality, it had been Ty I'd spoken about. I chewed nervously on my lip.

Lincoln stopped walking and faced me. "Isn't that who you were . . ."

I felt my cheeks heat and tears threatening to build, but I held them back.

Shaking her head, Lincoln took my hand in hers. "Oh, it wasn't John you were thinking about. I didn't mean to make you feel sad."

"I'm not sad—I feel guilty," I said, a bit too defensively. It was okay if I still felt sad about John. I knew that. I had loved him. I was going to marry him. But the feelings I now had for Ty were much more intense.

"You know he would want you to be happy, Kaylee. It's been years, and you haven't gone out with anyone."

"I've gone out on a couple of dates."

She raised a brow. "Did you feel anything for those couple of guys?"

"Well, no, but no one has caught my attention."

"Until Ty."

With a nod, then a sigh, I replied, "Yeah. Ty. The pain-in-my-ass brother-in-law of yours whom I can't stop thinking about. In every way. Every position. Hell, I even have weird, kinky dreams where he ties me up with a rope."

Lincoln laughed. "It's never been a secret you've found him attractive. I just thought you'd moved on."

"Yeah, so did I. Apparently my body hasn't gotten the memo. Even my heart is a little bit to blame as well. The bitch."

"Kaylee, have you thought about talking to him? Seeing where you both could go with this?"

I let out a humorless laugh. "No. I mean, yes. I don't know, Lincoln."

I stared out at the mountains again and let my mind drift to the past. A past I had worked so hard on keeping there. The emotions that went along with my past would be enough to drag me back into the water and pull me under if I let them.

"Talk to me, Kaylee."

I closed my eyes and took a deep breath, then let it out slowly, gathering my thoughts before I spoke. "My whole life, I've pretty much had everyone tell me what I was able to do, and what a girl like me just *shouldn't* do."

"You grew up with money—that was probably your folks' way of taking care of you."

Facing her, I laughed, this time finding humor in her words. "You do remember me trying to use a hammer to put screws up when you first moved here, right?"

She laughed and nodded. "Yes, I remember."

"Even with John, there were so many times when he would tell me I couldn't do something. He used to kid me about it, tease me. At first it was funny: 'Sure, make fun of me because I've never used an iron before, or never hung up a picture.' Then it started to get to me. Started to really tick me off . . ."

My voice trailed off. I hadn't ever shared this with anyone but my therapist.

"About three months before John took his own life, he told me he thought we were growing apart."

"What?" Lincoln gasped. "Kaylee, you've never told me this."

"At the time, I couldn't really believe it myself. I thought everything was fine. I instantly thought he was having an affair or was interested in someone else. He promised me that wasn't the case and that he felt like he was holding me back. When I look back on it, I think he was trying to save me from the pain of his suicide by trying to make me leave him."

"You think he had been planning it that long?"

I shrugged. "I don't know. I'd gotten angry with him because I was trying to put up wallpaper in the guest room. It was hard, but I was slowly getting it. He walked in and told me I needed to just hire someone because I was clearly not made for manual work. It hurt my feelings and felt like the last straw, so I told him that I was tired of the jokes, the little comments about me not being able to do things. He got angry with me, because he said he was joking and thought I had overreacted. He ended up leaving for a few days after he made the comment about us growing apart. It all seemed so surreal that I didn't know what to think of it. He apologized a few days later, and we made up like we always did. Sex and then more sex."

Lincoln gave me a sympathetic look.

"After he died, it took me months to get it out of my head that maybe I was the reason he took his life. Before you say I wasn't, I *know* I wasn't. John had some issues that went deeper than any of us knew. But at the time, I couldn't help but wonder if I had missed signs of his unhappiness. That perhaps he had said things, and I had simply brushed them off, thinking it wasn't important at the time.

"I honestly never thought another man would make me feel the way John did. And then Ty came along. The instant attraction I felt for him was both a relief and a shock. I don't feel guilty for my thoughts toward Ty, I really don't. For the longest time, I thought maybe I was somehow broken because I wasn't feeling anything toward men, and my therapist told me I had put up a wall to guard my heart. One look at Ty Shaw, though, and that wall came tumbling down, and I was ready to feel something for the first time in months.

"I remember that night at the Blue Moose, Lincoln. The way he was looking at me, the way he held me when we danced. I felt it, and I thought for sure he had too. It was that electric of a connection. I was finally ready to let go of that last little string that was holding me to my past.

"But when he finally kissed me that night, he acted like someone had just struck him in the face. He turned white as a ghost and took a few steps away from me. When a guy starts rubbing the back of his neck after a kiss and says things like, 'That was a mistake—I'm sorry I did that. Please forgive me,' a girl starts to worry. I worried for days that I had some weird bad-breath disease or I smelled bad, judging by how he'd acted."

Lincoln's lips pressed tightly together to keep from smiling. "Maybe he had a different reaction altogether. One that scared him."

"Scared him?" I asked. Wait, what? That was an interesting take.

"From what Brock's told me, Ty's been through a lot the last few years. The car accident, the pain-pill addiction, trying to find himself . . . maybe he felt something with that kiss that spooked him. You even said yourself that Ty made you feel things you hadn't felt in a few years. Maybe he felt something for you that he'd never felt before."

I stared at her for a moment. I wanted desperately to believe what she was saying. Then I laughed. "No, I think Ty saw I wasn't going to be a one-night stand, and *that* was what turned him off."

"Then how do you explain all the bickering? The way he looks at you sometimes, Kaylee? I see it. Brock sees it too. Hell, everyone sees it. He tries to hide it, and maybe he has his own reasons why. What about him being jealous over Channing?"

I went to speak, then snapped my mouth shut again. "Jealous?" I asked, more to myself than to Lincoln. "Do you honestly think he's jealous?"

"Yes. My gosh, Kaylee, it's obvious there's something between y'all! An attraction that you really can't deny. It's covered up by the attitude you both give each other, but it's clear you get under Ty's skin, and I don't think it's in the way you think. I think he likes you so much, but he feels like he can't act on it, and that agitates him. He then takes it out on you. I mean, you sorta do the same thing to him."

I let her words rattle around in my head. "This is interesting. I suddenly feel like I'm living in one of the romance books I edit. How had I not thought of it that way?"

She took my hand and squeezed. "Sometimes that old saying about not seeing the forest for the trees is pretty spot on, my friend. Talk to him. You're long overdue."

We started walking again and stepped up into the gazebo, where Lincoln sat down and let out a slow breath as her entire body sagged. "I'm exhausted."

"I bet you are, but you're a great mom—you know that."

Lincoln smiled and motioned for me to sit down next to her. I did and looked out over the pasture. Small patches of snow still covered the fields. With the recent warm-up, the snow had begun to melt. I loved that you could see hints of spring trying to be born, but winter was still holding on with an iron fist. I wrapped my scarf a little tighter around my neck and took in the peacefulness that was Montana.

Lincoln leaned her head on my shoulder, and it made me think of her asking about John a few minutes before.

It had been three years since John killed himself. I'd had no idea he had been so unhappy. No one did. And he left a note that simply said he was sorry. It was a complete shock to me and his family. Even his boss said that John had been excited about a new promotion at work.

That was the worst part about his suicide: I had no answers. Nothing that told me why. Could I have done something to help him? Was there something I missed that I shouldn't have? The endless what-ifs nearly drove me insane and were part of the reason it took me so long to come to grips with his death.

The first year, I felt like I was living in my own personal hell. I didn't even leave my apartment for months. Once I left Georgia, and the familiar stomping grounds I'd shared with John, I stopped having the nightmares. I didn't miss the feeling of waking up drenched in sweat, screaming for John not to pull the trigger. I wasn't even home when he took his own life, but the dreams always felt so damn real.

Of course, my therapist got me through most of it, especially the part about me keeping myself locked away from the world. It took me months before I could walk past the coffee shop we would stop at together every morning without breaking down and crying. And I hated myself for so many reasons. I couldn't save John, I was being weak, and all I wanted to do was forget. My chest felt like it was tightening just thinking back on it all.

There were so many times I'd thought about sleeping with someone, anyone, to take my mind off how lonely I felt. How hurt I was that John didn't trust me enough to tell me he wasn't happy, to share his suffering with me.

I shivered, but it had nothing to do with the cold weather. I pushed the negative thoughts about that time of my life away and closed my eyes. It was moments like this that I did what the therapist told me to do when I felt those old familiar feelings coming back.

One deep breath in, one deep out. Focus on the future.

In. Out.

Until the tightness in my chest loosened and all the bad feelings of anxiety and depression slipped free of my body.

Lincoln didn't say anything or even move. She knew the drill. Deep breathing meant I was fighting the memories, the fears and doubts. They didn't always show up as nightmares. No, sometimes it was a random panic attack. Or a crying fit for no apparent reason. Grief and sadness had a way of wreaking havoc on one's body. I could feel happy as a clam, then sad as fuck the next second.

"You know he would want you to move on, right?" Lincoln finally said.

"Yes, I know. It's just . . ."

She lifted her head and turned her body to face me, wrapping her own coat and scarf tighter around herself. "It's just what?"

"The first guy I let myself even think about moving on with rejected me and acts like being around me is a chore."

Lincoln smiled softly. "There are moments you guys get along. Remember when you found out I was pregnant before I even did?"

A wide grin broke out on my face. "Yes, I do remember that. It was one of the rare times Ty and I actually didn't fight. I think we were both too excited for you and Brock."

"Do you want a relationship with Ty?"

I tossed my hands up in the air and let them fall dramatically to my lap. "Hell, I don't even know anymore, Lincoln. I don't honestly think I could take another heartbreak, and I feel like Ty would not only break my heart but rip it up into a million pieces and stomp all over them if I let him in."

"He wouldn't hurt you on purpose."

Looking down at my hands, now folded in my lap, I saw how red they were getting from the cold. Why hadn't I grabbed my gloves?

"No, I don't think he would, either, and that's why he keeps me at arm's length. That day I kissed him in your kitchen, I felt it, and I know he did too. He tried to play it off by acting like he hadn't experienced the same rush of feelings I had. He chooses to ignore it, and I deserve someone who wants me—someone who isn't afraid to show me how he feels, someone who will treasure the love I have to give to him. That much I know."

"Like I said . . . talk to him."

I felt my chin wobble as I looked back over the mountains. "And if he tells me he isn't interested?"

"Then you move on, Kaylee. Like you said, you deserve happiness, but pushing your feelings to the side because you're afraid he won't want the things you want isn't healthy."

I nodded. "You're right. I need to talk to him. And if he truly doesn't have any feelings for me, I'll move on."

Chapter Four

*T*y

I tipped back the beer bottle and took a long drink.

Betty Jane walked up and tapped the bar. "Another one?"

"Yeah, one more."

She motioned with her chin to the dance floor. "The brunette out there with the shorter-than-hell shorts on is looking at you again."

"Not interested."

Her eyes widened in shock. "So the rumors are true. Are you slowing down on your playboy ways, Ty Shaw?"

With a smirk, I replied, "Hell no, haven't been in the mood for anyone here in town."

"That's because you've slept with nearly all of them."

I laughed. Hell if it wasn't almost true.

Betty Jane's eyes went to the entrance of the bar, and then quickly back to me. "No one has caught your attention lately? Not even our feisty local city girl, Kaylee?"

I let out a grunt. "Fuck, especially not her."

"That's too bad. She's making her way over to you as we speak."

With a groan, I looked over my shoulder and saw Kaylee walking my way.

"Fuck," I mumbled before I shouted to Betty Jane, "give me a shot of whiskey too!"

"Hey there, cowboy, drinking alone, huh?" Kaylee said, sliding up onto the barstool next to mine. The way my body instantly came alive when she was near agitated me. It also fucking thrilled me.

God, I'm fucked up.

"Not for long."

She smiled, and it made my throat grow thick. She had no damn clue the effect she had on me. Abso-fucking-lutely clueless.

"Are you waiting for someone?" she asked, nodding to Betty Jane holding up my bottle of beer.

"Yes."

"Date?"

"Are you working for the local paper now? What's with all the questions, Kaylee?"

Her smile faded some, and I instantly felt like an asshole because I was the reason the light had dimmed in her eyes.

With a half shrug, she answered me. "I was just curious is all."

"No, I'm not waiting for a date."

Betty Jane came back with Kaylee's beer and one for me, along with the shot I'd requested. I downed the shot first.

"Something wrong?"

I turned to Kaylee and stared at her. I tried not to let my gaze move to her soft pink lips, but I lost the battle before it even began. My eyes jerked back up to hers. "Nothing is wrong."

She took a drink of her beer. "Listen, I was sort of hoping we might be able to talk."

I looked out over the dance floor and caught the eye of the brunette. She was still eye fucking the hell out of me, not giving one single fuck that Kaylee was sitting next to me. I smiled, then looked back at the empty shot glass and pushed it away.

"Betty Jane, can I get another one, please."

Kaylee looked at the shot glass and then back to me. I'd yet to acknowledge her comment about wanting to talk. Another asshole move on my part. Her eyes filled with a look like she was unsure about something, and I sighed. "What do you want to talk about, Kaylee?"

She swallowed hard—and again, I could see it in her eyes. She was definitely unsure about something. Hell, she even seemed a little nervous.

"Well, I was . . . I mean . . . I wanted to ask you why you don't like me. Because I sort of feel like you don't, and I don't know what I did to you to make you feel that way."

That caught my attention, causing me to turn my entire body and face her. "Don't like you?"

"Yeah. I mean, it's pretty obvious I get under your skin, Ty. I don't know why, though, because when I first came to town, I thought maybe there was . . . um . . . there might have been something there."

"Something there?" I asked, knowing damn well what she meant and refusing to validate what she was saying.

Hell yes, there was something explosive between us, and my heart and my body were at constant war with each other over that fact.

"You know, an attraction between us. We kissed that night, and everything seemed to change immediately. Why?"

I stared at her, trying like hell to keep my breathing under control. Why was she bringing this up? This was so out of the damn blue. I had no clue what to say to her. How to explain what that kiss did to me . . .

I'd felt something I had never experienced before from just one kiss from her, and that scared me? *She* scared me?

Hell, she'd laugh in my face if I told her that.

Her eyes searched my face as I fought to find the words to speak. Should I tell her the truth, that she wasn't like any other woman I'd ever known? That she was the first woman I even dared to want something more with, but I wasn't sure I was able to give her what I knew she deserved? That I'd already failed in my professional life, that I'd failed my family the minute I'd started abusing the pain meds, and that failing in a relationship wasn't an option for me? It was something I didn't think I'd recover from.

Glancing back at my beer bottle, I pulled in a long, slow breath. I knew I didn't deserve someone like Kaylee Holden. She'd already had one guy disappoint her; she didn't need another loser. I was a player. A guy who hooked up with women for one reason only. Sex. That was all I had wanted with Kaylee, at first. It was all I had to give. Before the first kiss.

Then the second kiss . . . that one blew my fucking mind. I couldn't think straight for days after. She haunted my dreams and my thoughts.

I looked back at her, and that's when she smiled, as if she could read those thoughts.

Out of the corner of my eye, I caught the brunette making her way over to me. Fuck my life twice. Jesus, I couldn't catch a break tonight, when all I wanted was a damn beer or two.

"Ty? Are you going to answer me? Why did everything change between us?"

I swallowed hard and did the only thing I knew how to do. I put distance between us with a few harsh lies. "I wanted to fuck you, Kaylee. I thought you were going to be leaving, and when I realized Brock was into Lincoln and you were most likely going to stay, I knew I couldn't do that to Lincoln. So that's all you were to me, a good time, and I couldn't do that to my family."

Her eyes went wide and her mouth dropped open slightly. The pain that sparked to life in those baby blues of hers instantly made me feel sick. I wanted to take back my words, tell her it was all a lie. That she did, in fact, drive me crazy, and that I did want to fuck her, but just not in the way she thought. I wanted more than that with her; the sex would just be a bonus with this woman who had the power to destroy me.

"You couldn't do that to . . . *Lincoln*?"

I shrugged and put the last nail in my coffin by continuing to be a total asshole. "And you. I mean, I'm a dick, but I'm not that big of a dick."

When I saw the slight tremble of her chin, I lifted my hand, then stopped myself from touching her. Kaylee sat up straighter, reached for her beer, and took a long drink. Then she nodded and faced me. "Well, okay. I guess I got the answer I came here for." She let out a half-hearted laugh. "To think I was stupid enough to think that maybe there was something there between us. I was just being naive and foolish, but no more. You just made my decision for me, so thank you, Ty, for that clarity and frankness."

"Your decision?" I asked, confused.

Kaylee stood and was trying to walk off when I reached for her arm, which caused her to look back at me.

"What decision?"

Lifting her chin, Kaylee forced a smile. "Channing actually did ask me out, and I honestly wasn't sure what to do. I had these feelings . . ." She let out another laugh and shook her head.

"Feelings?" I asked, wishing I could take back every second of the last five minutes.

"Yeah, for you, but I see now that I was just being fucking stupid."

The ache in my chest burned. "Kaylee."

She held up her hand. "It's okay, Ty. I'm a big girl, and believe it or not, I was actually prepared for the rejection from you. I just didn't think it would hurt as much as it did."

I closed my eyes and cursed. "Fuck. Kaylee."

Opening my eyes, I saw the brunette standing a few feet away. For the life of me, I couldn't remember what in the hell her name was.

"Hey, Ty, you ready to get out of here?"

Lord, give me strength. I was seriously fucked now. This woman was clearly trying to give Kaylee the wrong impression.

The look on Kaylee's face nearly destroyed me. She looked from the girl to me. Then that blank face appeared. The one I had seen a time or two after she'd allowed herself to get too vulnerable.

Pulling her arm from my grip, Kaylee glared at me. "Enjoy your evening, Ty."

"Kaylee. Kaylee, wait!" I called out as I started to go after her.

The brunette stepped in front of me, her hands on my chest. "Ty, I'm horny, and you've been staring at *me* the last thirty minutes, not her. Let her go."

My eyes dropped down to meet hers. "What did you just say?"

"I said, I'm horny."

Looking once more at the door Kaylee had just walked out of, I knew I had a decision to make. Let Kaylee go and move on, or go after her.

◆　◆　◆

Light shone through the window and caused me to groan when I attempted to pry open my eyes. I scrubbed my hands down my face and slowly dared to give it a try. Instant panic set in.

This isn't my bedroom.

A feeling of dread and regret quickly rolled through me. What in the hell had I done?

Shit.

I looked to my left to see the brunette from last night, sound asleep next to me.

Fuck.

Another look back toward the window and I winced. My head was pounding.

How many shots did I have after Kaylee left?

"Son of a bitch," I mumbled as I tossed the sheet off of me and climbed out of the bed. It was then I noticed I still had my jeans on. I looked back at the brunette and saw she was dressed in yoga pants and a T-shirt.

I closed my eyes and whispered, "Please don't let anything have happened."

Quickly, I set off to find my shirt and boots. I needed to get the hell out of here.

The nameless woman stirred in the bed, and I picked up the pace. I couldn't find my socks, and in that moment I couldn't have cared less. I slipped on my boots, sans socks, grabbed my wallet, and then looked at the unused condom on the side table.

Rubbing the back of my neck, I let my gaze move back to the woman.

She was awake and looking at me.

"You may not know this, or maybe you don't want to admit it, but you're in love with her."

I frowned and tried to cover up her truth by laughing as I asked, "What are you talking about?"

She sat up and looked directly at me as she rested her chin on her knees. "Ty, the blonde from last night. The one talking to you at the bar. You're in love with her."

I scoffed. "You're crazy, and I need to leave."

"Why do you think I'm dressed, and so were you? You couldn't sleep with me last night. You said you couldn't do that to her. So either you're with her and you were about to cheat, or you're in love with her and won't admit it to yourself, or to her, for whatever reason."

"Remind me again, who in the hell are you?" I asked as I took a quick look around her bedroom before focusing back on her.

Her head tilted, and she flashed me a cute smile. "Lisa Waters."

Lisa Waters. Why does that name sound so familiar?

Then it hit me. Lord Almighty . . . it hit me like a freight truck. "Oh, holy fuck. You're Maria Waters's kid. I knew you looked familiar."

She laughed and crawled out of bed. "In case you hadn't noticed, I'm far from being a kid. I'm thinking the next time you meet with Mom for a therapy session, you need to tell her about these little hidden feelings you got going on."

"You don't know anything about it," I said. I picked up my phone and saw I had three missed calls. One from Brock, one from my mother, and one from an unknown number. I also had two voice mails.

"Maybe not, but I do know that you had a warm and willing body last night that was ready to do all sorts of naughty things with you, and you weren't the least bit interested in me." She gave me a wink. "I couldn't get your cock to harden no matter what dirty thing I whispered into your ear."

"I was drunk, and please tell me you're over twenty-one."

She flashed me a smile. "I'm twenty-two. How old are you?"

"Twenty-nine."

"I always did love an older man. Listen, I've got to go get ready—I'm having lunch with my parents. Show yourself out, will you?"

Groaning internally, I couldn't believe I had almost slept with my therapist's daughter. Thank God my wits, and not my dick, had showed up last night. "Yeah, sure thing."

As I walked past her, she reached for my arm, pulling me to a stop. "I won't mention this to my mother, but honestly, Ty, you need to talk to someone. You talk in your sleep—and believe me when I say I know what it's like to hold in the demons. You can only do it for so long before they start coming out any way they can. Your nightmares . . . they were intense."

I stared at her for the longest time. In all the times I'd hooked up with women, I'd never stayed with them all night. Not once. So knowing she had seen that side of me bothered the hell out of me, more than I cared to admit.

"I appreciate it, but you don't know what you're talking about. I'm not in love with anyone, let alone Kaylee Holden. And as far as any nightmares go, I was drunk and probably just dreaming weird shit."

She shrugged, then gave me another wink. "Good luck with all that, dude. I just know I wouldn't want to fight the battles your mind is waging with you."

The entire drive back to the ranch, I tried to figure out what in the hell I had been thinking last night, leaving with Lisa. And fuck me . . . she was Maria's kid. Just my damn luck.

After parking my truck, I decided to head to the barn and get a bit of work in before going back to my place. I lived in the foreman's house, which was about a mile or so from my folks' place and on the opposite side of the ranch from Brock. Once I was forced out of bull riding and worked the ranch full time, I spent a year adding on to the cabin that my granddaddy had built for the foreman and making it into a three-bedroom ranch-style house. It wasn't anything fancy, but it was home. And it was renovated by my own two hands, so that counted for something. Especially since I hated shit like that. But it had been good therapy at the time.

The moment I walked into the barn, I came to a stop. Brock and Tanner were in a stall, and both turned to look at me.

Tanner grinned, and Brock shot me a suspicious glare as he looked me up and down.

"Didn't even go home last night?" he asked.

"You keeping up with what I wear now, Brock?" I spat back.

He folded his arms over his chest and stared at me as I walked by. I looked into the stall to see that our horse Star was about to foal.

"She's ready? I figured it would be a few more days," I said.

Blayze popped up and gave me a wide toothless grin. "Hey, Uncle Ty! Star's gonna have her a baby, and Daddy said I can help deliver it and name him or her."

I reached over and rustled the brown hair on my nephew's head. "I like the sound of that plan, buddy."

"Who did you shack up with last night?" Tanner asked.

"Nice," I said, jerking my head in the direction of Blayze. "Remember, little ears."

Brock leaned over and smacked our younger brother. "Think before you speak, Tanner."

I shot my youngest brother a smirk as I replied, "And I didn't shack up with anyone."

"That's not what I saw. Dude, you were trashed and left with some hot chick who looked to be my age, if not younger," Tanner said.

I rolled my eyes. "She was twenty-two, and nothing happened."

"You left with her and stayed at her place, and you mean to say nothing happened?" Tanner asked as Brock shot me a look that said I was full of shit.

"That's exactly what I'm saying. Nothing happened." I looked at Brock. "Why are you shooting me death rays, Brock?"

"I hope you know what you're doing, Ty," Brock answered.

"What's that supposed to mean?"

He cast a quick glance to Tanner, then motioned down to Blayze. "You got this for a minute?"

Tanner nodded. "Yeah, go ahead."

"Where you going, Daddy?" Blayze asked, gazing up at his father with the same blue eyes Brock and I got from our own daddy.

"I'm going to talk to Uncle Ty . . . in private."

"You gonna talk about Aunt Kaylee and how she was mad at Uncle Ty last night?"

That caught my attention. "What?"

Brock rubbed the top of his son's head. "You sneak out of bed again, Blayze?"

He smiled and nodded his head. "Yes, sir. I already confessed to Mama."

I couldn't help but give the kid a knowing grin. Oh, how many times had my brothers and I sneaked down the steps to listen in on the grown-ups? Too many to count.

"Let's go," Brock said to me as he headed out of the barn.

"Listen, if you're going to give me a lecture, I'm not in the mood. I have a pounding headache, and I woke up in the bed of the daughter of my freaking therapist."

Brock turned and faced me with a stunned look on his face. "You're shitting me."

"I wish," I said, rubbing the ache in the back of my neck. "So what's this about Kaylee?"

He stared at me for a minute or two before finally speaking. "Kaylee stopped by last night. I guess she and Lincoln had a talk a few days ago about Kaylee speaking to you about a few things. She wanted to find out why you didn't like her."

I groaned. "I never said I didn't like her."

"Never said you did. Anyway, you got your point across to her, and she's going out with Channing this weekend."

Trying not to let it show how much that bothered me, I shrugged. "Good for her. It's about time she got out and socialized with folks. She's always holed up in that house, catching shit on fire."

He regarded me, trying to see if he could read me.

Not a chance, little brother. This place is locked up tight.

"Ty, are you really going to let her go like that?"

I swallowed hard. "I don't know what you're talking about, Brock."

He sighed and dropped his head, giving it a slow shake. "Okay, well, I thought you might want to know she's going out with him."

"Like I said, good for her, but it don't concern me any. Besides, she already told me Channing asked her out."

Brock's gaze caught mine. The corner of his mouth rose slightly into a smug expression. "It must be in our blood to be so damn blind. I get you're scared, Ty. I get this isn't what you thought your life would be like, but are you sure you want to push away the one thing that made you feel something?"

Anger pulsed through my veins. How in the hell did he know how I felt? Or who made me feel something? "Just because you're settled with a wife and kids now doesn't mean I want that, Brock. I've got enough shit in my life, and to add in a headstrong, stubborn-ass woman who would just drive me insane? Yeah, hard pass. Who wants to be tied down to one woman anyway?"

He nodded, a look of disappointment etched onto his face. "Right. Well, as long as you know what you're doing."

"I know exactly what I'm doing." The way the lie rolled off my tongue surprised even me. I had no damn clue about anything anymore.

"How's therapy going?"

That was *not* a subject I was wanting to talk about. "Fine. Now if that's all, I'd like to get some chores done and then get back to my place."

"Sure. Have at it, Ty."

I turned and walked away from Brock. It pissed me off that he was doing this to me. Pressuring me to do something I wasn't ready for. Sure, he had the wife and the new baby. He got to *make* his decisions. He went out on top as the best bull rider in the world. Retired after winning the PBR World Championship again. Hell, he still had people calling him to do sponsorships.

I'd also gotten calls after the accident to keep doing sponsorships, but I'd turned them all down. I wasn't interested. Not when I was trying to deal with the reality that I'd never climb onto the back of a bull ever again. It had been too difficult to even think of entering that world again right after the accident. Then, once the addiction started, I was so lost I didn't know what in the hell I wanted to do. I hadn't realized I'd never really found that lost part of me.

As I went about the morning, taking care of things around the ranch, one question kept popping up over and over in my head.

Who was I?

I had nothing to offer a woman like Kaylee. She deserved someone who wasn't broken. And I was as broken as they came.

Chapter Five

KAYLEE

The moment I opened the door and saw him, I knew I had made the right decision. Standing before me was a man who looked at me like I was his world. Of course, he had a bit of desire in those eyes; nothing wrong with that. For once I wasn't being given a scowl, and it made me feel really damn good.

"Channing, you look nice this evening."

The hot firefighter chief stood in front of me dressed in jeans, a nice button-down dress shirt with a dress jacket over it, and cowboy boots. He wasn't wearing a cowboy hat, and I had to admit, that made me feel sad. Ty always had his black cowboy hat on. Always.

Channing's eyes roamed slowly over my body. He had told me to dress casual, so I did my version of it. Jeans. A sweater that hugged my body, and high-heel dress boots.

"You look as beautiful as always," Channing said once his gaze met mine.

"Are the heels too much?"

"Not at all—we're going to Taste of Paris for dinner."

"I love it there!" I replied, grabbing my coat, only to have Channing reach for it and slip it over my shoulders. I wrapped the wool scarf around my neck and smiled.

Manners *and* good looking. The evening was starting off on a positive note.

"I've only been once, with Lincoln when we first moved here. The beef bourguignon was out of this world."

"It is a great place. I know the owners."

"Sounds perfect. Plus, I'm starving."

Channing placed his hand on my lower back and guided me out of the house. I turned and locked the door and took his arm while I navigated down the porch steps and to his . . . sports car?

I had to look twice. Channing drove a sports car?

Why did that disappoint me?

A vision of John in his BMW 5 flashed through my mind, causing me to slow my pace.

"Kaylee, is everything okay?"

I wasn't sure how long I stared at the Mazda Miata. Too long, apparently, because Channing looked worried.

"So, I take it you don't like sports cars?"

That pulled me from my moment of haze. "What? Oh, no. I mean, yes. Sports cars are fine. Sorry, I just had a memory take me by surprise, that's all. It's all good."

He nodded and opened the passenger door for me. "Good, let's get you fed, shall we?"

Before I got into the car, I looked out over the pasture—and saw Ty and Tanner.

Shit. Of all the times he'd have to be here. They were on horseback, riding the fence line that separated the Shaw ranch from the small parcel of land I lived on. He wasn't looking my way, so I quickly slipped into the car. My heart hammered in my chest, and I closed my eyes and took a few deep, deep breaths until I heard Channing open the driver's door.

"It's freezing outside. Do you have any gloves?"

I tried not to look at Ty as I answered. "I figured it would be okay, since we're walking from the car into the restaurant and that's it."

He smiled. "What if I made other plans for us?"

That made me turn and look directly at him. I smiled and said in a teasing tone, "What other plans? I only agreed to dinner."

"I thought maybe we could grab a drink after dinner at the Blue Moose."

Why was I not wanting to do that? What in the world was wrong with me?

Forcing myself to answer him, I replied, "That sounds like a good plan."

Channing was an easy person to talk to. Once we got to the restaurant, he ordered our meals, and we fell right into a conversation where he asked me about me. It was nice to have a man actually interested in me.

"So what made you decide to leave Georgia behind? I mean, I get that Lincoln had moved here and all, but that's a pretty big decision."

I shrugged. "Not really. I didn't have anything in Georgia holding me there. My family is there, but my parents travel a lot, so I didn't see them very often. My work is freelance, and I can do it from anywhere, anytime I want. I needed the change for a few reasons."

Telling Channing about John wasn't something I was ready to do.

"So what's the story between you and Ty Shaw?"

Okay, that came out of nowhere. I paused for a moment, staring at him with what was probably a befuddled look.

"The story?" I asked. I was hoping to stall for time so I could figure out why in the world Channing had asked about Ty . . . and how in the world I would respond to that question.

He laughed. "I don't think it was a coincidence he was out checking the fence when I came and picked you up earlier, do you? Is there something I should know there? A past between you two?"

I forced myself not to laugh. "A past between us? As in a romantic past?"

Channing nodded.

"No, not at all. Ty is a friend and that's it. I mean, if you can even call what we share a friendship. I'm his brother's wife's best friend, so we have to be somewhat nice to each other, but I'm pretty sure Ty can't stand me."

With a raised brow, Channing slowly let a small smile play across his face. "Well, then you haven't noticed the way he looks at you or gets jealous if another guy is talking to you."

I shook my head. "No, you're completely mistaken. Trust me." I desperately needed to change the course of this conversation, like yesterday. "So, shall we move on to that drink at the Blue Moose?"

He looked at me with a slightly surprised expression on his face. Yes, I knew that was a drastic change of subject, but Ty was also on my list of things I didn't care to talk about with Channing. But I guess I shouldn't have been surprised that Channing had brought up Ty, especially if he thought he'd seen an attraction there. In all honesty, Ty was a subject that I just wasn't ready to talk about. His rejection still left a bitterness in my mouth.

"Sure, the check is paid for, so I'm ready to go whenever you are. Did you like the quiche florentine?"

"Yes! It was amazing. How was the pasta?"

"It was great. I can safely say I am full."

Channing stood and took my coat, prompting me to stand and allow him to put it on me again. As we made our way out of the restaurant, I tried to push all thoughts of Ty Shaw from my brain.

Tried . . . and failed.

◆ ◆ ◆

When we stepped into the Blue Moose, I took a quick look around. No Ty, but I did see Tanner. I wanted to groan internally. Could I not go anywhere in this town and not see one of the Shaw brothers? I mean, it wasn't *that* small of a town.

"What would you like to drink?" Channing asked, taking my hand in his as he walked us toward the bar. My stomach did a little jump at the contact. It had been a long time since a man had touched me in any sort of intimate way. It wasn't like butterflies in the stomach, but at least my libido was waking up a little. She recognized a man's touch and liked it. Score one for me.

"I'll just have any local craft beer they have on tap."

He winked, and I couldn't help but smile. It looked like the evening was back on the positive again.

"Do you want to sit at the bar or at a table?" Channing asked as he motioned for Ralph, the bartender, to order.

"How about I go grab a table?" I replied while I gave his arm a slight squeeze. He smiled, and I turned and set out for a table. It didn't take me long to find one in the back corner. It wasn't tucked away, so it wouldn't appear we were attempting to hide, but it was a good distance from the dance floor and had a clear view of almost the entire bar.

"Here you are. I was looking all over for you," Channing said as he placed the beer down in front of me.

"Sorry, this one's sort of out of the way, yet we can still people watch and talk without competing with the music."

He sat down and gifted me with another wink and grin.

Another stomach jump . . . okay, this was promising. My body was certainly on board with Channing and his sexy little winks. I just needed to get my brain on board as well.

"Do you like to dance?" he asked, glancing out over the dance floor.

"I love to dance. I'm pretty good at the two-step, if I do say so myself."

He laughed. "Well, I figured, since you're from the South. No one would doubt it with that accent of yours."

I felt my cheeks heat. He didn't have to know I'd worked for years on my southern drawl, much to Lincoln's endless eye rolls when I threw out the words *fixin'* or *y'all*.

Having wealthy parents, I was always told to speak slowly and clearly around my father's business associates, or my parents' friends. Even though we were from the South, having a southern accent was very much frowned upon by my father. A well-educated woman would never say *y'all*. I did, more to spite them than anything. Well, and the fact that I loved how it sounded.

It was just another reason I was glad to be away from Georgia. Back then, anytime my mother called, it was usually to see if I was dating anyone yet, or if I could attend a fundraiser, or a wedding, or some other bullshit event where they wanted to put on airs for their peers and show off how great a family we were. The perfectly well-rounded, educated daughter. I was both those things, but somehow, I still lacked something in their eyes. Unfortunately, I had yet to figure out what that was.

I loved my parents, and I knew they loved me, but their money came in at a very close second to their daughter. Or maybe it was the other way around. I hadn't figured out where I stood in the ranking.

"So, you asked me about myself. Is it my turn now?" I asked, taking a sip of my beer and loving the way the music pulsed through my body.

"Have at it, Kaylee. I'm an open book."

I sat up a bit straighter and tilted my head some as I regarded him for a moment or two. "Okay, the most common one—why are you single? You're handsome enough, nice body, hot job, pun intended."

He laughed. "Well, I dated my high school sweetheart up until a year ago."

My brows rose. "Wow. What happened?"

Channing shrugged. "She wanted a different life that didn't include living in Hamilton. I wanted to be in Hamilton."

"Was there no compromise?"

His eyes looked sad for a moment. "There was. I tried for a little while. Told her I would move to Billings. She had gotten a nursing job there. I lived there for about a year and hated it. She knew I wasn't happy. So then I tried to commute. I work a split shift, so on my days off, I'd drive and stay with her in Billings."

"That's not too bad . . . it's what, five hours or so?"

"About that, closer to six, but take into consideration our winters, and there were more times I was stuck here in Hamilton. So I looked into taking a position with the Billings Fire Department because, honestly, being with her was what I wanted. I got offered a job and asked Lauren to marry me. She was surprised and didn't answer right away. That should have been my first warning sign. Then she said the words no man wants to hear after he's just gotten down on one knee and asked a girl to marry him."

"We need to talk?"

This time, Channing laughed. "Yep. Those words. She had met some doctor and didn't mean for things to happen, but she was attracted to him and was wanting to see where it would take her. So, instead of getting married, we broke up."

"I'm so sorry," I said, taking his hand in mine. "That must have been hard."

He shrugged and reached for his beer with his free hand and took a drink. "It was, at first, but I got over it."

"Do y'all still talk?"

"Nah, not really. I haven't heard from her in about five or six months. It's better that way. She got on with her life, and I'm doing the same."

I nodded and took another drink. "How many women have you dated since?"

Channing looked directly at me and gave me a panty-melting smile. Lord, this guy knew how to make a woman's body heat up. "Not many, maybe about four women. One was sort of long term, if you count five months as long term."

Laughing, I shook my head. "Not when your last relationship lasted years!"

"That's true."

"Someone local?" I asked.

"Yeah, Nellie Kesler."

My mouth fell open. "Nathan's sister? Like, Nathan as in the city manager?"

"Do you know him?"

I rolled my eyes. "Yes, he attempted to date Lincoln, and he is a grade-A jerk. No, the better word to describe him is a manwhore."

Channing tossed his head back and laughed. "That he is." His eyes drifted past me. "Like the Shaw brothers."

I tried not to let that statement get to me, but I couldn't help but wonder why he would say something so inappropriate. Unless it was his not-so-subtle way of trying to warn me off of Ty.

"How about we take a spin on the dance floor?" I asked, needing to change the very touchy subject.

He stood and reached for my hand. "Let's dance, cowgirl."

And boy howdy, did we dance. Channing wrapped me up in his arms, and we took off two-stepping. The guy was good, and I found myself comparing him to Ty. Of course, Ty had a bum leg, but he was still an amazing dancer.

Ugh. Stop this now, Kaylee. Ty is no longer in the picture. He was never *in the picture. He made it crystal freaking clear that we have no picture together.*

"Penny for your thoughts," Channing said, giving me a kiss near the side of my mouth.

I wanted my body to want more, but the slight nervous feeling in my stomach was all I got. Was it anticipation? I hoped it was. I needed to move on, and I needed to start to feel again. I swallowed hard and looked up at Channing. "I was thinking I'm sort of over this bar."

A wide grin erupted over Channing's handsome face. "My place or yours?" he asked.

"Mine, and this isn't an invitation into my bed, Channing. I want to make that clear."

"Okay, I wasn't assuming it was."

I raised a brow in disbelief.

He laughed and took a step back, holding his hands up in defense. "All right, okay, I won't lie and say it wasn't exactly on my mind. I'm a guy, after all. But I'm not going to pressure you in any way, Kaylee."

I gave him a soft smile. "That's not to say I only have talking in mind, Channing."

When he didn't say anything but just stood there, I continued. "Shall we leave?"

"Yes, I think that's an amazing idea . . . it's either that, or I may end up kissing you right here in the middle of the dance floor."

I chuckled as Channing wrapped his arm around my waist and guided us through the crowd. I may not have been having sex tonight, but there were plenty of other things we could do to take some of this sexual frustration away. *Lots* of other things to do, actually, and here I had at my disposal one handsome firefighter to help put out some small flames—or cause some others to spark to life.

As we headed out the door, I tried to push away the sudden feeling of panic that was churning my stomach. I drew in a few deep breaths as we walked to Channing's car.

Once we fell back into an easy conversation, I relaxed again. Channing had taken my hand in his and was rubbing his thumb over my skin as he drove. I hated that I felt nothing from that action. Not. A. Damn. Thing. And when we pulled up to my house, I let out a long exhale as I waited for him to walk around and open my door. He reached his hand in and helped me out.

"It's freezing!" I said as we quickly made our way up the steps.

After I unlocked the door, Channing decided to do something to warm me up. He kissed me. I turned to face him, and he cupped my face in his hands and pressed his mouth to mine.

At first I was stunned, not sure what to do. He pressed my body against the door and deepened the kiss. I opened to him and soon found my tongue moving with his.

I didn't feel a thing. Not one damn flutter in my chest or dip in my stomach. Nothing.

When he moaned, a flashback of Ty kissing me caused me to pull my mouth from his and shake my head. An emotion now took hold of my chest and squeezed like a damn vise. I wasn't sure what to make of this one.

Confusion? Guilt? Doubt?

Shit. Shit. Shit. I'm broken. That's it. I am a broken woman who will never, ever have sex again.

Channing looked at me with a befuddled expression.

"Are you okay?" he asked, taking a step closer and placing his hand on the side of my cheek. "I swear, Kaylee, I'm not pressuring you, it's just . . . I've been wanting to kiss you since I first laid eyes on you."

A weak smile lifted the corners of my mouth slightly. "Really?"

He leaned his forehead to mine. "Really. But if you're not ready, I'm a very patient man."

I sighed. "I'm sorry, Channing. I thought I was wanting this, but maybe what I really want is to jump back into the whole dating thing a lot slower than I planned."

"And that's fine with me. I had a great night tonight, and I really want to see you again."

We took a step back from one another, and our gazes met. "I had a great time too. I think we should call it a night."

He nodded. "Can I ask you one thing? And I swear this is not a ploy to get into your house."

I raised a brow. "I have Mace, you know."

Channing laughed. "I have to piss like a racehorse, and I have a thirty-minute drive home."

With a grin, I opened the door and walked into my house, Channing following me. "Down the hall, first door on the left."

"Thank you!"

After a minute or two, Channing walked into the kitchen. "Thank you again for the great night, Kaylee."

"No, honestly, thank you, Channing. It's been a while since I've been out on a date, and I really needed it."

I turned off the kitchen light and followed him back through the living room to the front door.

"Try not to set any more fires," he said with a grin that should have made me want to haul him up to my bedroom and have my wicked way with him. Instead, I opened the front door as I laughed.

"No promises. I have a new candle lighter I ordered from some girl on Etsy, along with her homemade soy candles."

Channing rolled his eyes. "Glad I'm not on call."

I slapped him on the chest and ushered him outside. "Be safe driving home."

He turned, and his eyes drifted to my mouth. I thought for a moment he might kiss me again, and I mentally prepared myself for it. Instead, he tipped his head and said, "Good night, Kaylee. May I call you?"

"Yes, of course!" I said, leaning up and giving him a quick kiss on the cheek. "Good night, Channing."

"Night, Kaylee."

I watched as he walked down the steps, then the pathway, and finally to his little sports car. He slipped in and took off down the driveway.

Letting out a deep breath, I turned and looked at the fence line that separated my rental property from the Shaw family ranch.

I focused a bit harder . . . was that two guys on horseback off in the distance?

When I stepped out on the porch and took a few steps, I squinted to see in the dark. Then I laughed.

"Who would be out on horseback after sundown?" I said, shaking my head and walking back into the house.

Chapter Six

Ty

I watched as Channing helped Kaylee out of the car. The lights from the front porch allowed me to see that he held her hand as they walked up the steps. When she turned and he kissed her, it took everything I had to keep from jumping the fence line and yelling for him to stop.

Instead, I watched in silence, tucked into the shadow of a tree. They broke apart, and Channing placed his hand on the side of Kaylee's face.

"Tell him to go home," I whispered, like I was the good angel sitting on her right shoulder.

When Kaylee opened the door and he followed her in, I closed my eyes and dropped my head. Fuck me, she must have listened to the little devil on her other shoulder instead.

"Kind of creepy as fuck, bro."

Tanner's voice made me look over my shoulder at him.

"What are you doing out here?" I asked, turning my horse and walking him toward my younger brother. The moonlight gave us just the right amount of light.

"Saw Mountie was still out, so I thought I would see what was going on."

Tanner looked past me toward Kaylee's place. "You ever going to tell her how you feel? Or just creep around like a super-freaky stalker on horseback?"

I laughed and started heading back toward the barn. Tanner turned his horse and caught up with me, walking his horse alongside mine.

"Advice about women coming from you, Tanner? What in the hell do you know about women?"

"Well, I know how to make them come in all sorts of creative ways, so there's that."

"That's because you used to listen to me, Brock, and Beck talk about that. We passed along all of our tips and tricks. Years of experience that we gifted to you."

He chuckled. "That is true. I know when a woman is faking an orgasm."

I looked at him and could barely make out Tanner's smirk. "So, I think what you're saying is that it's pretty clear you know a lot about sex, dude. Not women."

He shrugged. "Same thing."

"Hardly."

"Fine, so maybe I'm a little green when it comes to the romance shit, but Ty, you like this girl. Why can't you just admit it?"

"It's complicated, Tanner."

"Why?"

"It just is!" I snapped before kicking my horse into a gallop. Tanner did the same and followed me back to the barn, where we took off the saddles, got the horses brushed, and put a bit of hay in their stalls before we boarded them for the night. Tanner moved around pretty damn good for having a broken ankle.

"Where are your crutches?" I asked.

He shot me a look that said I knew damn well where they were.

I had figured Tanner was going to give up on the Kaylee thing, but he started again when I shut Mountie's stall door and locked it.

"I'm just saying, everyone sees the attraction there. Hell, even Blayze has a song about you and Kaylee."

Stopping, I faced him. "Is he still singing that stupid song?"

Tanner chuckled. "Well, he started to, and Brock put a stop to it, but even the kid sees it."

I rubbed the back of my neck. "You wouldn't understand, Tanner."

"Then talk to me about it, Ty. Come on, follow me."

I did as he asked and followed him into the tack room, where he opened the small refrigerator and took out two beers. "Let's head up."

"The barn loft?" I asked with a scoff.

"Hey, I've had some pretty fucking profound moments in that loft."

"Yeah, me too. I lost my virginity up there."

Tanner stopped walking and looked back at me. "Are you shitting me? That's my spot, dude. Why do you have to taint it with the sort of information that you could have easily taken to your grave?"

I shrugged and motioned for him to walk up the steps while I tried not to laugh my ass off. Once we got up there, we walked over to the double doors and opened them. There was a small balcony our father had added on years ago. We all used to sit up there, our legs hanging between the rails, and dream of what our lives would be like. Beck had always wanted to be in the marines. He followed his dream, and it had killed him. Brock, he was always the one arguing with me about who was the better bull rider. Truth be told, we were both good . . . damn good. And Tanner, he just wanted to be in the rodeo. Roping, women, and horses. The only three things he cared about.

We sat down, our legs dangling as we drank our beers in silence for the first few minutes before I spoke.

"You know the high you feel right before that chute opens and you go after that calf?"

Tanner took a pull of beer and nodded. "Yeah. Nothing like it."

"After my accident, I craved that feeling. Knowing I would never have it again did something to my mind. Fucked with me, big time. Then I discovered I could have a version of it with the pain pills."

I could feel Tanner's eyes on me. He remained silent, so I kept talking.

"It was a different high. A different rush, but hell, it was a rush nonetheless. It dulled the pain I not only felt in my knee but in my chest as well. Just like that feeling you get before a run—it was also addictive."

Facing Tanner, I took in a deep breath and let it out. "So addictive it scared the shit out of me. I got lost to it so fast. I spun out of control, and man, I thought I was smart. Hiding it from everyone, thinking I had the reins grasped tight on it. It took me a long time, Tanner, to realize I never had control. It almost . . . destroyed me. The rush I got from bull riding, yeah, it was dangerous, but I always knew I was the one in control, you know?"

He nodded. "Yeah, I know."

I rubbed the back of my neck. "Just when I thought I had beaten the addiction, another one came along. One I wasn't ready for at all."

"Ty, what do you mean?"

I heard the concern in his voice and put my hand on his shoulder and gave it a squeeze. "Not drugs, bro . . . Kaylee. She might as well be a damn drug."

His body relaxed.

I added, "I'm not going to lie: when she first showed up, with that little southern accent and those blue eyes, I wanted nothing more than to get her into my bed."

"You don't anymore?"

"Oh, I still do . . . and that's the problem."

He laughed.

"For the first time in my life, though, I've felt something for a woman that wasn't lust."

"Don't know that feeling, dude," Tanner said, taking a drink of his beer.

"Be glad you don't. It fucks with your head."

"So I've heard and seen. Chance is all caught up in some little barrel racer. Thinks he's in love."

"Wow," I replied, looking at Tanner. "What's going on with that?" I asked, hoping to change the subject from me and Kaylee. But it didn't work.

Tanner smirked. "We ain't here to talk about Chance. Keep going."

I nodded. "Anyway, Kaylee wasn't supposed to stay in town. I figured I could scratch the itch, she'd move on, probably come back into town a few times a year, we'd hook up, and that would be that."

"What happened?" he asked.

"I kissed her."

His brows pulled in and he stared at me. The only sound that could be heard was that of Mama's wind chimes blowing in the slight wind that enveloped us.

"You remember that rush? The high? I felt something like it for the first time in my life with a woman, and it was caused because of Kaylee Holden's damn kiss. My chest closed in on me, and I *needed* a woman—and it wasn't just for the sex. I don't even know how to explain it, but it felt like she had poured something of herself into me, and it left me craving more. So much more."

"And let me guess: you freaked out."

"Of course I freaked out. Wouldn't you have?"

He laughed. "Yeah, I probably would have, for a minute, and then I would have explored it."

I shook my head. "I can't let myself get attached to her. The idea that I had felt that much from just a kiss . . . who in the hell knows what making love to her would have been like if I hadn't walked away. I can't trust myself with those types of feelings. I don't know how else to explain it."

"I get it, but I think you're missing out on something if you don't at least try, Ty."

I pressed the beer to my lips and took a long drink. "I can't do it, Tanner. If I let myself even think about it, and then things don't work out or she ends up leaving? No, thanks."

He let out a confused laugh. "So you won't even give it a chance because you're afraid it might not work out or she'll leave?"

"Pretty much. I don't think I can handle another failure in my life, Tanner."

"*Another* failure? What in the hell are you talking about, Ty?"

"Bull riding, my drug addiction?"

Tanner grabbed my shoulder and gave me a push, causing me to look at him. "You did not fail at either of those things, dude. Ty, you were on your way to being number one again. It was a drunk driver who took that away from you. That was completely out of your control. And the drugs? You beat it—you recognized when the temptation crept up again after Brock's accident, and you started back up with therapy. You're winning that battle, Ty. Don't you ever fucking doubt that."

I swallowed the lump in my throat and nodded. "You should charge my therapist for this session, ya know."

He rolled his eyes and dropped his hand. "I'm serious, Ty. Listen, I'm going to be the first guy to say I have zero interest in tying myself down to anyone for a long time. My dick likes his playtime, and trust me when I say that we get a lot of playtime out on the road."

I laughed and shook my head.

"But I also believe in love. I see it in our parents. I see it with Brock and Lincoln. Hell, did you ever think Brock would open up his heart again after Kaci died giving birth to Blayze?"

"No, I honestly didn't."

"Then why won't you let yourself believe that you can also find happiness, Ty?"

"I'm not the kind of guy Kaylee needs."

"Who does she need?" Tanner asked, setting his now-empty beer bottle down behind him.

"Someone without a fucked-up past."

"But she has a fucked-up past of her own."

I rubbed the back of my neck. "Exactly. That's why she doesn't need someone like me. She deserves someone better."

Tanner let out a frustrated sigh. "Ty, you're never going to be able to move on if you don't stop thinking you're not good enough. Do you realize Dad couldn't run this place without you?"

I laughed. "He did fine before I worked here full time."

"He also never told you about all the ranch hands he had to hire on to help him out. You showed up and got everything organized and working like a fine-tuned machine, and Dad hasn't stressed at all these last few years.

"Ty, *this* is in your blood. This ranch. Being a rancher is what you were made for. And look at the work you do with the agricultural-education program. Look at what those kids are learning, what they're doing. Brock also told me you're looking into possibly raising some bulls for competition and have already been talking with Doug from the PBR. Damn, brother, give yourself some credit, will you, please?"

I finished off the last of my beer and set the bottle next to Tanner's. "Yeah, I guess so. It doesn't really matter anyway. I watched Channing walk into Kaylee's house after kissing her. Then, when I looked back, her kitchen light went off, so what do you think they're doing?"

Tanner scoffed. "Kaylee isn't going to sleep with him. Not on her first date."

"I'm pretty sure she would have slept with me if I had asked her." I pushed back and stood, stretching my stiff leg.

"Bothering you?"

"Nah, just gets stiff sometimes when I keep my knee bent too long."

Tanner stood and reached for the two bottles as I walked back into the loft. We walked down in silence and out to my truck, which was parked outside the barn.

"Let me give you a ride up to the house," I said. "And stop fucking walking on the ankle, dude. You want to get back out on the circuit, don't you?"

"Yeah, I sure as shit do." Tanner got into my truck and shut the door. I could tell by the expression on his face, something was heavy on his mind.

"Spill it, Tanner. I know you want to say something."

"Don't give up on her or your feelings for her, Ty. Maybe if you just talked to her."

I laughed. "Hell, we can't be in the same room for longer than five minutes before we're going at each other."

"And why do you think that is? Y'all just need to have sex and get all that pent-up tension out of the way and over with."

With another humorless laugh, I replied, "I wish it were that easy. Believe me."

We drove down the dirt road and to our folks' house in silence, everything Tanner had said to me replaying in my mind. I couldn't get my head to wrap around the idea of something with Kaylee. The woman drove me insane. Yet, at the same time, I ached to be near her. Ached so badly sometimes it hurt. And that was what scared me. If she broke my heart, I really didn't think I'd be able to handle it . . . and if I broke hers, I'd never forgive myself.

I pulled up and put the truck in park. "Thanks, Tanner. Who would have thought you had that in ya?"

He shot me a serious look. "I can be deep, bro. I can be deep."

With a roll of my eyes, I looked away. "Good night, Tanner."

"Night, Ty. See ya in the morning."

As I drove down the road that led to my house, I smiled. Snow started to drop from the sky. Maybe it would come down heavy and I'd be stuck at the house tomorrow. Then I wouldn't have to see Channing Harrell's little pussy sports car still parked outside Kaylee's house.

Chapter Seven

KAYLEE

I stood at my window and watched the snow falling. "What do you mean this is normal? Aren't the snowstorms supposed to start slowing down? It's almost April."

"We live in Montana now, Kaylee," Lincoln said. I could hear baby Morgan in the background, and a strange zip of jealousy raced through my body. I'd always known I wanted kids, but I'd never had the *urge* to have kids until recently.

I sighed and pushed those crazy thoughts away. "I know, but it looks like it's a blizzard."

"Brock wants to know if you have enough firewood. The wind is supposed to pick up, and he's worried the power might go out. There's a strong Canadian front moving down."

"What? Ugh! Let me get changed, and I'll go out and get some before Mother Nature decides to piss more snow out and block me in."

Lincoln laughed. "It happened once before and you thought it was fun, Kaylee."

"That was different. I was prepared for that snowstorm; this one I'm not. I can't be stuck in my house. I don't have any chocolate! A girl needs chocolate at times like that."

"Just go get some firewood, and then call me back so I know you didn't slip and fall."

"Gee, thanks for your vote of confidence. I'll have you know I put a new toilet seat on in the master bathroom." I heard a door shut, and the sweet sounds of Morgan were gone. "Where did the baby go?"

"Brock took her to put her down for her nap. Why did you change the toilet seat? There was nothing wrong with the one on there."

"Well, I'm still trying to connect it and everything."

The line went silent. Chewing nervously on my lip, I quickly kicked off my sneakers and slipped on my snow boots as I waited for Lincoln to press me for more information.

"Oh. My. God. Kaylee! You did not order that bidet toilet seat, did you?"

"It looks really cool! I miss having a bidet! You can take the money out of the girl, but you can't take away her desire for luxury and a warm seat to sit on when she has to pee in Montana!"

"You are ridiculous!" Lincoln said with a laugh.

"You say that now, but trust me, you're going to want one during a blizzard especially."

"The seat heats up, huh?"

I smiled. "So does the water."

She moaned a little. I knew that would get her. When we first moved here, we both fell in love with Montana. This was our first winter, and we were at what I hoped like hell was the tail end of it. I knew she was wanting it to end as much as I was.

"I need to come over and see how that works."

"Well, I have to hook up the water—that's the only thing throwing me."

"Good God, don't mess with the water. You'll flood the house!"

I reached for my winter jacket and put it on, zipped myself up, then grabbed my hat, scarf, and gloves.

"Hey, speaking of this house. I was thinking, since you're married to Brock now and I'm renting it, what if I buy it from you?"

"Are you serious? You want to buy the house?" I could hear the excitement in her voice. "Yes, you can buy it from me! Oh, Kaylee, this means you really are staying!"

Frowning, I put my hat on. "Did you think I wasn't?"

"Well, I mean, I didn't know."

"I like it here, Lincoln. Plus, now that I've got Blayze and Morgan in my life, I wouldn't want to leave them."

"Kaylee, I would love for you to buy the house. We can talk more about it later. Just go get some wood, then let me know when you get back inside."

"Will do," I said, opening the front door and stepping outside. "Give me a few minutes to call you back."

"Okay, talk soon! Love ya!"

"Love ya too."

I hit end and put the phone in my coat pocket, then quickly slipped on my gloves. I was about to turn and pull the door closed when Ty said hello from behind me, scaring the living daylights out of me. I jumped and slipped on ice on the front porch.

"Oh, no . . . no . . . no . . . no!" I screamed as I slipped and slid across the porch toward the steps. "Shit!"

But luckily, I came to a stop when his strong hands kept me from tumbling down the steps. I quickly turned and saw Ty standing there with a smile on his face.

"It was tempting as hell to let you fall, ya know."

I snarled my lip at him before giving him a good push. He didn't budge, of course, but I got an A for effort, even if it made me slip again, and he had to reach out and steady me. I ignored the zip of excitement that raced through my body. How in the hell did he do that—make me feel our connection—when I had layers of clothes on?

"Why are you here? There's a blizzard outside."

Ty laughed. "This isn't a blizzard, Kaylee. The snow we got right before Christmas? Now *that* was a blizzard."

I rolled my eyes and headed carefully down the steps.

"I need to get firewood. Brock said the power might go out."

"That's why I'm here."

Facing him, I felt a little flutter of excitement bubble up in my chest. Had Ty been worried about me and come to make sure I was okay? That thought really shouldn't have gotten me as excited as it did. Damn my vibrator. She was obviously not doing her job.

"Brock called me, since my place is the closest, and asked me to make sure you had enough firewood."

I was positive he could see the disappointment on my face, because he pulled his brows in ever so slightly. I quickly smiled. "That was sweet of him, but I am perfectly fine and more than capable of taking care of myself."

Continuing down the steps, I slipped and fell right on my ass. Hard. The pain shot through me, taking my breath away and causing instant tears.

"Shit, Kaylee, are you okay?" Ty asked, reaching down to help me up.

My tailbone hurt so bad I almost felt sick. The moment Ty saw tears in my eyes, I could tell something in him changed. He moved to lift me into his arms. I hated feeling weak and wanted to protest, but this was the closest my body had been to his since that night he'd kissed me . . . so, weak I would be. Plus, I still hadn't gotten my breath back, and the pain was verging on the unbelievable.

Ty quickly brought me back into the house and gently placed me on the sofa. He took off my hat, my gloves, and then my boots as I stared at him in shock.

Who was this man? Where did Ty the uncaring jerk go?

"Are you okay?"

I shook my head. I wasn't okay. I was in terrible pain, and I knew that if I talked, I would cry. Not to mention, I was feeling a bit emotional on top of the pain. Looking into his blue eyes nearly left me dizzy. His black cowboy hat always made his eyes stand out a little more, and he was mere inches away right now. It was all too much coming at me.

"Can you stand up and we'll get your jacket off?"

I went to stand and stopped, the pain radiating through my entire midsection. "Oh, God. Oh, God," I croaked out.

"It's okay, let me help you."

Ty carefully helped me out of the jacket. The way he moved so slowly, so gently, if I hadn't been in pain, I would have swooned.

Damn man.

"My, my phone . . . pocket."

Once Ty found which pocket, he took the phone out and handed it to me.

"Let me go get you some ice. Do you have any ibuprofen?"

I nodded. "There's some in the master bathroom."

"Let's get you to lie down. Sitting on your tailbone is going to be painful. Do you like lying on your side or your back?"

Normally, I would have made a smartass comment about him trying to get me on my back, but I was in too much pain to joke or make inappropriate innuendoes.

"Side, but I feel sick to my stomach."

"Okay, lean forward a little bit until I come back down." He looked around and reached for the little trash can by the front door. "If you get sick, use this."

And just like that, he raced up the steps. I closed my eyes and tried to take in a few deep breaths, but even that made my tailbone hurt.

"Please, please don't have cracked or broken anything. Please . . . ," I mumbled.

After about two minutes, Ty was coming back down the steps with a pillow and ibuprofen. He turned and went into the kitchen. I heard the ice machine and a few drawers open and close.

"Dish towels?" he called out. Before I could answer, he added, "Never mind, you have a gel ice pack. This is perfect!"

I couldn't help but smile. This was a side of Ty Shaw I had never seen. He probably felt guilty since it was his fault I fell. Of course, had he not been there to catch me the first time, I might have broken an arm or even a leg.

Then he was in front of me again, and my heartbeat picked up ever so slightly simply because I could smell his cologne. Or his soap, or whatever that delicious manly scent was that he had. I was going to guess it was soap. Ty didn't seem like the kind of guy to put on cologne. It was a mix of leather and a clean, fresh scent, as if he bathed with Irish Spring. Or maybe that was just Ty's own unique smell. Regardless, I loved it . . . a lot.

And why is my mind fixating on how Ty smells when I'm in so much pain? Good Lord, if I don't have sex soon, I'm going to combust.

"How about we get you to lie on your back."

I nodded, not wanting to talk because I could feel the tears simmering just under the surface, and I was feeling overwhelmed with pain and Ty's stupid smell.

He handed me the ibuprofen and a glass of water and then placed the gel pad on the sofa. The pillow he had brought down was on the coffee table.

"Let's stand you up really quickly, and then I'll help you lie down." I shook my head.

"Kaylee, I need to get the ice pack under you."

My chin trembled, and I felt a warm tear slip down my cheek.

Ty dropped down and sat on the coffee table, his face white as a ghost. He removed his cowboy hat and set it to the side. When he cupped my face in his hands, I felt an instant rush of butterflies in my stomach, but then the pain in my lower back took care of that feeling and replaced it with nothing but throbbing.

"Fuck, does it hurt that bad?"

The only thing I could do was nod.

"Okay. Okay. Do you think you can lean back, and I'll do my best to get the pad under you?"

"I'll try," I said, my voice sounding so weak, I wanted to punch myself, but, considering I was already in pain, I didn't want to deal with any more.

Ty helped me to lean back as he gently tucked the gel pad under me.

"Let me put the pillow under your knees."

Once he'd finally gotten me settled, Ty hit his watch. "I'll set a timer for twenty minutes."

"How . . . do you . . . know . . . all this?" I asked.

He smiled, and my heart felt like it skipped a beat. For one brief moment, I didn't feel pain. I only saw that smile. That dimple. Those eyes that sparkled when he allowed himself to just be . . . Ty. Happy, not on guard, and willing to let me see him without the walls. I'd seen that side of him before. When we found out Lincoln was pregnant with Brock's baby. When it was just the two of us, a secret only we knew. It had been fun, seeing him so carefree. Seeing that sparkle in his eyes. It was rare, so anytime I could see it felt like a gift.

"I've cracked my tailbone a few times and bruised it more times than I can remember. I'm pretty sure you just bruised yours, but it hurts like a son of a bitch no matter which one happens."

"Bull riding?" I asked.

"Yeah," Ty replied with a nod. "And once getting bucked off a stubborn mare."

"What is it with you and women?"

He winked, and I was pretty sure I sighed, but that was okay in this instance because he would simply think it was from the pain.

"They either love me or hate me. It's a curse I have to live with, I guess."

I stared up at him as he looked down at me, that smile still on his face. His brown hair looked like he had run his fingers through it at least a dozen times today. It was messy, but in a clean-cut sort of way. Ty kept his hair short, but a little longer on the top. Countless nights, I'd come to visions of my hands running through his hair as he brought me to orgasm. God, he was sexy as hell.

Our eyes were still locked, and I couldn't help but wonder if he could read my mind. Maybe he knew where my thoughts were going, because his gaze fell to my lips and stayed there a beat too long.

Ty cleared his throat. "Let me go get some firewood for you. Here's your phone."

He stood. For a moment I forgot all about the pain in my tailbone and focused on the pain in my chest instead.

"Thank you," I whispered as I took the phone from him. The moment he shut the front door, I called Lincoln. The ice was already helping to dull the pain.

"Wow, that was fast. You really are getting good at doing things on your own," Lincoln said.

"Well, apparently your husband doesn't think so," I said, trying to sound like I wasn't dying, or Lincoln would be sending Brock over here next.

"What do you mean?"

I sighed and tried to adjust some, and gasped.

"Kaylee, what's wrong?" Concern laced Lincoln's voice.

"Hold on, give me a second." I let the moment of jarring pain slip away before I spoke again. "Brock sent Ty over here to check and make sure I had enough firewood. Ty scared me, I nearly fell, then I pushed him, and then I really *did* fall on the steps. He thinks I bruised my tailbone."

"Oh, no! Do you need me to come over?"

"No, I'm on the sofa, and Ty gave me some medicine and put ice on it. Apparently he's bruised his tailbone a time or two."

"Oh, Kaylee, I'm so sorry."

I felt the tears burn against the back of my eyes, but I refused to let them spill. Keeping it together, I said, "It's okay."

"You're hurt."

"I'm fine. I just need to rest here for a bit, and then I'll be back to normal."

"Brock is asking what's wrong . . . give me a second and let me fill him in."

Lincoln relayed everything to Brock as I hit mute on my phone, closed my eyes, and focused on a happy place. A warm beach with a good book, a hot guy rubbing suntan oil on my back. Yes . . . yes, that's where I wanted to be.

"Mmm, yes, that feels good," I softly said.

"Did you dial 1-800-We've-Got-Porn?"

My eyes snapped open to see Ty standing there with an armful of wood. How had he done that so fast?

"No, asshole, I was trying to picture myself on a warm beach. A happy place, by myself . . . where you're not there."

He winked again, and I paused what I was about to say. As a matter of fact, I think I forgot how to breathe.

"Kaylee? Hey, are you there?"

I unmuted the phone and said, "I'm here."

"Um, Brock just said he didn't tell Ty to go over there."

"What? Are you sure about that?"

"Yes. He said he hasn't even talked to Ty since earlier this morning."

I raised a brow and looked at Ty, who was currently putting the wood on the little iron wood rack I had bought in one of the cute little stores in downtown Hamilton. Ty had bitched and moaned the entire time he was in the store with me, because we had been sent there originally to find a cute birthday present for his mother. A task I had willingly agreed to help him with until I realized Ty was not a fun shopper. At all.

"Okay."

"Okay? Is that all you're going to say?"

"Yep."

"He's right there, isn't he?"

"Yep."

"Well, isn't this interesting."

"Yep."

"Make sure he gets you all settled before he leaves. I'll be over in the morning when the snow clears."

"Will do. Thanks."

I hit end and studied Ty as he piled up the wood. He had taken off his jacket and was in a long-sleeved black T-shirt that showed every muscle in his arms and back as he stacked the wood. Each time he leaned over, I got an ass shot. I bit my lip and looked away.

Why, dear God above, could Channing not make me feel this way? Why did you have to make my body desire this man? Why!

"Why, what?" Ty asked, making me glance his way.

"Huh?"

"You said, 'Why?'"

"Oh . . . I, um . . . I mean, why did I have to fall? It's a terrible time to get hurt. I was going to help Mrs. Kennedy plan her daughter's baby shower."

He grinned. "Ever since you planned Lincoln's wedding, you've become sort of the hot party planner in Hamilton."

I laughed, but I stopped when it made my tailbone ache. "Well, I don't do it often, but when I do, it's a lot of fun."

"Have you ever thought about opening up your own event-planning business?"

I just stared at him. When I once mentioned the same thing to my parents, they both had the same negative reaction—that I wouldn't be able to run my own business.

It never occurred to them that I actually *did* own a business, my editing business. I worked on some of today's hottest-selling romance and historical writers' manuscripts, yet, in their eyes, they had paid for me to go to college to read books all day. In my father's voice, I heard, "What a waste of a college education with a degree in journalism. Why you couldn't get a business degree is beyond me."

Looking down at my phone, I shook my head. "I don't know. It's really just for fun."

Ty went back to the wood, but this time he was building a fire in the fireplace. "You should really think about it, Kaylee. You've got the eye for it. I mean, look at Brock and Lincoln's wedding: it was beautiful, and everything went smoothly."

I felt my cheeks heat. "Are you actually giving me a compliment, Ty Shaw? I figured you would have some smartass remark about me being better suited to planning funerals and such."

He chuckled as he lit the fire starters. "That would have been a good one—too bad I didn't think of it first."

I rolled my eyes and tried not to smile.

Soon a large fire was going, and I could feel the warmth. It balanced out the cold ice pack on my lower back and tailbone and helped take my mind off the pain I was still in.

Ty stood and dusted off his hands as he looked at me. "Do you want me to make you anything to eat? Some soup or something?"

"Soup?"

"Yeah, do you have any?"

I shook my head. "I don't."

"Okay, well, do you have any veggies? Some broth?"

The way he was behaving was throwing me for a loop. "Ty, why are you doing this?" I asked, looking at him and trying to read every emotion that passed over his face. The damn man was good at hiding his feelings. Very good. I was also very intrigued about why he'd said he was sent here instead of fessing up that he had come over on his own.

"Why am I doing what?"

"Being so nice to me?"

He laughed. "As much as you want to think I don't like you, Kaylee, we *are* friends. I feel guilty that it was my fault you just got hurt."

And there it was. He felt guilty because he thought I'd fallen because of him.

I sighed. "It's not your fault, and you don't have to stay. I think I can get up now."

Trying to prove my point, I went to move—and froze when the pain hit me.

"Don't move!" Ty said in a stern voice. "Damn it, why do you have to be so stubborn? I want to be here, Kaylee. Let me try to make you something to eat, will you?"

My stomach chose to growl right at that moment. Damn betraying body of mine.

I rolled my eyes and tried to seem put off. "Fine, but just so you know, I'm making you eat whatever you make for me too. I don't trust you won't put some hot sauce or something in it."

The way he was looking at me was exactly how he had looked when we'd first kissed. That night at the Blue Moose. Something in his eyes said he did indeed want to be here. Be with me.

The other thing I saw in his eyes was at war with those feelings. My breath felt shallow, and I swallowed hard.

"It's a deal. Now, please just lie back and rest for a bit. I'll round up something to eat for dinner."

I did what he said, and once I closed my eyes, it didn't take long for me to drift off to sleep.

Chapter Eight

Ty

When I opened Kaylee's refrigerator, I couldn't help but chuckle. The girl was a super-healthy eater. I could give her that. She had a ton of vegetables. One quick check in her pantry and I had everything I needed to make my mom's vegetable soup.

I pushed up my sleeves and got to work cutting up the veggies while the stock heated up with the onions and a few cloves of garlic.

Once everything was in the pot, I looked around her kitchen and found a bottle of shiraz. I'd save that for dinner. Kaylee also had some sourdough bread and fresh rosemary, perfect for when the soup was finished.

Looking into the refrigerator again, I smiled when I saw the six-pack of beer. I opened one and took a drink.

"You want a beer?" I called out.

She didn't answer me, so I walked into the living room . . . and came to a stop. Kaylee was sound asleep. I shook my head and set the beer on the coffee table as I gently removed the gel pack from underneath her, then laid a blanket over her.

"Ty?" she whispered, opening her eyes only long enough to see me before she shut them again.

"Yeah, baby. It's just me. Get some sleep."

Inwardly, I cursed myself for slipping and calling her an endearment. I'd never fucking called anyone *baby*. But this woman wasn't anyone, and it was clear my heart was feeling more than I wanted to admit.

She nodded and went right back to sleep, a slight smile on her face.

My heart raced in my chest, and I took a few unsteady steps back until I hit the chair. Sitting, I stared at Kaylee as she slept. When she had fallen earlier, I'd seen the pain on her face, the tears in her eyes, and it felt like my whole world had tilted. I hated seeing her in pain. I hated seeing the way those blue eyes looked at me, as if she was wanting so desperately to tell me something, but couldn't.

After about ten minutes of just watching her sleep, I got up and checked on the soup. Then I pulled out my phone and sent my father a text.

Me: I came over to Kaylee's place to make sure she was set for this storm. She fell on the steps and I'm pretty sure she bruised her tailbone.

He replied almost instantly.

Dad: Poor thing. You didn't leave her, did you?

Me: No. She's asleep on the sofa and I made her some vegetable soup.

Dad: Have you checked the weather, Ty? It's gotten worse, the snow is coming down even harder. I don't know if you want to leave her tonight, especially if she's hurt.

My eyes widened in shock as I read his text. "Stay the night?" I said with a laugh. "Is he insane?"

Me: I'll make sure she's set up with everything, then head back to my place. I'm sure once the ibuprofen kicks in, she'll be fine.

When my phone rang, I knew I was about to get a lecture.

"Hey," I said, wincing as I prepared for his verbal reprimand.

"Ty Shaw, you cannot leave that girl there alone with a huge storm coming and a bruised tailbone. You can stay there one night . . . the girl doesn't bite."

"That we know of," I shot back.

He let out a frustrated sigh. "What is it with you two?"

"Nothing. I'll stay, don't worry."

"Thank you. Tell her that your mother will be over in the morning. She has a new knitting project she wants to start Kaylee working on."

I rolled my eyes. Not only had Kaylee infiltrated all my thoughts but she'd also made my mother fall in love with her. She was actually teaching Kaylee how to knit, getting her prepped for her spring garden, and teaching her to make soap. How she had time to undertake all these projects on top of remodeling this house was beyond me.

"You still there, Junior?"

"Yeah, I'm here, Dad." I rubbed the instant ache in my neck. "Maybe I'll run back to my place and grab an overnight bag."

"No, you can't risk getting stuck and then leaving Kaylee alone."

Laughing, I walked over to the back door just off the kitchen. "It can't be snowing that hard. I just—"

I stopped midsentence as I saw the snow coming down in sheets.

"The power might—"

My father's voice cut off.

"Dad? Dad?"

During heavy snowstorms, our cell coverage sucked. I sighed and dropped my head back as I gazed up at the ceiling.

A moment later, the power went out.

I closed my eyes and cursed. "Fucking great."

No power meant no heat. That meant I'd have to keep the fire going and stay in the living room with Kaylee all night.

Glancing over to the stove, I let out a sigh of relief. At least the stove was gas, and that still worked without power.

I turned on the flashlight on my phone and got busy looking for candles. This was going to be one hell of a long night.

I placed a few more logs onto the fire and sat back down in the chair. The one that faced Kaylee. She was out, which was probably good. I knew she was in pain, so the longer she slept, the better.

Taking a long pull of beer, I kept my gaze on her. She was so damn beautiful.

Finally, her eyes opened, and in the firelight I could just barely tell she was looking directly at me.

"Ty?"

"Yeah, it's me."

"Why are you sitting in the dark?" she asked, slowly trying to sit up. "Oh, wow, okay, that hurts."

I stepped over to the sofa and helped her to stand. Once she was up, her body relaxed.

"It's probably only going to hurt when you go to sit and then stand back up—at least from my experience, that is," I said.

"Great," she replied as she looked around the house and pulled a deep breath in through her nose. "So, I have to ask again, why are you in the dark, and what is that amazing smell?"

"The power went out, and that would be vegetable soup."

She turned and looked at me. The flames from the fire danced in her eyes, and my cock hardened. Bastard.

"We're going to have to sleep down here if the power doesn't come back on."

Kaylee's mouth opened, then closed. Then she shook her head and asked, "We?"

"I'm not leaving you when you're hurt, and the snow is coming down so bad I wouldn't even be able to see to drive back home. Roads are already snowed over anyway, and not a chance in hell snowplows are out in this mess."

She stared at me with a confused expression, as if she was trying to piece together a puzzle or something. "So, you're staying here? All night?"

"Until my mom comes over in the morning, or whenever Dad or Brock can get the ranch roads cleared. She said she has some knitting project she wants to show you."

"I don't need to be looked after, Ty," she said as she turned, then walked to the stairs. She looked up the stairway, then back to me. "I'll just use the bathroom down here."

With a smile, I nodded. "I'll make you a bowl of soup if you want. I have some more ibuprofen and a fresh ice pack."

"How did you get the one out from under me?"

With a smirk, I replied, "I had to get creative."

Her lips snarled. "Pervert."

Laughing, I watched as she headed toward the guest bathroom. I made my way into the kitchen and took out two bowls and filled them both almost all the way up. Kaylee had some onion jam she must have bought from one of the local farms, so I put some of that on the sourdough bread and put it on a plate.

I waited for what seemed like forever, then finally went to the bathroom in the hall and knocked. When I didn't hear a reply, I leaned in and heard what sounded like a sniffle.

I knocked again. "Kaylee, what's wrong? Are you hurt?"

"I'm fine, Ty."

Her voice cracked, and I knew she wasn't fine.

"Did you fall again?"

She didn't answer. Fuck.

I reached for the doorknob and was surprised to find she had left it unlocked. I pulled out my phone and turned on the flashlight and opened the door. Then I froze.

Holy. Mother. Of God.

Kaylee was standing there, naked from the waist down.

When she looked up at me, my breath caught in my throat. She was crying.

"I can't sit down on the toilet. Leaning down hurts too bad," she said softly.

"Let me help you."

Shaking her head, she held her hand out. "Please, don't. I'm so embarrassed and was two minutes from trying to step into the bathtub to pee."

I couldn't help the slight smile I was trying to hide. "Let me help you, Kaylee."

My heart hammered in my chest as I walked to her and wrapped my arms around her, helping her sit.

"Jesus, that hurts."

My legs were spread apart as I gently lowered her onto the toilet. "I think maybe we should have an X-ray done: you might have cracked your tailbone, not just bruised it."

Kaylee dropped her head toward my body and cried, causing me to stay right where I was. Her half-naked body between my legs and her head lying on my stomach.

Son of a bitch. Don't get hard . . . please don't come up, pleeease don't come up. Think of anything else but the position she is in right now.

Thank Jesus, she peed, and all hopes of my cock coming to life quickly vanished. I'd never been so damn happy for a woman's full bladder than I was right in that moment.

"I have to wipe . . . will you look away?"

"Um, yeah, of course."

I took two steps away from her, turned, and stared ahead. There was a painting on the wall, and it looked like the mountain range to the north of the ranch. I leaned in closer and saw four men on horseback riding toward the ranch.

Why had I never seen that painting before? The details were hard to make out in the semidarkness, but the painting was amazing.

"Where did you get this painting?" I asked.

The toilet flushed, and she said, "Can we just get through this extremely awkward moment before I answer that? I need your help getting up, Ty."

Turning, I looked back down at her. "Right. Let me help you up."

After getting her back up, we both looked down at her yoga pants and—fuck me—her pink thong. It might've been dark in there, but I sure as hell could see a pink thong.

"I don't think I can bend down to get them, and I swear to God, if you make eye contact with me or so much as glance at my female parts right now, I will cut off your dick. Well, I'll do that once my tailbone isn't hurting anymore."

My eyes snapped back up from her panties, but I didn't make eye contact.

"I won't look," I said, my voice cracking like that of a teenage boy who's gotten his first glimpse of boob.

Why, God, why are you punishing me? Why?

Chapter Nine

Ty

I squeezed my eyes shut, leaned down, and felt for her panties.

The dryness in my throat made me feel like I was about to die from dehydration. I couldn't have produced spit in my mouth to save my life right then. This situation had literally robbed me of my breath.

I slid her panties up high enough so that she could reach them. Pulling that pink lace over her luscious thighs and possibly grazing her ass with my hands would've caused me to stroke out, that much I was sure of.

"Okay, pants now," she said.

Doing the same thing, but this time opening my eyes, I lifted her pants and got a view of her pink panties covering all the parts that I was fixated on. The dryness in my throat was immediately gone, and I was pretty sure I was drooling now.

"Ty?"

Holy shit, I could see her blonde curls through the lace of the fabric. Fuck, I shouldn't have looked. I. Should. Not. Have. Looked. When I'd walked in, I'd done the gentlemanly thing and kept my gaze away from anything below her waist. But now? Now it was right there, in my face.

The urge to push that lace to the side and lick her from stem to stern swept over me. It was almost an urge I couldn't fight anymore.

"Ty!"

What would she taste like? I couldn't even imagine. It would be sweet . . . it had to be. Kaylee cared deeply for people, and that made her sweet.

I swallowed hard, my mouth moving closer to her core. A magnetic pull that I wasn't strong enough to fight.

"Ty Shaw, stop staring at my pussy and give me my pants!"

Oh, fuck. I snapped out of it and lifted her yoga pants.

"Shit, sorry. Sorry!" I said as I stumbled to a standing position. I buried my face in my hands and groaned.

"That groan could go either way, so I'm hoping my vagina doesn't repulse you like my kissing did."

I dropped my hands and looked directly into her eyes. Her words didn't make any sense, and I wondered if I had heard her right. "What did you say?"

"Can we please leave the bathroom now?"

"Oh, yeah, sure. Sorry."

I took a step back and let her walk out first.

"It doesn't hurt too bad when I walk, but trying to sit down or stand up hurts like a bitch."

My eyes focused on her ass. She had a great ass, even in the dark, and those yoga pants hugged it in all the right ways.

"That smells so good. I forgot I had this jam!"

Forcing myself to stop staring at her ass, I pulled out a chair at the dining room table. I was glad she had little cushions on them so she wouldn't have to sit on the hard wood. "You okay sitting here, or should we go back into the living room, where it's warmer?"

She shook her head. "No, this is good."

She reached for my arm and slowly lowered herself into the chair. Once she was settled, I got the two bowls and placed them on the table, then put the bread down.

I sat opposite her and watched as she took her first bite. I had lit a few candles in the kitchen, so I had a better view of her than I had in the bathroom. Kaylee also had a few oil lanterns. One was in the kitchen, one in the living room, and those were lit too.

"Ty, oh my gosh, this is so good! Who would have thought you knew how to cook!" Her eyes closed, and she let out a moan as she pushed another spoonful of soup into her mouth.

Fuck me every which way to Sunday. At this rate, my cock was going to combust if she didn't stop whimpering and moaning. I mean, it wasn't like I hadn't just seen her half-naked and had my face mere inches away from heaven.

"Are you having sex with it, Kaylee, or eating it?" Holy shit, that just slipped out. I just made a bad situation even tougher by bringing up S-E-X.

She looked at me, hurt in her eyes. I hadn't meant for my words to come out so cold and harsh, but my still-hard cock was pissed with me for not taking care of him.

With eyes downcast, she focused back on the soup and took another bite, quietly eating, and I wanted to tell her I was sorry. But my pride and pent-up frustration wouldn't allow it. So, I didn't.

"So what's with the bidet up in your bathroom? I saw it when I ran up there earlier," I finally said, hoping to move on. The problem was, I kept picturing those panties, the smell of vanilla from her soap or maybe from some lotion she probably used. It made my damn head feel foggy and put me on edge.

With a shrug, she answered, "I wanted one, so I ordered it."

"I can hook up the water for you once the sun comes up. I wasn't sure where your tools were, and I already felt like a jerk looking around your place for candles."

A small grin played at the corners of her mouth. "They're in the laundry, under the sink. I'm still learning what is what, but I'm getting the hang of it."

"Okay, I'll take a look at it in the morning. It's too cold up there right now, and obviously pitch black."

"Honestly, I can take care of it. YouTube has been a lifesaver for me when I don't know how to do something around here," she said, still giving me a slight grin.

There was no sense in arguing about it with her. I'd just do it, and she'd have to deal with it.

We finished the dinner in silence. After I took our bowls and put them into the sink, I helped her stand up.

"I think I'm going to try and walk up the steps and shower. Maybe the hot water will lessen the pain some."

"Kaylee, there's no power. The pump on the well can't bring any water up to the house, and not to mention the water heater is off."

Her lower lip jutted out into a pout. It was the cutest thing I'd ever seen. "Then what do we do?"

"Do you have any board games?"

Her eyes seemed to light up at that, or maybe it was simply the candlelight flickering in her eyes. "Ty, you don't have to stay."

I handed her more ibuprofen and a bottle of water. "I honestly am stuck. I went outside before you woke up to go get more firewood. It's really bad out there. I could hardly find my way to the barn to get the wood and back to the house, it's snowing so hard."

"Yikes. What happens if you can't leave in the morning?" she asked, chewing nervously on her lip.

"It'll be fine. Tanner or Brock will get the plow out and make a path. Don't worry."

She nodded, then said, "I'm going to go find some warmer clothes. I don't have anything for you to wear. I'm sorry."

"No worries, I'll be fine. I've got some sweatpants in my truck. I'll run out and get them. You might want to make any calls you need to, especially before your phone dies. If the cell coverage is even working. It's hit or miss when it snows this heavy. Maybe to Lincoln, or to

Channing—let him know you're all right. My signal wasn't working earlier, so I had to use your phone and saw you had some missed calls, but it's working now."

Kaylee stood there for a moment just staring at me before she finally spoke. "Right. I'll do that."

Then she walked out of the kitchen, and I closed my eyes and internally cursed myself. Why did I have to bring up Channing? Probably because he'd called her earlier while she was asleep. My phone wasn't working, so I borrowed hers, and when I'd glanced down at it, I'd seen his name.

Dick. Asshole jerk.

I used to like the guy until I saw him kissing Kaylee and walking into her house. The thought of him with her made my stomach roll with nausea.

After using a bottle of water to rinse out the two bowls, I stacked them in the dishwasher, then put on my jacket to head out to my truck. When I got to the front door, I heard Kaylee talking to someone, and my curiosity got the better of me. I quietly made my way up the steps. It was freezing upstairs.

"I'm fine, honestly. No need to bring the fire truck, but it's sweet of you to offer to come warm me up."

Rolling my eyes, I made a silent gagging motion. I hated the thought of that asshole being in her bed. Warming her up. Inside her. My fists balled at my sides.

"No, it's painful to sit or stand, but walking seems to be okay. I'm going to stay down in the living room tonight where the fire is. Yes, I've got plenty of firewood."

It wasn't lost on me that she hadn't mentioned I was there.

"No, Ty started it for me a few hours ago. He stopped by to make sure I had enough."

Still no mention of me actually still being there. Interesting . . .

"Honestly, Channing, I'm fine. I don't need you hauling out the fire department simply for me. It's dangerous on the roads, anyway. Besides, I'm not helpless."

Even I could hear the frustration in her voice. Kaylee didn't like to feel useless, or be made to feel weak, and I admired that about her. She could own up to her weaknesses when she wanted to, which wasn't often, yet she wasn't prideful either.

"Let me go ahead and let you go; I don't want to use up all my battery. I'm going to shut off my phone, so if you try to call or text, you'll know why I'm not answering."

Turning, I quickly headed down the steps to the front door, seeing as she was getting off the phone. Once I stepped outside, I sucked in a breath, then coughed.

"Holy crap, it's freezing out here," I said out loud.

I carefully made my way down what had once been the steps, but they were covered with so much snow I couldn't see them. The snow was now already halfway up my tires. I opened the back door and smiled when I saw my gym bag.

"Thank you, God."

Now I had a change of clothes and a sweatshirt I could wear. I grabbed the bag and trekked back up toward the house. I looked to my left and couldn't see anything but white, everywhere. Thank God I didn't park that far away from her front porch. We were in a whiteout, and I made a mental note to check the weather on my phone.

When I got back into the house, I shook the snow off, removed my jacket and boots, and made my way to the guest bathroom to change. I was ready to get out of these jeans and into some more comfortable clothes. Sleeping in the living room wasn't looking so bad after all, now that I knew I wouldn't have to wear my jeans.

As soon as I got into the bathroom, I slipped out of my jeans and tossed them to the side, then removed my boxers. Kaylee had some of those little wipes, so I thought I might as well clean myself up a bit before getting dressed again.

Reaching behind my back, I pulled the shirt over my head and dropped it next to my jeans. I grabbed a couple of wipes and started to clean off my body . . . but my damn mind betrayed me once again. I couldn't help but think back to Kaylee in here and those pink panties right there in my face—

The door to the bathroom swung open, and Kaylee walked in, quickly coming to a stop when she saw me. Standing there. Naked. With a few wipes in each of my hands.

"Wh-what . . . why . . . what's . . ." Her gaze drifted down. "Oh, my . . . okay, *wow*."

Her eyes were now locked on my cock, which had already started to come to life from my dirty thoughts only seconds ago. He appeared to really like having her eyes on him, so he decided to amp up his game a bit. I almost passed out from all the blood rushing directly to my dick.

Traitorous bastard.

"Is that a bad *wow*, or a 'Holy shit, you're the biggest I've seen' *wow*?"

My voice pulled her eyes off my dick and to my mouth, then up to my eyes. "What? Oh my gosh, you really are an asshole, ya know. Why are you holding wipes in your hands?"

"I was cleaning myself off. What did you think I was doing with them? Did your perverted mind have other ideas?" I looked at her and smirked.

She looked down at the wipes in my hands and quickly zipped her gaze back to mine. Then she frowned and looked pissed off. "Nothing . . . I, um . . . that's actually a good idea."

"I do come up with them every now and then."

Kaylee stood there, staring at me.

I leaned my head a little toward her. "Kaylee, was there a reason you just walked into the bathroom?"

"Um, I don't really remember why I came in here."

There was no way I could stop the smirk, nor did I want to. "Maybe you want to strip naked, too, and clean yourself off. We could help each other out, ya know. I wash your back, you wash mine." I couldn't help it. I had to go there and watch her get flustered.

Even in the dim light, I could see her cheeks had turned as red as a tomato, and I couldn't help but laugh.

"You wish," she spat back.

"Probably for the best, since your boyfriend wouldn't like that, now would he?"

Her mouth opened to say something, but then she shut it. A slow smirk moved across her face. "Are you jealous of Channing?"

The fact that she hadn't denied she was seeing him did something to me. A painful squeezing sensation nearly took my breath away. I grabbed my sweats and pulled them on.

"Are you not putting underwear on?" she asked, complete shock lacing her voice. God, I was enjoying this little encounter more than I should.

"No," I said as I reached into my bag and pulled out a T-shirt. I slipped it on before I reached for my jeans and the other shirt and stuffed them into the bag. As I walked out of the bathroom, I stopped and looked at her. "And to answer your earlier question, no, I'm not jealous of Channing. You make a good couple."

Her mouth opened slightly; then she licked her lips and pressed them tightly shut. She stepped out of my way.

"If you need help using the bathroom, let me know."

I headed into the living room and dropped my bag at the front door, then reached for my phone on the coffee table and pulled up Tanner's number. I sent him a quick text, thankful to see it went through.

Me: Do you think you could get into the plow and make a road for me to get the fuck home?

Tanner: Dude, have you seen it outside? It's a blizzard. Where are you?

Me: Stuck at Kaylee's house.

The bastard sent me a text back that was six or seven laughing faces, and maybe a GIF—or ten—of different people falling over in laughter.

Me: You're dead to me.

Tanner: Man, I needed that laugh. Well, if you two can't work out the shit between you now when you're stuck together in a storm, you never will.

Me: Did I mention you were dead to me?

Tanner: Yes. You did. But I'm still laughing my ass off. Stay warm. I'm sure you can think of a few ways to do that.

Me: Fuck you, Tanner.

I turned off my phone and dropped it onto the coffee table. Kaylee walked into the living room, and it was then I realized she had changed into sweatpants and a sweatshirt. I knew it must have hurt like a bitch for her to change on her own. I couldn't help but wonder if she would rather suffer and do it alone than ask me for help. The idea hurt more than I wanted to admit. She was holding the ice pack.

"This sofa actually pulls out into a bed. I mean, we could put the sofa pillows down the middle, to keep to our own sides."

"Don't worry about it. I'll sleep on the floor in front of the fire so I can keep it going all night. If you want the bed pulled out, I can do that for you, though."

She shook her head. "No, the couch itself is more comfortable. I put the soup into a container and in the refrigerator."

"I was going to do that. You didn't hurt yourself doing all that walking, did you?"

"No, it's fine. I needed something to do so I wouldn't feel completely helpless."

I nodded and then walked over to the fire, moving the logs around and adding another one.

"I was thinking we could watch a movie, then remembered that wasn't possible."

"Definitely need power for that."

Her cheeks turned a slight pink, or maybe it was from the chill in the air. "Ty, I . . . I just wanted to say thank you for helping me."

Standing, I turned to her. She was making her way over to the sofa. I quickly followed and helped her sit. She was able to get the ice pack situated as she lay down, which sort of disappointed me. That meant I couldn't touch her, and touching her was one of my new favorite things to do.

"Let me get the pillow under your legs," I said.

"I brought down another pillow and some extra blankets. They're on the bench by the stairs."

Facing the bench, I saw the blankets. "I'll grab you another one."

I walked over and picked up the three blankets. Dropping two on the floor, I took the other one and draped it over Kaylee.

"Thank you," she whispered, her eyes looking at me as if she was trying to tell me something but didn't know how.

I turned away from her and dropped the one pillow on the floor, then lay down, pulling both blankets over me.

It was going to be a long fucking night.

Chapter Ten

KAYLEE

I had no idea what time it was. All I knew was that I'd woken up and I was freezing. The more I shivered, the worse the pain became in my tailbone. Ty was sleeping on the floor, and the fire was slowly burning out.

I thought about getting up to put more wood on, but at that very moment, Ty stirred and quickly stood. He grabbed the poker and moved the wood around, causing a big flame to shoot up. He placed three more pieces of wood into the fire and then turned. I was positive my teeth were chattering.

"Sorry, I didn't mean for it to get that low."

"S'okay," I managed to get out.

Ty reached down and grabbed another blanket and walked over to me.

With a shake of my head, I said, "N-no. I just need it to warm up a bit and . . . and . . . I'll be fine."

He frowned. "Jesus, Kaylee, your lips are practically blue. Do you have any quilts?"

I nodded and pointed upstairs. Ty moved quickly up the steps and soon reappeared with the quilt from my bed and one from the other bedroom upstairs. When he draped one over me, I pulled it over my head.

"Do you need me to warm you up?"

Every inch of me stopped moving. I think even my heart paused for a moment.

Say no. Say no. Say no. Say no, for Pete's sake, Kaylee!

When I didn't answer, I felt the quilt and covers move down. "Can you move forward and get on your side? I'll slip in behind you."

I was so cold, I couldn't even argue with him. The idea of any kind of heat was something I cared more about at the moment. I carefully moved, placing a pillow between my legs as I turned to my side.

Ty placed the now-warm ice pack on the coffee table and carefully climbed over my body and slipped down onto the sofa. He wrapped his arm around me, bringing my body flush against his.

My heart raced in my chest and my teeth chattered, but I wasn't so sure it was from the cold anymore, because my body instantly heated at his touch. At the feel of him against me. His dick was pressed into my ass, and I could feel it better than I should have thanks to his going commando.

Ignore the large penis pressed against you. He's not even hard. See, you don't do anything for him. Not. A. Thing.

My mind went back to a few hours ago, when I'd walked into the bathroom and found him butt-ass naked. The man had a body to die for. His abs had abs. He was toned in all the right places. His chest was broad, and his muscles . . . I was getting warm just thinking of them.

Let's not forget his dick—Lord Almighty, he was thick and long. The way it got so hard, so fast, and then jumped against his stomach had my panties instantly soaking wet. It had been a long time since I'd been with a man, and I'd wanted to drop to my knees and taste him so badly, I hadn't been able to think straight. Good thing my tailbone hurt like a bitch and I hadn't totally lost all my senses in that moment, or I might have.

"Are you okay? Lying like this doesn't hurt you, does it?"

The concern in his voice caused tears to fill my eyes. I forced myself to keep my voice calm and steady as I answered him. "I'm good—it doesn't hurt."

He held me a bit tighter, and this time a tear did fall. Then another. I squeezed my eyes shut and wished more than anything that Ty felt the same way about me as I did him.

"Good night, Kaylee," he whispered in the softest voice.

Determined not to let him know I was upset, I spoke clearly. "Night, Ty."

He soon drifted off to sleep, his breathing slow and rhythmic, me in his arms, tucked nicely against his body. It was a terribly romantic moment, one you would read about in a romance novel. It might as well have been fiction.

I cursed myself for being so foolish. There was a man out there willing and ready to have a relationship with me, yet I couldn't seem to let go of my feelings for Ty.

I willed myself not to cry again. Instead, I closed my eyes as sleep overtook me and soon got lost in a dream.

A dream that would soon turn into a nightmare.

◆ ◆ ◆

John stood before me, a gun held in his hand.

"I'm not happy, Kaylee. I haven't been for a long time."

Tears streamed down my face. "John, please, we can figure this out."

He shook his head. "No, it's too late."

I wrapped my arms around my body and cried harder. "It's never too late. Please don't do this. Please!"

The sound of the gun firing caused me to scream. I covered my eyes and prayed it wasn't real. I hadn't just seen my fiancé take his own life. It was a dream. Please, dear God, please let this be a dream.

"Kaylee? Kaylee, wake up."

My eyes shot open and I gasped for breath. Ty was crouched in front of me, concern etched all over his face. His beautiful blue eyes were looking directly into mine.

"You had a nightmare. A very intense one. Are you okay?"

I reached out and placed my hand on the side of his face. Was this a dream still? I was so confused. Pain engulfed me. Both physical and emotional. My head, my lower back, my heart. It felt all consuming.

When his hand covered mine, tingles zipped through my body, and I knew in that moment that I wasn't dreaming.

"I haven't had that dream in a long time," I finally said.

"Do you want to talk about it?"

Normally my answer to that question was no. But I was tired of saying no. Tired of keeping it all inside. Tired of being alone and pretending that my life was completely normal when it was so far from normal.

I slowly moved to sit up, my lower back still hurting something fierce, but it wasn't as bad as it had been earlier. Ty moved back, still crouched down, now looking up at me.

"I have this dream that I'm in the room with John." Ty had a confused look on his face at the mention of him. "John was my fiancé. He took his own life a few years ago. Anyway, I'm in the room when he kills himself. It's so vivid, and there are moments I can't tell if it's a dream or a memory. It's really odd, because I wasn't there when he killed himself. But in the dream, I'm right in front of him, begging him not to pull the trigger, and it feels so real. It's unnerving."

Ty took my hands in his but didn't say anything, which, oddly, I appreciated. I hated when people said they were sorry or that it wasn't my fault. I just wanted someone to listen. Someone other than the therapists.

"I had been out of town when John shot himself. My parents had this benefit dinner in the Hamptons, and they had asked me to fly to New York. I had no idea John was so tormented. So unhappy. A few months before he took his life, he had mentioned splitting up but then changed his mind. I didn't see any signs. No one did. For the longest time, I blamed myself. My thinking was that I wasn't good enough for him, didn't pay him enough attention. Maybe he'd met someone else, someone who loved him better than I did. I still don't know why he did it, because he didn't say much in his note. Not knowing has been the worst kind of torture."

My eyes met Ty's. "I was pretty fucked up after it happened. I didn't want to leave my apartment; I didn't want to see anyone who was connected to him in any way. I lived in seclusion until Lincoln forced me out of the house one day and took me to see a therapist. She saved my life . . . truly, she did. I haven't had that dream since I moved to Montana . . . until tonight."

Ty looked down and then back up at me. "Do you think it was because I was here?"

My eyes widened in shock. "No. Not at all."

Honestly, I had no idea if his presence had anything to do with the dream's returning, but I certainly wouldn't put that on Ty.

"Is it because you've moved on?"

"I haven't moved on with anyone, and even if I had, I wouldn't feel guilty. I know now I deserve happiness, and I know John would've wanted that."

"But you *have* moved on. You're with Channing."

Laughing, I rolled my eyes. "I'm not with Channing. For fuck's sake, Ty, I went out to dinner and to a bar with him. Did a bit of dancing, and that was it."

Something that looked like anger flashed over his face.

I studied him, narrowing my eyes. "Did Channing tell you something happened between us? Because nothing did."

"You kissed him."

I jerked my hands out of his, causing a sharp pain in my lower back. "How do you know that?"

He shrugged. "I saw you kissing him; then he followed you into your house."

"Are you stalking me or something? Oh my God, was that *you* on the horse that night?"

Ty rubbed the back of his neck, then stood and walked over to the fire. "I happened to see you that night when he brought you home—that's all."

"Well, you obviously only saw part of what happened," I said, slowly getting up from my sitting position while I ignored the pain and walked over to him. He put a few more logs on the fire. "What you didn't see was him leaving a few minutes later, after he used the restroom. Nothing happened."

"You don't owe me any explanations, Kaylee."

I stared at him. Confusion whipped around my head, making me feel dizzy. I wanted to hit him. This man was going to drive me insane. One moment he acted jealous; the next he acted like he didn't care. Which one was it? Because I was sort of getting whiplash here.

"Then why did you bring it up, Ty?"

"I was only trying to help, by telling you it's okay to move on."

With a scoff, I grabbed his arm and made him turn around to face me. "I don't need you or anyone telling me that. I know it's okay to move on. The only problem is, the guy I want to move on with has zero interest in me."

Ty's blue eyes turned dark with lust, and a bubble of desire flitted through my stomach. I wanted him to kiss me more than I wanted my next breath.

Something in the air changed between us, and I knew he felt it as much as I did.

He took a step closer, his lips parted slightly, his eyes focused on my mouth, then up to my eyes and back to my mouth.

Kiss me, Ty! For the love of all things, kiss me!

Right as he leaned in closer, there was a loud cracking sound on the front porch.

Ty and I both turned to look. He moved away from me and walked to the front door while I closed my eyes and cursed internally. The universe was trying to tell me something. Maybe it was time I actually listened to it.

"Holy shit!" he gasped.

"What? What's wrong?" I asked, making my way over to him.

"I don't know how much snow has fallen, but the weight of the snow on your porch roof caused part of it to collapse."

"Collapse!" I shouted, looking out the window. He was right: the steps were now blocked with part of the porch roof and more snow than I had seen in a long time. "Well, shit, it's a good thing I haven't bought the place from Lincoln yet."

Ty turned and looked at me, a smile on his face. He looked so young and carefree in that moment that I couldn't help but smile back. Then we both laughed. Actual belly laughs at the absurdity of our situation.

It felt so amazing to share this moment with him. It reminded me of when we had found out Lincoln was pregnant. Ty had hugged me and spun me around, both of us giddy, knowing that we knew something neither Lincoln nor Brock knew yet. Lincoln had been only a few weeks pregnant and had fainted in the hospital after Brock had been hurt when a bull charged him after a ride for a charity at a local rodeo. They'd run a pregnancy test, and it had come back positive. I might have told the hospital a little white lie that I was Lincoln's sister. That was how Ty and I found out about the baby.

I had so much fun with him that afternoon. We talked about the baby and came up with different ideas of how to break the news to Lincoln. We went on about how excited we were to see Lincoln's shocked face. I had felt that connection between us and thought Ty had as well. It didn't take long before he was pushing me away from him as he fell back into the routine of making his silly insults and pretending we hadn't had another amazing connection.

Just like then, I knew it wouldn't be long before he returned to his normal behavior and I became the annoying girl whom he couldn't stand to be around.

I turned away and walked over to my phone to check the time. I had a message from Lincoln I'd somehow missed.

"Lincoln wants to make sure we haven't killed each other."

"Why is she up so late?" Ty asked, making his way toward the kitchen. Our little moment appeared to be over.

"Probably the baby."

I typed back that we were fine and I was feeling better. She didn't reply, which told me she had fallen back asleep.

As I slowly made my way to the kitchen, I took in a deep breath to prepare myself for things to go back to the way they were only hours ago. Things between Ty and me were civil, and I wanted to keep it that way. I wasn't in the mood to argue or spit back and forth with him. I was cold and tired. If he wanted to pretend that he hadn't almost kissed me only minutes ago, then so would I. I'd continue to play the avoidance game like a master.

"Do you want some tea? I saw you had some in your pantry."

I rubbed the sides of my arms to warm myself up some. "Hot tea sounds good. How are you going to light the stove?" I asked.

He held up the candle lighter I had bought from Etsy and winked at me. My breath stalled in my throat, and I gave him a nod. The light from the lantern cast a glow that made him look even more handsome than he was. It wasn't fair. I probably looked like shit, and he still looked deliciously hot in the shadows.

Once he had the stove going, he poured some of the bottled waters into the teapot and put it on the fire.

"When do you think the power will come back on?"

"I don't know," he said, rubbing the back of his neck and trying not to look worried but doing a piss-poor job of it. "Probably not until at least midmorning."

I sighed and looked at the chair. The thought of sitting again made me wince.

"You need help sitting down?"

I shook my head. "No, it's feeling better. I'm sure I just bruised it. It's just tender."

He nodded.

Then the silence returned, before Ty broke it just as the water started to boil. "So you're going to buy this place, huh?"

Smiling, I replied, "Yeah, Lincoln clearly doesn't need it. I thought maybe I could turn the little room in the barn into a workroom."

"For editing?" he asked, clearly puzzled by that.

I laughed. "No, for setting up my painting studio and such."

Ty paused for a moment and turned to me. "So it was you who painted that painting in the bathroom?"

"Yeah."

His brows pulled in some, and he regarded me for a moment or two. "Kaylee, I didn't know you could paint."

With a shrug and a half-hearted chuckle, I replied, "I can't. That's just something I've always dabbled in. A little hobby, if you will. I like staying busy."

Ty poured the water into the two mugs he had gotten out and handed me one. I wrapped my hands around it and groaned in pure delight.

"So warm."

He grinned and did the same. "How long have you been painting?"

"I don't know—since I was around ten, maybe? Once my parents saw I was interested in it and that it kept me busy for hours, they had an entire room set up with easels and paints of every different type. It was a good way to keep me out of their sight."

He tilted his head as he tried to read my expression. "Did you take lessons?"

Laughing, I shook my head. "Hell no. I just painted what I saw. Sort of like authors who write what they see in their minds. They use words; I use pictures. It's an outlet for me."

"Has my mother seen that painting?" he asked.

I thought about it. "No, I don't think so. I just finished it a few weeks back and hung it up. It's a picture of you, Brock, Tanner, and Beck. I've seen pictures of him at your folks' place. Your mom was telling me a story about you three older brothers riding out one day toward the mountain range, and how Tanner had begged y'all to let him go. She said the three of you pretended not to notice him behind you, but it was clear you knew he was there."

Ty's breath hitched. "I remember that day like it was yesterday." He looked into his tea, his smile fading just a bit. "I'm surprised my mom talked about Beck. She normally doesn't."

"I asked her about him."

Ty's eyes snapped up to mine. "You did?"

Taking a sip of the tea, I let the warmth slide down my throat and heat my entire body. "Yes. I know what it's like to hold something inside, to fear talking about it, because then it becomes too real again. It didn't take me long to see that your mom never spoke about Beck. Your daddy does when it's just him. He's mentioned Beck a few times, and I see the hurt in his eyes. Tanner talks about him too. You, Brock, and your mama, y'all keep it all inside. You both take after her in that sense. Keeping your feelings inside, locked up nice and tight where they're safe. Where the vulnerability can't get to you."

Ty stared at me for the longest moment. Then he chuckled.

"I think there's just something about you, Kaylee, that makes people open up. You have something very special inside of you, and they see that."

"What about you?"

He huffed. "What about me?"

"That day, in the kitchen . . . you wouldn't have taken them. You know that, right?"

His entire body went stiff. His blue eyes turned sad, but he never broke the contact his gaze had with mine. "I'm not so sure you're right. I almost did, but you did a helluva good job at distracting me."

I smiled, feeling my cheeks heat as I glanced down at my tea and then back to him. My smile faded, and I could practically feel my heart beating out of my chest. "You wouldn't have taken them, Ty." My voice was barely a whisper.

In that moment, he looked so lost and confused. A million different emotions swept over his face before he finally swallowed hard and shrugged. "I know my desire to *not* take them was stronger than the urge I had to take them."

The corners of my mouth rose slightly, and I nodded.

He took another drink of his tea and then stood. "I think I'm going to go stoke the fire and climb back under the covers. You need help going to the restroom again? I wouldn't mind taking another peek at those cute little lacy panties of yours." He waggled his brows before walking over to the sink.

"I think one peep show is plenty for you in a twenty-four-hour period. I'm fine. But if you want to sleep on the sofa with me, you can."

He looked like I had just jabbed him with the hot poker he used on the firewood. "Um, I mean, if you're cold I can. Otherwise, I'm fine."

"It's freezing in here, and I'll be honest: I slept better with your body next to mine."

Oh. My. God. What had I just done? I could practically feel my cheeks turning six shades of pink. I lied—okay, maybe it wasn't all a lie. I *had* slept better in Ty's arms.

I'm pathetic, I thought. *I can't seem to let this man go.* It looked like I was ready to use any excuse to have him near me.

"Um. Okay, yeah."

I slowly stood; the pain in my tailbone was easing up. "Maybe I'll take a few more ibuprofen also."

Ty quickly got a bottle of water from the refrigerator and handed it to me, then a couple of pills.

"Do you need me to put the ice pack between us?"

Oh, man, I really could've come back with a smart-ass answer about him needing to have it there to keep his dick down, but I let it go. I swallowed both pills and shook my head. "We didn't put it back in the freezer, but I think I'm okay."

He nodded and gave me a befuddled, possibly anxious look. Why did sleeping with me on the sofa make him so nervous? Maybe Ty really did have feelings for me, and he didn't know how to deal with them? It wasn't a secret he had been a player, but from what I'd seen the last few months, he'd hardly gone out with anyone.

There was the girl from the bar the other night, though. That memory caused my stomach to feel a little sick.

I followed him into the living room and watched as he messed with the logs and got the fire going again. He put two more on the fire and then looked back at the sofa. Was that hesitation?

"You get on first—that way you don't have to crawl over me," I said. I couldn't help the small smile that was tugging at the corners of my mouth. I was rather enjoying this side of Ty Shaw. Unsure. Nervous. Scared, maybe? From what I'd heard from other women in town, the man knew his way around a woman's body, but the thought of being near me seemed to make him want to run out into the snowstorm.

I frowned at the thought. Hadn't he almost kissed me earlier? And what about his issues with Channing? Because thinking I was with another guy had clearly bothered him.

Ugh. I needed to stop with all of this. Why did I let my emotions get so out of whack around this man?

"I mean, if it makes you uncomfortable, then you don't have to. I understand," I said, giving him an out, although reluctantly.

He frowned at me and released an exhale before turning away. That was the Ty I was used to. The one who frowned, scoffed, rolled his eyes. He was back. It had taken a bit longer for him to show up, but I knew eventually he'd be here.

I moved toward the sofa and carefully sat down, wincing at the pain. I tucked the pillow between my legs and lay on my side so that I could feel the heat of the fireplace on my face. I willed my breathing to be normal and steady. I didn't hear any movement from Ty, and I wasn't about to open my eyes and look. For all I knew, he'd taken me up on my offer and was on the floor already, sound asleep.

It seemed like an eternity before I finally heard him move. My curiosity would be the death of me: I opened an eye to peek, only to see him sitting in the chair, gazing into the fire. He looked as lost and confused as I felt.

I closed my eyes and prayed that when morning came, Tanner or Brock would have cleared a path and Ty could leave right away.

I needed him to leave. For my own sanity, I needed him gone.

Chapter Eleven

Ty

I knew the moment she finally fell asleep. Her breathing slowed and evened out, and her body relaxed. I could see her perfectly, the light from the fire casting a beautiful glow that seemed to make her even more stunning, if that was possible.

My gut ached as her words replayed in my head.

"I mean, if it makes you uncomfortable, then you don't have to. I understand."

I hadn't said anything in reply. Not a damn word. I watched her get settled on the sofa and stood there like a complete idiot. I'd almost kissed her earlier and then pretended it hadn't happened. Then again, so had she. But what had she meant about the guy she wanted to move on with not wanting her? I knew she wasn't talking about Channing; I saw the way that asshole looked at her. He'd climb into her bed in a heartbeat if given the chance.

My fingers jerked through my hair as I took in a deep breath and then slowly blew it out. I focused on the fire, unable to sleep. The early morning was knocking on the door, and I prayed like hell that Brock or Tanner would be making his way to Kaylee's place once the sun came up.

Kaylee moaned, causing me to look over at her. She pulled the quilt up farther, then trembled.

"Fuck," I whispered as I stood and put another log on. Then I carefully made my way onto the sofa, making sure I didn't bump her tailbone.

It was like she knew I was there. Once I was lying down, I started to pull her body to mine to warm her up. She rolled over, facing me on the sofa.

Why in the hell did she have such a deep fucking couch?

Her hands went to my chest, and I stilled. The corners of those pretty little lips of hers rose into a smile, and she whispered my name.

"Ty."

It sounded more like a plea than anything else. Then she nestled in closer, her body pressed against mine. She was still asleep and had no idea what she was doing to me.

My cock instantly reacted when she threw her leg over mine. If I pulled her closer, my dick would be pressed against her pelvis. I closed my eyes and prayed for strength, or prayed for her to realize what she was doing and put some more distance between our bodies.

Her hand gripped my T-shirt, and she moaned.

I closed my eyes and fought for breath. This woman had no fucking idea how hard it was to keep my hands off her. One touch, one kiss, and I knew I would lose all self-control.

Then she moved closer, and my cock pressed into her, making her hips move against me. I was seriously regretting my decision to not put my boxers back on. I fought to stay still, to not press into her heat.

Then she moved again.

Holy shit. She was trying to get on top of me.

"Kaylee," I whispered. "Please wake up."

The feel of her body pressed to mine was seriously fucking with my mind. I wanted her like I had never wanted anything in my entire life.

"Mmm," she said, moving more, grinding her pussy against my hard dick.

"Fuck it," I said as I moved, pulling her body on top of mine.

Her eyes opened and our gazes locked. She was on me, her legs straddling me, her pussy pressed down on my hard-as-fuck cock.

I swallowed hard, not sure what in the hell I should do. Then she did the one thing I so desperately wanted her to do, and the one thing I so desperately needed her *not* to do.

She pressed harder against me, rocked herself on my dick, and pressed her mouth to mine.

Fucking hell.

My heart slammed against the wall of my chest. Her lips were as soft as I had remembered. She tasted like mint tea and honey. Our tongues moved slowly at first, until I lost control and laced my fingers in her blonde hair, deepening the kiss. Kaylee rocked faster, causing my cock to throb with the need to push inside her.

I pulled my mouth from hers. "Your tailbone."

"Hurts like a bitch. Please don't talk. Just keep doing what you're doing."

Her mouth was back on mine; then her hand trailed down my chest and slipped inside my sweatpants.

If she touched me, so help me God, I was flipping her over and fucking her.

Then I heard a truck door shut and voices outside.

I pulled my mouth from Kaylee's. "Someone's here."

Her hand instantly came out of my pants, and I carefully moved her to the side as I got off the sofa and went to look out the front window.

Fuck me. I was hard as a steel beam, wearing sweatpants, and my family was outside, interrupting our moment.

I wasn't sure if I was pissed or happy as hell. I was leaning toward the first but knew the latter would be the better outcome. My father and Tanner were there, both of them looking at the part of the porch roof that was covering the steps.

I moved to the door and opened it, letting in a blast of cold air. "Well, if it isn't the rescue squad!" I said, trying to make my voice even. On the inside, I was a fucking mess, though. I knew it would take months for this to fade from my memory, if it ever did.

With a quick look to my left, I saw Kaylee sitting on the sofa, a blanket wrapped around her body and a look on her face that nearly made me fall to my knees. She slowly stood. Our eyes met, and I couldn't tell if what I was seeing was regret, embarrassment, or hurt. All I knew was, I was the cause of it . . . again.

I'd let my weakness for her take control and nearly made a decision I knew we would both regret. Or at least one of us would. The moment she found out how wrong I was for her, she'd wish it would have never happened.

"My dad and Tanner are here."

Kaylee forced a smile and nodded as she walked past me, still in obvious pain, and up the stairs, not saying a word.

If I had thought that night at the bar had been hard, this was a thousand times worse, because in my heart, I had wanted to be with her more than I had ever wanted anything in my life.

Chapter Twelve

*T*Y

One month later

I stood in the middle of the pasture outside the high school with fifteen high school students, all of them focused completely on me. I was grateful for the mild weather today, a balmy sixty degrees, which meant the kids were all out here in jeans and T-shirts, and I still had on a jacket.

"Bull management and nutrition is essential in the development of bulls, especially bulls being bred to perform in the PBR."

Hank Williams raised his hand. I liked this kid—he was named after one of my favorite singers, after all—but he was starting to wear my patience thin today.

"What about fertility?" Hank asked. "The bull has to play a major role in that?"

I nodded. "Yes, but today we are talking about nutrition. Not the bulls . . ."

My voice trailed off.

"Having sex?" Katelyn Murphy added with a giggle.

That made them all laugh. Crossing my arms over my chest, I couldn't help but notice that two of the girls, Missy and Gina, were staring at me. I was pretty damn sure they'd signed up for this class only to ogle me. I was really hoping they would move their attention to Ron, the ripped senior football player who I knew for a fact had a thing for Gina but was too shy to ask her out.

"Are you all done going through puberty? Can we move on?"

The timer on my phone went off right then, alerting me that it was time to send them all back to the campus. This was an off-site program. Once a month I met with the kids during their last period, which was their 4-H class. I knew Mr. Haven appreciated the break, and I was pretty positive he and Ms. Perry, the senior English teacher, were hooking up and taking advantage of the forty-minute time slot with no students. It was, after all, Ms. Perry's off period.

"That's it for today. I'll see you guys Saturday morning, and don't be late. You know how much it pisses me off."

"You're not supposed to swear in front of us," James Walker said, a smile on his face.

"That's not a cussword. Now get the hell out of here. Tell Mr. Haven I'll get the bulls put back up in their pens."

"Bye, Mr. Shaw!" Missy and Gina called out.

I waved but didn't look at them. "Later."

It was the same reply I gave all the kids.

Once I had the two bulls our ranch had donated to the school put up and away, I made my way back to the school parking lot. I took my time, since I knew the kids took a while to file out of school and get to their cars.

My phone vibrated with a message. I pulled it out to look at it. My stomach dropped a bit.

Kaylee.

I hadn't talked to her since the morning of the snowstorm. She'd gone to the doctor, and it turned out she'd only had a bruised tailbone. I'd found out from my mother, who had been over to her place a few times since that morning. I hated that I was avoiding her, and everyone knew I was. Kaylee included. I normally saw her around town, but I had purposely avoided the places I knew I might run into her. I had let myself get dangerously close to giving in to my need for her that morning, and I couldn't do that again. Not when I knew I wouldn't be able to give her more, and Kaylee deserved more.

I drew in a deep breath and opened the text message.

Kaylee: A package came to my place addressed to you, it's too big for me to bring it over to you.

With a frown, I stared at her message. A package? I hadn't ordered anything.

Me: Who is it from?

Kaylee: I'm not the freaking post office. Come get it and you'll be sure to find out.

Okay, so she was indeed pissed at me for avoiding her. Best to keep it short and sweet.

Me: I'll be by in a bit to pick it up.

She didn't reply, which was fine by me. I wasn't in the mood to deal with bickering back and forth on text messages. The memories of that morning before my dad and Tanner showed up still rocked me to my core.

Once I got into my truck and started it, I called Brock.

"Hey, big brother, how was the class today?"

I groaned. "It would be fine if they stuck to the lesson for the day."

He laughed.

I added, "Did you happen to order something big that might have gone to Kaylee's house?"

"No. Let me ask Lincoln if she did. Are you heading back to the ranch now?"

"Well, I had another errand to run but thought if the package was yours, it might be better for you to go and get it."

"She's still pissed at you?" Brock asked.

"Of course she is—it's Kaylee we're talking about."

He sighed. "Ty, the two of you need to talk about what almost happened."

It was my turn to sigh as I scrubbed my hand down my face, then stroked the stubble on my chin. I hadn't felt like shaving this morning, so I had a heavy five-o'clock shadow going on.

I'd told Brock about what had almost happened between me and Kaylee, and about how, by the grace of God, our father and Tanner had shown up and stopped anything from progressing between us.

"Nothing happened, so why talk about it?"

"You do know that sometimes you're a real asshole?"

"Yes, I do, and that's why it's better to keep my relationship with Kaylee as nothing more than friends."

"And that's what you truly want?"

No.

"Yes."

"You always were a terrible liar, Ty."

"Can you just ask your wife about the package?"

I heard the screen door open and shut. "Hey, baby, did you order anything big that might have gone to Kaylee's house?"

Blayze was in the background, laughing. He and Lincoln must have been outside enjoying the nicer weather.

"Is Morgan sleeping?"

"Yeah, she's been taking longer naps lately. It's been kind of nice, I'm not gonna lie."

I chuckled.

"Lincoln said she hasn't ordered anything."

"Shit," I mumbled. "Did you want to head on over and pick it up?"

"Who's it from?"

"I don't know—she wouldn't tell me. Said something about her not being the post office."

He laughed. The fact that he found any of this amusing pissed me off.

"I'm glad you think this is funny, Brock."

"Sorry, dude, but it is. If only you would just—"

"I've got to go. Talk to you later."

I hung up before he could say anything more about talking shit out, then tossed my phone down. "Shit."

I put the truck in drive and headed back to the ranch. When I got to the driveway that led down to Kaylee's house, I almost didn't make the turn, my nerves getting the best of me.

"Stop being a pussy," I said as I floored it and raced down the driveway. I knew it might be something Dad had ordered for the ranch.

After parking right in front of her place, I got out of the truck and took a look at the newly repaired roof. Lincoln had offered to pay to fix it, but Brock had said Kaylee told her no: she had already committed to buying the house, and it was hers to fix. I admired the shit out of her for taking responsibility for it.

I walked up the steps and looked around at the plants on the porch and smiled. What was it about women and the first signs of spring that made them start putting flowers out?

Sitting next to the door was, in fact, a large package with my name on it. From a saddle company in Billings.

"Damn you, Tanner."

There was no doubt in my mind that my little brother had sent this to Kaylee's house on purpose. I picked up the box and carried it down to my truck. It was large and awkward, and I almost fell twice. My leg was bugging me for some reason today, and the dull ache seemed to show up anytime I went a few days not thinking about the accident. It was like a bitch slap to remind me yet again of my past.

After putting the saddle into the back of my truck, I went to get in but stopped. It would be pretty damn shitty of me to leave and not even let Kaylee know I had gotten the package.

With a frustrated sigh, I shut the door to my truck and walked back up to her door. I knocked, but she didn't answer. Glancing back toward the barn, I saw her BMW SUV parked there, so I knew she was home. I knocked again, this time harder.

Nothing.

I pulled my phone out of my pocket and called her.

"Hello?"

She sounded like she had me on speakerphone.

"Why do you sound like you're in a can?"

"Probably because I'm trying to stop this leak."

"What leak?"

"It's nothing."

I rolled my eyes, then reached for the door. It was unlocked.

"You really need to lock your front door."

"Are you in my house? I didn't invite you in, Ty Shaw."

"Clearly you did by leaving your front door unlocked," I said, making my way up the steps.

"Damn it, Ty. Go away."

I hung up the phone and pushed it back into my jeans pocket. I walked into her bedroom and straight into her bathroom. I'm not going to lie: I was hoping she'd be in nothing more than those lace panties again.

Instead, what I found was Kaylee sitting on the floor, trying to use a wrench to stop the spray of water coming from the hose she had hooked up from the wall to her bidet.

"Shit, I forgot to hook that up for you," I said, trying to take the wrench from her.

"I got it!" she shouted, water now spraying both of us.

"Obviously, sweetheart, you don't. Let me have it."

Kaylee shot me a dirty look. "I'm not your sweetheart. You can leave, Ty. I've got this."

"Kaylee, will you just let me help you with that?"

She looked up at me, pure determination in her eyes. "I can handle this. I don't need your help."

"Clearly you do. You're going to flood this whole bathroom, and then it's going to leak downstairs, and you haven't even let the ink dry on the contract from buying this place yet."

Kaylee tried harder. If she ended up breaking it, things were going to go from bad to worse.

"Shit! Come on, you stupid thing!"

"Just let me help."

"I've got it!"

She jerked again, and again it didn't move. I could see the frustration beginning to build on her face.

"For fuck's sake, will you just stop being afraid to admit that you need help and let me get it tightened? You're being childish."

She let go of the wrench to say something to me, and I grabbed it. "Let me get in there."

When she moved, she shot me a look that said a million and one things, number one being to fuck off.

When I got the water to stop spewing, I stood and wiped my face off with my shirt. I was frustrated as fuck that she just couldn't have moved over and let me fix the damn thing.

"I don't understand why you're so afraid to ask for help."

Her fists balled up at her sides, and her face turned red as a tomato. Oh, hell. I just poked a little too hard at the bees' nest.

"I'm not afraid to ask for help! My whole life, I've never *had* to ask for help, because no one ever let me do a fucking thing! I'm capable of doing things, you know!"

This was a side of Kaylee I'd never witnessed before. The girl on the verge of losing her shit.

She threw up her hands and let out a frustrated scream, causing me to take a step away from her. If I wasn't careful, she might start swinging.

"It got stuck, that's all. If you'd given me a minute and let me think, instead of trying to do it for me, I would've gotten it. I've managed to do plenty on my own, and I don't need . . . I don't need . . ."

I smirked, and I had no idea why. But I couldn't stop myself from poking her a little more. "You don't need what, Miss Independent?"

Tears filled her eyes, and I instantly felt like a dick. A big fucking dick who needed to have his ass kicked.

"I don't need *you*. I can do this if you would just have faith in me, John! Why can't you just believe in us!" She shook her head. "I mean, in *me*! Why can't you just believe in me?"

She turned around and wrapped her arms around her body, clearly trying to keep from crying. Then she started to breathe, deeply. One deep breath in, one long one out. I knew that technique all too well. She was trying to keep herself from losing her shit. It was something I had done a number of times after the accident. My physical therapist was all about breathing techniques to calm yourself down and to relax the mind.

I slowly walked up to her and put my hands on her shoulders. Her body tensed. After turning her to face me, I placed my finger under her chin and lifted her face to meet my gaze. There were so many things I wanted to say to her. How much she meant to me. How much I wanted to hold her in my arms and tell her everything was okay.

But how could I, when my own mind was filled with so many doubts?

"I have faith in you, Kaylee. Please don't ever doubt that."

She was one of the strongest women I'd ever met. The fact that she'd picked up and left her family to start a new life in Montana alone showed what an incredible woman she was. A single tear slipped free and made a slow trail down her cheek. It killed me to see her cry. I didn't like knowing I was the cause of that tear.

This was why she was better off without me. She deserved someone who didn't make her cry or piss her off.

Another tear fell, and I used the pad of my thumb to wipe it away.

Kaylee licked her lips and gazed up at me like all I had to do was kiss her and everything would be all right. And it would, for a little while. We'd forget all the shit in the world for a little bit. Get lost in each other. Then reality would set in. She'd see the side of me that no one ever saw, that no one knew. The side that hid all the pain and hurt. The doubt and loneliness.

If I showed her that side of me, what would she do?

I wasn't about to open myself up for more hurt to find that answer.

"I'll go ahead and go. I'm sorry I upset you."

Before I took a few steps back, I kissed her forehead and turned to leave, but I stopped and looked at her once more and said, "I'm not John."

She sucked in a breath and took a step away from me. "Wh-what?"

"You called me John."

"I . . . I didn't mean . . . I didn't mean to call you that."

With a nod, I turned and headed out of her room and down the stairs.

When I reached for the front door, her voice stopped me.

"Wait. Don't go."

I closed my eyes. I knew if I stayed, and she asked me to do anything, I'd do it. Whatever she asked, I'd fall at her feet and beg her to let me in. And with the way she had been looking at me a few moments ago, I knew what she would be asking.

Her hand gently lay over mine on the doorknob, causing me to open my eyes and look down at her.

"I'm asking you to stay."

"Why?" My voice was rough and broken sounding.

"Because I need you, Ty."

I shook my head. "No, you don't need someone like me, Kaylee. I'm pretty fucked up."

Her teeth dug into her lower lip as she looked down at the floor and then back up at me. Her eyes were filled with the same heat as that night at the Blue Moose. I'd almost taken her that night, but the searing kiss she'd given me had pulled me out of the haze this woman seemed to be able to put me in. It made me realize that Kaylee had the power to completely destroy me if she wanted to. I couldn't think around her, and I needed to have a clear head.

She removed her hand from mine, and I tried hard not to let the disappointment show on my face. I expected her to step aside and let my sorry ass leave.

Instead, she stepped between me and the door and pulled her wet T-shirt over her head.

My eyes drifted down her beautiful body. Her nipples were straining against her white lace bra, making my cock instantly hard. I'd never in my life wanted a woman as desperately as I wanted Kaylee. Those blue eyes seemed to penetrate straight into my fucking soul.

"Kaylee," I managed to get out, my voice sounding shaky, like my self-control was balancing on a thin wire.

Then her hands went to her sweatpants, and she pushed them down.

"Me fucking you isn't going to fix anything," I said, looking directly into her eyes.

"Then I'll fuck you, because it might not fix anything, but I'm tired of wanting you. Needing you."

A low growl formed at the back of my throat as she said that while pushing her bra straps down her shoulders, placing those perfect tits on display for me.

I shook my head and took a step back.

The fight was over when she shimmied out of the lace panties.

My self-control shredded into a million tiny pieces as I took two steps toward her and pressed my mouth to hers.

Her arms wrapped around my neck, and I picked her up, her legs instinctively wrapping around me.

"Yes, Ty. God, yes," she panted.

This was wrong. So fucking wrong, and at the same time, so damn right.

One thing I knew for sure: this woman deserved to be in her own bed, and not fucked against the front door of her house.

I turned and headed toward the stairs, then raced up them. She held on to me tightly, her body pressed against mine. The heat between us electric.

After walking back into her bedroom, I stopped long enough to shut the door. It wasn't like anyone would be walking in on us, but you never knew when my family would magically appear.

Slowly, I laid her on the bed, then reached behind me and pulled my shirt over my head, tossing it to the floor. "I'm no good for you."

"So you keep saying, but so far what I'm feeling from you is very, very good," she replied, giving me a sexy smirk.

"I can't do a relationship, Kaylee, so if you aren't looking for just sex, tell me to stop now, because that's all I can give you. One night. I can only give you one night."

Her eyes moved over the upper part of my body with pure lust. She got on her knees and started to unbuckle my belt, then undid my jeans. I'm pretty sure I stopped breathing momentarily as I watched her every movement.

"Kaylee."

"Stop talking, Ty."

She pushed my jeans and boxers down all at once, causing my cock to spring out. She licked her lips, her eyes never leaving my dick, and my knees shook.

Then, before I could even get my thoughts straight, she took me in her mouth—and my whole body jerked in response to her heat.

That perfect mouth wrapped around my dick, and she moaned like I was the best thing she'd ever tasted.

I closed my eyes and prayed I wouldn't lose my load in her mouth right that second. It had been too damn long since I'd been with a woman, and only one woman had been on my mind for months. Now the subject of my thoughts was on her knees, sucking me off, and it was taking Herculean strength to not blow my load in record time.

"Fucking hell," I whispered, slipping my fingers into her blonde hair. She wrapped her hand around my shaft and took me slow, like she was savoring the taste of me on her tongue. I groaned and let her do what she wanted. I needed her to slow down—hell, I actually needed her to stop altogether. But this felt so damn good. Too damn good. Sinful, almost.

Grabbing her hair, I tugged her off my cock.

"Fuck, baby, I'm going to come if you don't stop, and this can't be over before I even get started with you."

She looked up at me and smiled as she crawled back onto her bed. I kicked off my boots, then the jeans and boxers she'd pulled down, and joined her on the bed.

"My turn," I said in a husky voice. I needed to take back some semblance of control here so I could slow this train down and enjoy her body. Every last inch of it.

Kaylee bit down on that lip and spread herself open to me. Her confidence in bed was a huge turn-on. I loved that she knew exactly what she wanted and wasn't shy about it. At all.

I knew I should have stopped us; she deserved more than a casual fuck. But I couldn't deny myself. Tasting her, fucking her, making love to her. I wanted all of it. All of her, even if just for one night. If I could get just one taste of her, one feel of her, it would appease the want that seemed to grip my chest every time she was around.

Just. One. Taste.

The moment my tongue swept over her, though, I knew I would never be satisfied with any other woman again.

Kaylee Holden was going to destroy me in one night.

"Oh God!" she panted, her fingers digging into my scalp, pulling me.

I licked and sucked, my hands holding her hips in place as she attempted to get closer, only to draw away when her orgasm became too much.

Ultimately, she gave in and welcomed everything I was giving her. She cried out my name, and I freaking loved the sound of it falling from her lips as she tumbled over the edge with her moans and whimpers of pleasure. It was like music to my ears.

I'd always paid attention when giving a woman pleasure. What did they like, what made them come harder? What sounds did they make as they were getting ready to come? It wasn't for my own pleasure, though. It was for theirs. But with Kaylee, her sounds did something to my chest. To my beating heart, which seemed to beat faster and harder as she cried out my name.

With soft kisses placed on her velvet skin, I moved myself up her body. I took one nipple into my mouth as I twisted and pulled the other, causing her to whimper my name again. God, the way she responded to every single thing I did to her. A soft moan, a whimper, my name whispered from her lips. I fucking loved all of it.

"How long has it been, princess?"

Her eyes met mine, and for a moment, everything seemed to pause. I was stunned I had used an endearment on her, and she seemed equally stunned. I'd never in my life called a woman *princess*, or *honey*, or *baby* while having sex with them. But Kaylee was different. She *was* a princess. Royalty, in my eyes. Someone who deserved a man who treated her like the queen she was. I'd try damn hard to be that man for her tonight.

"A long time. John was my last."

My eyes widened in shock, and I started to back away. She hadn't had sex with any man in over three years? I was positive she could hear the pounding in my chest.

Kaylee reached for me, drawing me back to her. "I want you, Ty. Please don't turn me away again. Please don't do that to me."

Her pleading words were my undoing. Every sense of logic I had drained right from my brain, and I moved up her body, pressing my mouth to hers. We both moaned as our tongues intertwined. Her kiss exactly how I had remembered it from the two other times we'd kissed.

It was addicting. A drug that I felt myself giving in to. Something I knew I would crave the rest of my damn life.

When she wrapped her legs around my body, she urged me to push inside her. I positioned myself at her hot, wet entrance. Ever so slowly and carefully, I pushed inside—instantly realizing my freaking mistake. The feel of her heat and tightness around my cock nearly had me coming on the spot.

I froze and was about to tell her we had forgotten protection.

She placed her hands on the sides of my face, drawing my gaze to hers. "Do not stop, please."

"I don't have a condom on, Kaylee."

"Please don't stop."

I closed my eyes and groaned. It was irresponsible for both of us to do this, but in the moment, I wasn't sure either of us was thinking clearly. "Fuck, you're so tight."

Her hands moved to my shoulders, where she dug her nails into me when I pushed in more. The last thing I wanted to do was hurt her.

"Are you . . . are you okay?" I managed to ask.

"Yes. Yes, I'm fine. Ty, please move. I need you to move."

With my face buried in her chest, I groaned. "Can't. Feels so good. I'm going to come if I move."

Her body shook as she giggled. "That would really be a bummer, because I was sort of hoping for at least another orgasm."

I lifted my head and met her gaze. How was it that each time I looked at her, she left me breathless with her beauty? It was like she grew more beautiful as the days went by. The most beautiful woman I'd ever seen, and would ever see, and I was currently balls deep inside her. If I died right now, I would die a happy man, knowing that my life would never be this amazing again.

"Just one more?" I asked, one brow lifted.

Her eyes narrowed, and she gave me a look that said she was about to throw out a challenge. One that I knew I was up for.

"Are you saying you can deliver *more* than one more mind-blowing orgasm?"

I pushed in farther, making her suck in a breath, then let out a delicious-sounding moan.

"Oh, baby, I can deliver as many orgasms as you can stand."

With a wink as her legs wrapped around my body tighter, she replied, "Let the counting begin."

Chapter Thirteen

KAYLEE

On my knees, my hands gripping the sheets as Ty took me from behind, I was on my way to my fourth—yes, *fourth*—orgasm. The man was like the damn Energizer Bunny. His stamina was unbelievable. The way he knew how to make love. How to fuck. My God, it was mind blowing. I'd never had sex this hot. One minute he was sweet and gently making love to me, pulling a long, blissful orgasm out of me; then he was flipping me over and fucking me from behind, building up another orgasm that I knew was going to pick me up and throw me right on over the ledge.

"Ty!" I cried out. "I'm so close. God, I need . . . I need . . ."

He leaned over and kissed my back while he moved his hand to my clit. I wasn't sure what he did—pinched my clit, rubbed it? Hell, whatever he'd done, I fell. Hard.

Stars exploded in the room, and I thought for sure the bed had spun out of control. I was having another orgasm, this one with my entire body shaking. I could feel my insides contracting and squeezing his cock. What was it about sex with Ty that made everything ten times more intense?

"Fuuuck. I'm going to come," Ty said in a gravelly voice.

Then he pulled out, and I whimpered in protest.

"Turn over," he commanded. I quickly did as he asked.

He pushed back inside me, and it dawned on me what he was doing. He wanted to come while he looked into my eyes. His gaze met mine—and I couldn't believe what was happening.

I was about to come *again*. No freaking way.

"Ty, I'm coming again. Sweet Mary, mother of Jesus, you have a magical dick!"

He moved faster, a smile on his face that quickly turned to something more serious as his own orgasm drew near. He laced his fingers with mine and pushed them into the mattress. His weight on mine was both punishing and unbelievably blissful. We moved together in perfect harmony, as if we were made for each other. I knew he felt it too.

I hadn't been with a whole lot of men, but I wasn't inexperienced either. Sex with Ty had ruined me for any other. It had erased all past lovers from my memory forever, and all future ones—well, they were simply screwed. I felt something deep within me that I wasn't sure how to describe. It felt like a part of my soul had been missing, until now.

Then he said my name, and it made my heart feel like it was going to explode inside my chest.

"Kaylee."

God, it was so sweet sounding, yet it fell from his lips like he needed to say it in order to even breathe.

Damn it all to hell. Do not fall for him, Kaylee. You can't.

"Baby, I'm going to come."

"Yes!" I cried out, feeling him get bigger inside of me as my fifth orgasm still rolled through my body.

He pressed his mouth to mine and poured himself inside me.

The moment Ty had first pushed into me, then looked at me with panic in his eyes, I realized he hadn't put on a condom. The feeling of us connected as one, the emotions running rampant in my mind; I couldn't have made him pull out if I'd tried. And truth be told, I didn't care. I wanted him. All of him.

And his words to me before he pushed inside were still rattling around in my head. He wasn't looking for a relationship. This was a one-night thing. He didn't do commitment.

Ty buried his face in my neck, his breaths coming fast and hard. My body was deliciously sore, and I knew I would feel him for days. That made my lower stomach tighten with the need to have more of him. I was greedy like that: it had been years, after all.

When he didn't move off me right away, I ran my fingertips softly over his back. I wanted him to stay like this, stay inside of me forever, but I knew that fantasy wasn't going to come true. Ty was tormented by something, something he hid from everyone he loved. I wanted desperately for him to let me in, but I knew one romp in my bed wasn't going to do it. He would soon drift out of the postsex fog and leave my bedroom, probably never looking back, now that he'd scratched the itch to have sex with me. That thought caused my eyes to build with tears.

Would he go back to treating me like a friend? Would he want to hook up again? God, I hoped so, because my vagina was going to demand more playtime with his dick. I could force myself to ignore my feelings for him. A friends-with-benefits arrangement sounded good to me.

What did I say to him, though, when this night was over? I was afraid of spooking him, and I didn't even know the words to avoid it.

Ty pulled out of me and rolled over, drawing in one long breath after another. I could see his heart beating rapidly with each rise of his chest. I rolled onto my side and placed my hand over his heart. He laid his hand over mine, and that gesture nearly sealed my freaking fate.

"You ruined me for all other men, you know that? Five orgasms?"

He smiled. "I don't like odd numbers."

My brows drew in. "Huh?"

Ty rolled over, giving me a sexy smirk as he pushed me back onto the bed, his dick still semihard as he pushed in and out a few times, then pulled all the way out. "You need one more to make it six."

I laughed. "I'm exhausted, Ty. There is no way—"

His hand went between my legs, and he groaned when he slipped his fingers inside. "That's so fucking hot, my cum between your legs. I've never had sex without a condom before, and I think you might have broken my dick, because I don't think I can ever use protection again."

I chuckled.

Okay. So he oddly didn't seem to be freaked out about the no-condom thing. Had he assumed I was on the pill? It was irresponsible for both of us to let things get carried away like that, but right now, his fingers moving inside me were making all my worries slip away.

"Oh my . . . ," I panted.

"I want to taste you again."

My eyes snapped open. "You just came inside me, Ty. With no condom on—which, by the way, we should probably talk about."

He winked. "We will, after I make you come again."

Moving over me, he pressed his cock against me.

"Have you been bit by some super-sex-powered spider, because there is no way you could be hard again."

Laughing, he pushed inside me. "He hasn't gone down yet."

My eyes widened in pleasant surprise. Oh yes, my vagina was going to need more of his super-powered cock.

Each thrust inside of me had my body aching for another release. This was insane. I was exhausted. My orgasm maker had to be out of order after five.

Then he reached between us, his thumb making soft circles around my clit, and I moaned in delight.

"Come again, Kaylee."

"O-okay," was the only word I managed to get out between heavy pants.

And boy did I come. Ty watched me the entire time. His blue eyes smoldering with something that looked a hell of a lot more intense than lust.

That's when it happened. The moment I knew. With his eyes locked on mine as I whispered his name. "Ty."

He smiled and whispered, "That's it, princess, come for me."

I gave him what he asked for . . . and then stupidly fell head over heels in love with him.

I am so fucked.

When my body had finally settled, Ty pulled out of me. "God, you are so beautiful when you come. It takes my breath away."

He kissed me so passionately I almost wanted to cry, and then he crawled out of my bed.

"Let me get something to clean you up with."

Tears pricked at the back of my eyes. No man had ever treated me like that before. Not even John. Sex with him was good, but when he came, he pulled off the condom, tossed it in the trash, and slipped on his clothes and went about his business while I made my way to the bathroom to clean up. After-sex with him was uneventful. No holding me, no kisses, no telling me how beautiful I looked when I came.

My head was spinning. I needed to stop comparing John with Ty. What in the hell was wrong with me?

Ty walked back into my room from the bathroom, his naked body on full display as if he didn't have a care in the world. I sure as hell didn't mind. He was a beautiful specimen. He had scars on his body that made him even more beautiful. The one on his leg was the most beautiful of all, but I knew in his mind he didn't look at that particular scar the same as he did the others. Maybe some were prizes from bulls he had ridden and beaten, or some that had beaten him. Not that one scar, though. That one spoke volumes. I knew it was a reminder of what he had lost.

His muscles were defined, and the way they moved when *he* did . . . Lord, I could come for the seventh time if I thought too hard about it.

He crawled onto the bed, spread my legs open, and stared at me like my vagina was some masterpiece of art that hung in a famous museum. The way it made me feel was incredible. I should have been embarrassed, but I wasn't. I loved the way Ty looked at me. The way he studied my body, learned what I liked during sex and what I didn't like. Almost as if he was planning on doing all this again. Which I most certainly would be down for.

Then the warm cloth touched my sensitive skin, and I moaned in pure delight. "That feels so good."

He softly cleaned me off, and I relaxed even more. Exhaustion started to kick in, and I fought to keep my eyes open. When I lifted my head and looked at him, he smiled and then winked.

I dropped my head and groaned. The man was not only insanely handsome but was a good lover as well. "My vagina is forever ruined, thanks to you." When I felt his warm breath down there, I held my own. "Yes. Please."

"I don't think so, baby. I don't like odd numbers, Kaylee," he whispered before his tongue licked me like I was his favorite dessert; then he withdrew, leaving me aching and feeling empty. "But I do like the taste of you."

"Tease," I whimpered, trying to lift my hips to meet his mouth.

He moved up next to me, wrapping me in his arms as I snuggled against him. I had figured Ty for the type of guy who would have sex and leave. I wasn't going to complain, though. Instead, I buried my face in his chest and drifted off to sleep.

I woke up at one in the morning, not believing I had fallen asleep in Ty's arms and slept right through dinner and the girls' night out I'd planned with Mary Kate and Lynn. I had met them in a knitting class Ty's mom, Stella, had talked me into going to. And it didn't take long for me to realize a very naked Ty slept next to me. Still. He hadn't left, and I hated how insanely happy that made me feel.

With a smile, I crawled on top of him.

His cock instantly hardened, and the man wasn't even fully awake. A few rubs of my oh-so-ready lady bits against him had him coming fully awake, and fully hard.

Without a word, I moved and adjusted so I could slowly sink down onto him. He felt insanely big this way, and I knew I was going to be sore for days. I didn't care, though. It would be a delicious sort of sore. One that would make me think of every single orgasm this man had pulled from me.

"Ride me, Kaylee."

"No odd numbers, remember?" I said as I slowly ground myself against his body. My clit was pulsing, and I knew if I moved the right way, I'd be coming.

"Right now I don't give a fuck. Ride. Me."

His commanding voice made my entire body tremble. I did as he asked and came in record time. It was almost embarrassing how fast my body reacted to his.

Ty flipped me over and set his own record. He thrust inside me only a few times before he grunted into my neck and came.

The feel of him inside me was one of absolute bliss. Fear gripped my chest when I realized again that I would never want another man besides the one currently still inside me, kissing me softly on the neck, on my jawline, and finally my lips.

When he stopped kissing me, he looked into my eyes. "I guess it *has* been pretty fucking reckless to be having sex without a condom so many times."

"You think?" I asked, a little bit of snark in my voice.

"I saw your birth control pills in your bathroom last month, after you fell and got hurt."

My mouth opened slightly, and I stared at him. "So you assumed I was still taking them?"

"You're a smart woman, Kaylee. If you weren't on the pill, there was no way you'd let me fuck you without a condom. I saw it in your eyes when I first pushed inside you."

I was on the pill, sure, but even I knew there was still a good chance for an unplanned pregnancy, especially when you kept having sex.

"What about diseases?"

"I've been tested, and I haven't been with a woman since last spring."

That little bit of information had my attention. "Really? Why not?"

And who is the bitch so I can track her down and throat punch her?

Okay, I couldn't really ask that last question, but it was burning in my mind nonetheless.

His mouth went back to mine, giving me another mind-blowing kiss. When we finally needed air, he drew back and looked directly into my eyes. "I'm clean, and I wouldn't have done it if I had been unsure."

I swallowed hard. "You didn't answer my question. Why haven't you been with anyone since last spring?"

Ty grinned, and my heart skipped a stupid little beat. "Haven't been interested in anyone since then, and I've been busy."

My brow lifted. Should I have been flattered, knowing Ty had been interested in me enough to have sex with me? Lots and lots of sex? I decided to leave that part of his statement alone.

"Busy?"

Ty laughed. "Yes. Busy. But I am clean, I swear to you. I would never do that to you, princess, and I know you wouldn't do that to me either."

The flutter in my chest radiated through my whole body at his endearment. I couldn't help but wonder if he called other women he took to bed *princess*. Or *baby*. Or *sweetheart*. The thought made me feel sad, so I pushed it away.

"You're right, I wouldn't. I'm clean too."

He kissed the tip of my nose, then pulled out of me. "Let's shower, then get some sleep. I have to help Brock and Dad plow the south and west pastures tomorrow morning and need to be at the barn by six."

I snarled my lip. "Why do y'all get up so early? It's not like it's getting hot midday."

He reached for my hand and pulled me out of bed. I followed him into my bathroom like this was our normal routine. How was he acting so casual about all of this?

I, on the other hand, had already begun to slowly fall apart. One night wasn't going to be enough for me. Would I actually be able to go back to the friend zone after tonight? The best sex of my life, and I was supposed to act like it had never happened. Supposed to accept that one and done was my only option.

No freaking way.

"Early bird catches the worm."

With a roll of my eyes, I stepped into the shower, then turned it on, staying out of the spray until it heated up. "I never was a fan of fishing."

Then I was pressed against the cold tile. I gasped, letting a string of foul language fall from my lips.

"That's it, baby. Talk dirty to me. I like it."

I laughed but quickly stopped when he used his foot to push my leg out.

Turning to face him, I asked, "Ty, seriously, does your cock never get tired? And how many times are we going to tempt fate?"

His eyes looked almost hopeful, and I had the strangest feeling Ty Shaw *wanted* to tempt fate. Like this was going to be his only shot at something, and only I was going to be able to provide it.

"If tonight is all I get of you, I'm taking full advantage of it."

I smiled, but the pain in my chest ached a little more. He hadn't changed his mind, not even after the most amazing night ever.

Ty lifted my leg, then pushed inside me. He held nothing back, like he knew this was the last time he'd ever be with me. If I had anything to do with it, though, this wouldn't be the last time.

When I felt him grow bigger, I dropped my head back against the wall. He reached between us, his finger working my clit with the expertise of a man who had done this to me for years.

I came again. He'd gotten his even number with eight orgasms. Then he pulled out and came on my stomach, the water soon washing his cum away but not the overwhelming grief that instantly hit me. The reality that this night was quickly coming to an end. The bubble I'd let myself fall into was about to pop.

Chapter Fourteen

KAYLEE

The sounds of nature caused me to open my eyes and stretch. Instantly, I felt the pain between my legs and grinned like a little girl.

After Ty and I had sex in the shower, we returned to my bed. He pulled me against his body, and we both fell asleep the moment we closed our eyes.

I looked to my right and saw the empty bed. I wanted to ignore the instant rush of sadness, but it gripped at me like a vise, and for a few brief moments, I thought I might have a panic attack. I took in some deep breaths and calmed myself down.

I sat up and noticed a folded-up piece of paper on the pillow. My name was written across the outside, and I couldn't resist a smile. The tension in my body instantly melted away.

Reaching for it, I held my breath as I opened the note and read what Ty had written.

Morning, Kaylee.
I wanted to wake you up to say goodbye, but you were
sleeping so peacefully I couldn't do it. But I also couldn't

*sneak out of here like last night didn't mean anything to
me, because it did. More than you'll ever know.*

I closed my eyes and took in a deep breath. His *but* was fixin' to
come. I could feel it. I needed a moment to just let this first set of words
settle into my memory. Last night had meant something to him, and
deep in my heart, I had known that all along. I saw it in his eyes. In the
way he made love to me.

With one deep breath, I opened my eyes and kept reading.

*Thank you for a night I will never forget. I wish I could
give you more.
Ty*

I swallowed hard and clutched the note to my chest. Then I dropped
my hands to my lap and shook my head. "Damn you, Ty Shaw!"

After throwing the covers off me, I quickly got out of bed and got
dressed.

*He tells me he can't do a relationship, that it's a onetime thing, yet he
sleeps next to me all night long. Then he leaves me a sweet note in the morning!* The man was confusing as hell. I knew he'd said he couldn't give me
more, but Lord, a part of me knew he hadn't meant it.

"You jerk! You asshole! You . . . you . . . you confusing man," I
raged, plopping down on the end of my bed while I buried my face in
my hands. Then I let out a scream of frustration.

"You're so stupid. You knew from the beginning, Kaylee Holden.
You knew. He told you he couldn't give you more than one night. You.
Knew."

Dear Lord. I was talking to myself. This was bad.

I jumped up, tracked down my phone, and sent Lincoln a text
message.

Me: We need an emergency shopping trip right now.

Lincoln: In case you forgot, I have a baby who is barely over a month old, and a five-year-old son who hears and repeats everything to his father. What's going on?

Me: I slept with Ty.

Lincoln: Let me call Stella to come sit with the kids. I'll be there as soon as I can.

I stood, looked at my sheets, and quickly yanked them all off my bed. I needed to wash them and get Ty's scent off them as soon as possible; then I needed to think about everything that had happened last night, including all the unprotected sex we'd had. In some strange way, that part was the one thing I didn't regret. I regretted that I had somehow managed to let a piece of my heart fall to Ty Shaw.

"Stupid! Stupid! Stupid!" I ranted, pacing across my living room floor while I waited for Lincoln. My hand moved to my stomach, then to my mouth and back to my stomach. One minute I thought I might throw up; the next, my stomach was dipping in delight as memories of last night came back.

The door opened, and Lincoln took one look at me. "Do I need to go hurt him?"

With a smile, I shook my head. "No. But you need to take me into town so I can spend some money. Then I need you to get me drunk."

"Done. You'll have to get drunk fast, though. I can only be gone for a few hours. I pumped enough breast milk for Morgan's next feeding, and that's it, and I hate being away from her for very long."

"Fine. We'll skip the getting-drunk part and just go shopping."

She smiled, then motioned for me to follow her. I grabbed my purse, and an hour later, we were sitting in the coffee shop on Main Street. Lincoln knew not to ask any questions until I'd gotten in a good shopping session. This wasn't her first rodeo when it came to retail therapy with me. After John died, and I had finally gotten myself out of the house, I spent a lot of trust fund money from my grandparents on stupid shopping trips. She made out on them as well, though, so really we both sorta won.

I took a sip of my flat white coffee and set it on the table. Lincoln watched me carefully, taking a sip of her chai tea. Then . . .

"I can't stand it anymore! What happened?" she blurted out.

"So, Ty got a package."

She rolled her eyes. "I don't want to know about his package. I don't tell you about how insanely large my husband is."

I snarled my lip at her. "First off, yes, you do, and you just did, bitch. Second, I said he *got* a package. Not that he has a package—which, by the way, he has a huge cock. It's pretty too. I don't think I've ever seen a dick that I could say was pretty, but his is. Lord, it's really big too. Did I mention that already?"

Lincoln quickly looked around the coffee shop, her cheeks red. When it was clear no one had heard me, she waved her hands around. "I know about the stupid package! Skip to the sex part."

I let out a long breath. "He walked into the house after he picked up the package, and I was in the middle of trying to fix a . . . problem . . . I had with the bidet."

"What was wrong with it?"

With a half shrug I said, "There might have been a small water leak."

Her eyes widened, then she said, "I'm so glad I sold you that house."

I chuckled, then went on. "Anyway, Ty insisted on fixing it, and I really wanted to do it on my own. It was a bad day, because, you know . . ."

"It was the anniversary of John's death."

Which explained my outburst with Ty and the fact that I had called him by another man's name.

"Yeah. So, anyway, I blew up at him and yelled, and then I accidently called him John."

Lincoln gasped. "Yikes."

"Yeah, I hadn't realized I did until he said something. Then he got all sweet on me, and nice, and he looked like he was going to kiss me, and then he did what he always does. He pushed me away and headed downstairs to leave. I stopped him and asked him to stay. He said he wasn't any good for me, that he was fucked up. I responded in a way that might have been careless."

Her brow rose and she picked up her tea. Before she took a drink, she said, "Keep going."

"Well, I sort of stood in front of the door and started to take my clothes off."

Lincoln coughed. Then hit her chest a few times. "You took your clothes off!"

I leaned in and shot her a warning look. "Why don't you stand on the chair and yell it a little louder? The people in the back didn't hear you." I looked around the coffee shop; no one appeared to have heard my loudmouthed friend. Everyone was buried in their computers or phones.

"Sorry! Sorry!" she whispered.

"It was the only thing I could think of doing. So yes, I threw myself at him. Of course, Ty being a man, all his senses went right out the door, and he kissed the living shit out of me. Let me just pause here to say the man can kiss. Like, whoa, he can kiss."

Lincoln smiled.

"Then he informed me that he wasn't good enough for me, or some bullshit like that. He warned me that he wasn't looking for a relationship."

"That doesn't surprise me."

"It didn't me, either. He said if I was looking for something more than just a night of sex, he wasn't the guy."

"And you obviously told him you were fine with that, I'm assuming. Since, you know, you guys did the deed."

"We did more than the deed, Lincoln. The man made me come eight times. Eight! He has some weird fetish about odd numbers."

Lincoln seemed confused, but her look was quickly replaced with shock as she leaned across the table and whispered, "Wait, you had *eight orgasms?*"

I leaned in closer so I could whisper back, "Over the course of the afternoon and night. Yes! The man is good, I'm telling you. I don't think his dick went down all night."

Giggling, Lincoln covered her mouth and looked around the coffee shop again. Then she focused back on me. "Wow. Okay, so it's pretty damn clear the two of you have been wanting *that* for some time."

I nodded. "He said he hadn't been with a woman since last year. Spring, or something like that."

Lincoln narrowed her brows and thought for a moment. "Probably that woman he hooked up with in Billings."

"What woman?" I asked, surprised by this bit of information.

Lincoln froze.

"You knew he hooked up with someone and didn't tell me, Lincoln?"

"Would telling you have made you feel good about it at the time?"

"No."

She waved her hands in front of me. "Well, okay then, there you go."

I dropped back against the chair and let out a groan. "Oh, God, Lincoln. I'm in so much trouble."

"Because you're not okay with the one-night-only thing, are you?"

I shook my head. "I'm so far from okay with that. I think at some point last night, when he whispered how amazing it felt being inside me, or the way he made love, or when he told me how beautiful I was when I came and it took his breath away . . . yeah . . . I might have fallen in love with him. Or maybe I already *was* in love with him and hadn't wanted to admit it."

Lincoln reached across the table and squeezed my hand. "Oh, sweetie."

My eyes closed, and I forced myself not to cry. I had agreed to Ty's conditions, but I had done so because I'd wanted him so desperately. Needed him. It had clearly clouded my better judgment.

"Does this have anything to do with yesterday being the anniversary?"

"No!" I said, opening my eyes and looking at Lincoln. "I mean, the anniversary always makes me feel sad, but I wasn't trying to sleep with Ty to make things better. Okay, that's a lie, maybe I was . . . but not about John. I needed him, and I was tired of us always fighting, and I saw it in his eyes how much he wanted me too. And last month, we messed around on the sofa for, like, three minutes before we got interrupted, and I haven't been able to stop thinking about him. How close we had almost come to sleeping together that morning. I've been going insane thinking about it."

I dropped my gaze to my coffee. The silence between us spoke a million words. Lincoln knew I had messed up, but she would never tell me. She knew how I felt about Ty, and I was a grown woman who had made my own choice to jump into bed with a man who flat out told me he didn't want anything other than sex. The same man whom I'd had unprotected sex with. This was ridiculously messed up on so many levels.

Lincoln cleared her throat. "Okay, let's back up. What happened when he left? When did he leave?"

"This morning. He had to meet Brock and Ty Senior at the barn. He didn't wake me up, but he did leave me a note. It was sweet, yet frustrating as hell."

She frowned. "That doesn't make sense."

I raised a brow at her.

With a slight smile, she tilted her head. "It's Ty, so maybe it does make sense."

Letting out a sigh, I explained. "He told me how much the night meant to him, about it meaning more than I'll ever know. Then he thanked me for the night like it was just some casual fuck and said that he appreciated it."

"Oh, Kaylee, at least he left a note and didn't sneak out."

I nodded. That had been a relief. For those few moments when I'd thought he'd just left, I had been crushed.

"Lincoln, I don't know what to do. I have feelings for Ty, and I know he has them for me. I've never had a man touch me the way he did, so him telling me he can't give himself to me is just bullshit. The way he kissed me . . . I mean, if he does that with all of his hookups, they probably have some secret club where they all go and meet for fucking therapy because their va-jay-jays will never want another man."

The corners of her mouth rose slightly as she took a sip of her tea.

Now it was time to really drop the bomb on her. It was bad enough I was freaking out because I had let myself fall in love with Ty; that was nothing compared to what I was about to drop on her like a bad STD.

Gazing down at my cup, I circled the rim of it with my finger as I cleared my throat and said, "Oh, and one more thing. We didn't use a condom . . . like, at all."

The sound of a teacup hitting a saucer filled the coffee shop as I glanced up and saw my best friend looking at me with not only shock but anger.

Chapter Fifteen

Ty

The time I'd spent on the tractor all morning left me alone with my thoughts. I wasn't sure if that was good or bad. When I woke up in the morning, and everything from the night before came back in one mad rush, my first urge was to get the fuck out of there. That didn't last long, though. I turned and saw Kaylee sleeping. Her hands were tucked under her face, and she had the sweetest expression on her face.

She looked content. Like she had been fucked thoroughly and well.

I smiled at that, because it was me who'd put that look on her gorgeous face. Even I had to admit I was surprised by all the sex we'd had last night. Of course, we'd crawled into her bed around four in the afternoon and never left it but to get something to drink and to use the bathroom a few times. Oh, and there was the shower time.

I smiled.

The shower. God, the shower.

Fucking her in the shower was now on my list of top favorite things I'd ever do in my lifetime. The number one thing on my list was watching her face as she came and called out my name. She was beautiful.

At some point during the night, her demeanor changed. The lust in her eyes turned to something different. Something I wanted to acknowledge so fucking badly but knew I never could. She couldn't fall in love with me. I wasn't the right guy for her. I might have been able to give her multiple orgasms, but that didn't mean I could make her happy. The way she'd looked at me that last time I had been inside her made all the alarms go off in my head. My dick hadn't cared; he would be perfectly happy spending the rest of our days buried inside Kaylee Holden.

I pulled in behind Brock and turned off the tractor. Once I jumped down, I turned to ask him a question, but before I could even get a word out, he punched me.

Stumbling back, I grabbed my jaw and looked at him. "What in the fuck was that for?"

Brock looked pissed. More than pissed; he looked downright furious. "You had sex with Kaylee without a condom? More than once? What in the fuck were you thinking?"

I stared at him in total shock.

How in the hell did he know? Had he seen my truck parked outside Kaylee's place this morning? Even if he *had* seen my truck, how in the world would he have known about the unprotected sex?

"What is wrong with you, Brock?" I asked, working my jaw back and forth. He took a step toward me, and I stood up straighter, ready for his next move. "You come after me again, I will beat the living shit out of you, ya little fucker. Let's not forget which one of us won every single wrestling contest we ever had, Brock."

Brock stood planted firmly in place. "Start talking before Dad gets here, because I can promise you, he will be just as pissed at you for being so careless."

"I'm sorry, but in case you forgot how this works, two people make that decision."

"And you thought it was okay to do that? Do you want to run the risk of having a kid with a woman you informed you didn't want a future with?"

My brows pulled down, and anger coursed through my body. "How in the fuck do you know all of this?"

"Lincoln."

I groaned and closed my eyes; instant tension built, and my head ached. Of course Kaylee would have run off and told Lincoln about last night. "Why is Lincoln telling you about my sex life?"

"Because she's worried about her best friend. The two of you obviously took fucking stupid pills last night."

With a sigh, I nodded. "I agree, it was stupid. Very stupid."

"Oh, you think?"

I shot him a dirty look. I didn't need my younger brother lecturing me on something I knew I had fucked up on. "I know. But I don't know how to explain it. At the time, it felt right. Good. Hell, it felt so good . . ."

He rolled his eyes. "Do you make this a habit? Fucking women without a condom?"

I took a step toward him and grabbed his shirt. "Don't talk about her like it was some casual fuck."

His brows lifted, and he gave me an incredulous look. "Really? Then what was it, Ty?"

I stared at him, unable to answer his question.

"I . . . I don't know what it was, but nothing else is going to happen. I told Kaylee before we even started I wasn't looking for anything more, so she knew what the rules were."

Brock shook his head and then dropped it as he sighed. "Ty, dude. Lincoln got pregnant with me wearing a condom, *and* she was on birth control. What were you thinking? If you aren't looking for something serious with Kaylee, why would you risk that?"

I swallowed hard and looked down at the ground. The sound of another tractor rolling up had both of us looking over to our father.

Brock faced me again. "Let's finish up here and then go grab some lunch and beer. It's time we talked, Ty."

With a nod, I reached down and picked up my cowboy hat, which had been knocked off my head when Brock punched me. I knew I'd deserved it.

As our father approached us, Brock said in a low voice, "Dad doesn't need to know about this."

"If you think I'm going to fucking announce it, you're wrong."

He shot me another dirty look, then headed over toward our dad.

Brock was right. If my parents found out how reckless I'd been, and with Kaylee, of all women, they would be angry and disappointed. I'd already disappointed them enough.

"Fields are all plowed . . . good job, boys. We can plant them tomorrow. Tanner called your mama and said he'd be in town for a few days. We'll put him to work as well."

I smiled, as did Brock.

Our father's gaze bounced from me to Brock. "Everything okay with you both?"

Brock and I exchanged a look and then nodded at our father. I would never be able to figure out how the man seemed to know when something was off with his sons. He'd always had some weird sense when we were fighting or upset with one another. He especially knew when it was between me and Brock. Before, it had always been about bull riding. Arguing which one of us was better, fighting about God knows what. We'd try to hide it from him, but he always seemed to know.

"Yeah, everything is fine. We're going to head off and grab some lunch and beer. You want to come with us?" Brock asked. We both knew our father would say no, but inviting him would ease his mind about something being wrong between us.

He frowned. "What happened to your mouth?"

I reached up and flinched when I touched it, then tasted a small amount of blood. Immediately, my gaze went to Brock, who was smirking. The bastard had gotten me good.

"Brock and I got into a bit of an argument," I said, causing Brock's eyes to widen in shock. After the whole shit with my drug addiction, I'd sworn to my folks I'd never lie to them again. I meant it. "We worked it out. No worries, Dad," I added with a smile.

Our father nodded, took another good look at both of us, and laughed. "You two will never change—always settling things with your fists."

"It's quicker that way, right, Ty?" Brock smiled and patted our father on the back as he turned and headed over to his truck.

"You boys stay out of trouble. You got a newborn to look after, Brock Shaw."

Brock's mouth fell open, and he turned back to me. "And he assumes it's my fault?"

I shrugged. "You're the one who punched me, dude."

With a snarling expression, Brock shook his head. "Where do you want to eat?"

"Filling station sounds good to me."

He nodded. "Ride together?"

I laughed. "Hell no. I'll meet you there."

Brock beat me to the filling station and was sitting at a table talking to Kristin, a waitress who'd been working there since they'd first opened. As I made my way toward the table, a few people said hi and some nodded a silent hello, and I responded with one of my own. A few women gave me sexy smiles; those I ignored and kept on walking.

"Hey, Ty. Something to drink?" Kristin asked.

"Anything on draft, Kristin. Thanks."

She nodded and smiled before turning and walking off. Brock took a drink of his bottled beer and slowly set it down.

I looked around the restaurant, stalling.

"Okay, I'll start first, since you're not. Why don't you want something more with her?"

My gaze shot back and locked on his. I laughed. "Are you seriously asking me that?"

"Yes, I am, Ty. It's about fucking time you say it out loud so the rest of us can understand where the hell your mind is in all of this, not to mention your dick."

I frowned. "Say what?"

"Tell me. Tell me whatever the hell it is you have in your mind that makes you think you're not cut out for a relationship."

Laughing again, I dropped back in my seat. "So you fell in love, got married, and, what, earned your license in psychology all at the same time?"

He rolled his eyes. "Listen, Ty, I get that life fucked you over, and I'm not going to pretend I know what it was like to walk away from bull riding. I had the choice and left on my own. I understand you went through some shit, and I, of all people, get why you're keeping her at a distance. But you've already told me there's something about her that's different. It's fucking obvious that you're scared of your feelings for her."

I scoffed.

Kristin walked back over with my beer and set it down, then looked at both of us. "Ready to order?"

"I'll have the gas hog burger," Brock said, handing her back the menu.

"Ty?" she asked, waiting for my order. Brock's words were tumbling around in my head. I was unfocused as shit and hadn't given a second thought to food.

"Um, I'll take, ah . . . um . . ."

I glanced up to see both of them watching me. The corner of Brock's mouth twitched with a smirk he was at least attempting to hold back.

"I'll have the same thing as Brock," I finally said.

"Sounds good. Both well done, right?"

We both replied yes together. Once Kristin was gone, I let out a breath, shook my head, and closed my eyes for a moment before speaking.

"There's a side of me, Brock, that is scared shitless to let myself even think I could be happy. With anything or anyone. If I let someone in, the darkness will eventually swallow up any happiness I feel, and I'm going to end up right where I was that morning after the accident. Lost, confused, hurt. Angry. Kaylee's had enough heavy bullshit in her life—she doesn't need mine."

"So you're going to make that decision for her? You ever think maybe she's the one person who is capable of making you happy? That she can make that decision on her own *because* of the heavy shit she's already been through?"

My gaze met his. "That's the problem, Brock. Something about Kaylee Holden gets to me. In a good way . . . a damn good way. The first time we ever kissed, I knew she would become my new addiction if I let her. And I can't let her. I fought this battle for almost a year, and one move on her part and I was practically on my knees with need for her. I can't . . . I can't do it."

"Why not?"

"I can't lose her. If I did, it would destroy me."

He let out a half-hearted laugh. "What makes you think you'll lose her? How is that any different than what you're doing to yourself, and to her, right now? And maybe it was just an itch y'all needed to scratch? You ever think of that?"

It was my turn to laugh. "Nah, that wasn't no itch. I've never in my life felt that way with a woman. I didn't want to leave her bed, Brock. I did and said things to her I've never done or voiced to any other woman. I thought I couldn't get her out of my mind before, and now, after being with her? Hell, I'm never going to be able to forget the way she felt in my arms. But it will end badly, because I'm not the guy she needs."

"And why do you think that?" he asked.

I stared at him like he was an idiot. "She's already had a guy who was messed up in the head. He hurt her and left her devastated. I won't be the one to do that to her again."

He sighed. "Damn it, Ty, why do you think you're going to hurt her?"

"I'm not going to ask Kaylee to fix something that's broken. It's me. I'm the one who's broken. I won't do that to her. She deserves more."

"What if you ain't broken, Ty? You just need someone to help you heal? I thought the same thing with Lincoln. She changed my entire life. She healed what was hurting. You've got to take the risk, Ty."

I shook my head. "I can't. This morning when I woke up next to her, I had the strangest feeling in my chest, something I have never experienced before, and Kaylee was the cause of it. She makes me want something I'm not ready for. Hell, I don't know if I will ever be ready for it, truth be told."

"You won't ever be able to move on if you don't learn to take the risk, to open up your heart and let something good in," Brock said— and fuck me if I didn't consider buying what he was selling.

Anger ripped through me because I knew he was right, but I didn't want to admit it. I didn't want to take the jump. I was scared; I was so fucking scared of being hurt again. Of hurting Kaylee.

Brock sighed and shook his head. "So explain something to me. Why did you not wear a condom?"

My heart dropped in my chest, and we stared at each other. There was no way I could tell him the truth. Judging by the way he was looking at me, though, he already knew the answer to that question.

"Holy fuck, Ty. You can't give yourself to Kaylee . . . so were you hoping to give her a part of you? Are you out of your damn mind, bro?"

Kristin walked up at that moment and set our food down in front of us. "Anything else you boys need?" she asked.

I shook my head, and Brock answered. "We're good, thank you. Although, now that I think about it, Kristin, Ty here needs a new brain, if you've got any there in the back. He seems to have lost his."

She just smiled at us both while I shot him a pissed-off look.

When she walked away, I met his hard stare. I didn't need to answer his previous question; he saw it in my eyes. The only thing he did was shake his head and look away. Leaving me to let the guilt and regret of last night settle right into the middle of my chest.

Chapter Sixteen

KAYLEE

Three weeks later: May

I stood on the front porch and smiled as Blayze bounced down the sidewalk toward me. He had an overnight bag and a huge smile on his face.

"Aunt Kaylee! Are you ready for our sleepover?"

Returning his smile, I nodded. "I most certainly am!"

Blayze raced up the steps and wrapped his arms around my waist. My heart jumped in my chest, and I attempted to control my tears. These stupid emotions lately were going to be the death of me. I didn't even know why I felt the urge to cry right then.

When Lincoln walked up and stopped, she took one look at me and her smile faded.

"Blayze, why don't you run on in and put your bag in the guest room. I need to talk grown-up stuff with Aunt Kaylee."

"Okay, Mama!" He raced into the house as we both watched. When I turned back to Lincoln, I saw the love in her eyes for her son. She might not have been his biological mother, but she loved and adored that little boy so much.

Then her gaze met mine. "What's wrong? Did you finally see Ty?"

I blew out an exaggerated breath and waved my hand in front of me in a nonchalant manner. "No, he has totally ghosted me."

It had been three weeks since that night we'd spent together. That wonderful, incredible, sex-filled night.

"You haven't seen him at all?" Lincoln asked, concern in her eyes.

I shook my head. "No. I think he's put some sort of GPS on me, and it alerts him whenever I'm within a one-mile radius, because I haven't run into him in the normal places I usually do around town. Either that, or he's not leaving the ranch, which is possible. Stella said it's been a busy beginning to spring."

Lincoln nodded. "Yeah, Brock's been up early every day to head on out and help his dad and Ty."

I forced a smile.

"Has he texted you at all?" she asked, glancing over my shoulder, looking for Blayze.

"Once. He asked how I was doing and if I had plenty of wood for that front that moved through a couple weeks ago."

Her mouth dropped open. "That's it?"

Smiling, I drew in a deep breath and let it out. "What do you expect, Lincoln? We agreed it was a one-night thing."

"That's fine, but to totally avoid you is just him being a dick."

I shrugged. "Whatever. Doesn't matter anyway."

She tilted her head. "It does matter. What if—"

Knowing what she was about to say, I cut her off. "I started this morning, so all is fine."

I couldn't help but notice the relieved look on her face. It was quickly replaced with a confused expression. "Wait, is that why you're feeling down? Kaylee, you didn't want . . ."

Lincoln's voice trailed off when I broke our eye contact and looked back into the house.

"Blayze? What are you doing?" I called out, hoping to see him coming down the hall and saving me from this conversation. He wasn't, though.

Damn it.

"Oh. My. God. Is that why you didn't want him wearing a condom?"

I turned back to face her. "Scream it, why don't you, Lincoln?"

Her hands covered her mouth as she gasped. When she dropped them back to her side, she slowly shook her head. "Kaylee Holden, have you lost your ever-loving mind? You were trying to get pregnant?"

"Of course not!" I said in a hushed voice.

"Then why do you look upset about this?"

"I'm not upset," I shot back. *At least not really upset.*

"You are! I see it all over your face. You were hoping Ty got you pregnant."

My eyes burned with the threat of tears. As crazy as it sounded, when he didn't put a condom on, then thought twice about it, I knew I wanted him to *not* wear one for two reasons. One, I needed to feel him bare, and two, I actually *had* lost my ever-loving mind.

A small part of me hoped he'd left a piece of himself behind that night. In my crazy mind, I knew Ty had meant it when he'd said one night would be it. I needed more. I needed something of him, and as crazy as it sounded now, a baby would have been fine with me.

I wiped away a tear that had managed to slip free. "Is it so wrong that I maybe wished for something from him? That if he couldn't give me himself, then at least I'd have a part of him?"

Her eyes closed as she let out a breath. "Kaylee." Then she wrapped me in her arms, and I let the tears fall.

"I know it's stupid, and irresponsible, but a part of me was hoping like hell it had happened, Lincoln. Does that make me crazy? I think that makes me crazy!"

"Shh, it doesn't make you *that* crazy, sweetie. Just a whole lot crazy."

I laughed and sobbed at the same time.

"What's wrong? Why are you crying, Aunt Kaylee?" Blayze asked from behind me.

Drawing back from Lincoln, I quickly wiped the tears away. "Nothing is wrong, buddy. Everything is exactly how it should be. What should we do first?"

Blayze smiled. "I have practice tonight."

I drew my brows in and gave Lincoln a wondering look. "Practice for what?"

She sighed. "Blayze here thinks he wants to be a professional bull rider. His daddy couldn't be more proud; his mama, on the other hand, is a nervous wreck. Anyway, in his attempt to help him pursue this career goal, Brock signed Blayze up for an event at the rodeo next month."

"Surely not bull riding!" I said in a horrified voice.

Lincoln shook her head. "Oh, no. Close, though. Mutton busting."

Unable to hide my laughter, I placed my hand over my mouth and attempted to cover it up with a cough. After clearing my throat, I asked, "And where does one go for mutton-busting lessons?"

I swore Blayze puffed his chest out some.

Lincoln replied, "They don't have lessons for that, but Brock doesn't give up easily. He talked to Brad Littlewood, who owns some sheep, and asked him if they could practice on them." She looked at her son. "Did you bring your helmet?"

"Yes, ma'am," Blayze said.

My heart melted a little. These crazy urges to have a baby were beginning to worry me. I'd understood how strong those emotions were when I'd held Morgan in the hospital when she was a few hours old. She was a baby. With the whole sweet smell and precious fingers and toes. I thought the desire would fade away. It hadn't. It felt like it was growing stronger and stronger with each passing day.

"I'm not surprised Brad was on board with this," I said with a chuckle.

Brad Littlewood was the father of Brock's best friend and fellow bull rider, Dirk Littlewood. Dirk and I had grown pretty close after I'd moved here with Lincoln. Nothing sexual between us, just friends. He was easy to talk to and wasn't the least bit interested in trying to get into my pants, for reasons that were still unknown to me. It was nice, though, having a guy friend whom I *didn't* want to impregnate me. Of course, if I'd asked him, he might have been down for it.

Oh God. I am going crazy.

"What time do I need to have him there?"

"Six, if that's okay? Brad said he'd meet me down at the barn, but I called and told him you'd be bringing Blayze today, and not me and Brock."

"Sure, that's perfect."

"Great!" Lincoln said as she bent down and held out her arms for Blayze. "Now, you have fun tonight with Aunt Kaylee, and you mind your manners."

"Yes, Mama, I will."

I smiled as I watched the two of them. Brock had begged Lincoln for a night on their own. She was hesitant at first, but with Morgan being two months old now, she was more willing to spend a few hours away from her. I was keeping Blayze for the night, and Stella and Ty Senior had Morgan.

I was almost positive that if I kept Morgan, my ovaries might send out an SOS to Ty—or any other hard and willing man, for that matter.

"I love you, little man," Lincoln said, kissing Blayze on the cheek and then hugging him again. His little arms wrapped around her neck.

"I love you too. And don't worry, I'm sure Aunt Kaylee will remember to feed me."

Lincoln's eyes shot up to look at me, a frown on her face. My hands went to my hips, and I stared at her with an open mouth.

"Seriously, Lincoln, it was one time I forgot to feed the kid! He lived!"

Blayze laughed while Lincoln rolled her eyes and stood. "You sure you're okay? Do you want to talk some more?"

I glanced at the time on my watch, then smiled down at Blayze. "We need to make some dinner, then head on over to the Littlewoods' place. I'm good. I just needed a cry, I think."

She nodded and then stepped closer to me. She pulled me into her arms again.

"Wow, breastfeeding is working out for you!"

Lincoln laughed, then pulled back and winked. "Brock thinks so too."

I snarled my lip. "You had to take it there, didn't you?"

With a half shrug, Lincoln kissed Blayze once more and headed to her car. Glancing back at us, she waved her hand. "Bye, Blayze! See you tomorrow morning!"

"Have fun!" Blayze and I both said at once.

Once Lincoln drove off, Blayze and I faced each other. "Pizza and ice cream in town, and then mutton-busting practice?"

Blayze fist-pumped. "Yes! I love spending the night with you, Aunt Kaylee!"

Grinning, I took in a deep breath and proudly let it out in one whoosh. I may have been his only aunt, but I knew I was his favorite.

The moment I pulled up to the Littlewoods' barn and put my car in park, Blayze was trying to jump out the door.

"Hey! Your helmet!" I called after him.

"Gosh dang it, that darn helmet," Blayze said as he reached back into the car and grabbed his helmet.

"The apple didn't fall far from the tree, I see."

Blayze gave me a look that said he had no idea what that meant.

As we walked toward the corral, Blayze reached up and took my hand, causing a fluttering sensation to take hold in my stomach.

Brad stood there with a huge smile on his face. Too huge. Something was up.

Right at that moment, out from the barn appeared Dirk. Blayze dropped my hand and ran directly for him, jumping into his arms.

"Uncle Dirk!" he cried out as Dirk lifted him up and gave him a hug.

I couldn't help the smile that grew across my face as I walked up to Brad. "Nice secret you kept there, Brad."

He laughed. "Hell, the boy surprised me."

I focused back on Dirk and Blayze. Dirk was currently handing something to Blayze. They were both looking at it intently.

When I first met Dirk Littlewood, I was taken by him, but not because he was handsome as hell with his dark hair and dreamy green eyes. I liked him because he was just a nice guy. A manwhore, but a nice guy who treated his friends with love and respect. Dirk was the type of guy who would drop everything to help out a friend.

Dirk hadn't come home to Hamilton very often since Brock retired. I knew that bothered his folks, and his mother had said more than once she wished Dirk would follow in Brock's footsteps and retire. I didn't see that happening anytime soon. He was on a roll and seemed to have slipped right into the number one spot Brock had walked away from. From what I'd heard, Dirk was already on fire this season, and there was no way he would walk away when he was on top.

Then he looked over and saw me. He shook his head. "Damn, girl, aren't you a sight for sore eyes."

I laughed as he pulled me into his arms and spun me around before placing me back on solid ground.

"Aunt Kaylee was sad earlier and crying."

Everyone looked down at Blayze; then two sets of adult male eyes were on me.

"You all right, Kaylee?" Brad asked. Dirk wore a scowl and appeared ready to kick the person's ass who had made me cry.

I rubbed the top of Blayze's head. "Gosh, way to sell a girl out, there, Blayze," I said, chuckling. "I'm fine, Brad. Honest. It was just a girly thing."

He nodded. When I looked at Dirk, I could tell he clearly wasn't convinced.

"Dad, you got this with Blayze? I think Kaylee and I need to exercise those two mares in there."

Brad nodded. "I've got this. Blayze, let's get on your helmet and have us some fun with the sheep."

"Dirk, I'm fine, and I need to keep an eye on Blayze."

"Dad's got Blayze. Come on, girl." He took my hand and pulled me toward the barn.

"Blayze, do you want me to stay?" I called back.

"Nah, girls make me nervous when they watch me. I need to perfect my sport without the pressure of a woman watching."

My eyes widened, and I looked back at Dirk. "What in the hell did he just say, and when did he learn to use his words like that? Lincoln's going to freak!"

Dirk let out a roar of laughter. "Apple didn't fall far from the tree."

I giggled. "I just said that to him not more than two minutes ago. That boy is exactly like his father."

"Hearts will be breaking all over Hamilton when that kid gets older."

I glanced back at Blayze and smiled. It was true. A mirror image of his daddy, he would certainly have the attention of girls everywhere.

The next thing I knew, I was saddling up a horse and climbing on.

Dirk and I rode in silence for a bit before he finally spoke. "You feel like talking about it?"

I scoffed. "Not really."

"A guy?"

My head snapped to my left, and I laughed. "You automatically think I cried over a guy? How sexist of you."

Dirk laughed. "Well, yeah. You're a woman, and you chicks do shit like that."

I rolled my eyes. "Well, not that I agree with you, but it *was* over a guy, and I had a moment of weakness. That's all."

"That guy wouldn't happen to be Ty, would it?"

This time I was positive my eyes nearly bugged out of my head and my mouth dragged along the dirt path we rode on.

Dirk winked. "Your expression and lack of vocal response is my answer."

"You think . . . me and Ty?"

He looked at me, his face serious. "Why do you think I always kept our relationship strictly in the friendship zone? I see the way Ty looks at you. I went down that road with Brock and Kaci once upon a time. I wasn't about to do it again. I also figured at some point, Ty was going to get his head out of his ass and realize how much he liked you. He is a Shaw, though, and bound to fuck things up."

I forced my eyes straight and stared at the trail in front of us for a few moments before I spoke. "There's nothing between us, Dirk."

"Okay. Do you want there to be something between the two of you?"

Our gazes met. "Ty's not looking for a relationship. I understand that."

I couldn't stand the look in his eyes. It wasn't pity, but it spoke volumes. He knew the truth, just like Lincoln did. I may have talked the talk, but that was about as far as it went. I was positive I had a sign above my head that blinked, I'VE FALLEN IN LOVE WITH TY SHAW.

"Kaylee, I need to let you know something. The real reason I'm here in town, and it has to do with Ty."

He stopped his horse, which made me stop mine. "Is everything okay?" I asked.

"Yeah, but I don't think what I'm about to tell you is going to make you very happy."

My heart felt like it jumped to my throat. "Why would you say that?"

Dirk rubbed the back of his neck while he struggled with what to say. Finally, he came out and said it. "CBS wants to offer him a broadcasting position on the Unleash the Beast Tour. He'd be gone . . . a lot."

"A broadcasting position?"

He nodded. "They asked once before, but he turned it down."

"Why did he turn it down?"

Dirk shrugged. "Only he knows why. He said he wasn't interested at the time. I think he was still dealing with not being able to ride, and the thought of being near it all was too painful. But with him being at the PBR World Finals last November and reconnecting with some folks, they want him again. They asked me to bring him the offer, thinking with me being friends with him, he might take it a bit more seriously and give it more thought."

My eyes widened. "Wow. What do you think he'll do?"

He smirked. "That depends. Is there something going on between you two?"

I swallowed hard. Then shook my head. "No. Nothing."

Dirk lifted his brows, evidently not missing the sadness in my voice. "Nothing?"

"We slept together, but Ty told me the rules . . . he's not interested in being in a relationship."

Both of our horses decided they were tired of standing there and started down the trail again.

"You know he's just lost in himself. I don't really know any other way to explain it. Bull riding for Ty was exactly how it is for me. It's my life, the dream I always envisioned I'd live. If it was ripped away from me like it was from Ty, I honestly think I'd lose myself as well. He thinks he's broken and unrepairable."

I chewed on my bottom lip before I replied. "I understand that. I do. I don't think he's broken, though. I think he's scared, but I saw something in his eyes when we were together, Dirk. A longing for something more, and I felt this connection between us. If I'm being honest, I think I felt it the first time he smiled at me. I don't want to fix him, because I don't think he's broken. The man that he is, is the man I . . ."

My voice trailed off.

"The man you love?"

I closed my eyes and shook my head before turning back to focus on Dirk. "Do you think if he took this position it would help him to let go of some of the pain and hurt he's holding on to?"

"Hell, I don't know, Kaylee. I honestly don't know. I think it's more than just the bull riding. There's something else Ty is holding on to. Something that makes him fear allowing something good to come into his life. Maybe he thinks if he's happy, the rug will be ripped out from under him, and he's not sure he's capable of another sucker punch like that."

"And that is no way to live your life."

"I agree," Dirk said.

"If the roles were reversed and it were you in Ty's shoes, would you take the CBS gig?"

Dirk thought for a moment as the horses made their way down the path in a lazy trot. "Honestly, if it were me, and there wasn't anyone holding me back, I'd do it. I'd want to be immersed in the world, because I fucking love it. But, at the same time, if I met someone who made me feel something I haven't ever felt before, then that would change things. I may not want the type of life Brock has, but that doesn't mean I don't dream of it one day. One day . . . far, far away."

I nodded and smiled at the same time.

"Listen. Stella and Ty Senior's thirtieth wedding anniversary is tomorrow night. There's going to be a big party. Why don't you go with me, as my date?"

Tilting my head, I gave him a hard look. "Your date? You do know I'm not sleeping with you, right?"

He laughed. "Let me rephrase it—go with me as friends. It will be fun."

I didn't want to tell Dirk that I had been secretly hoping Ty would ask me to go with him. It was stupid to even wish it, but I had let my silly heart dare to believe he might. It was tomorrow night, so the chances of Ty asking me at the eleventh hour were slim to none.

"Tanner will be back in town. I was sorta holding out for him to ask me," I replied with a wink.

Dirk threw his head back in a fit of laughter, which in turn made me laugh. It felt good to laugh and smile.

"Damn those Shaw boys."

"I'd love to go with you, but you do know it's going to be fancy? Stella is going all out, and I'm the one who's been in charge of getting it all put together. It's formal."

"I heard that rumor. Looks like you're starting to become quite the party planner in Hamilton."

Lifting my shoulder in a half shrug, I replied, "I have done a party or two."

He smiled. "Go with me, because it's last minute and I don't have a date. And considering you haven't flat out told me no, I'm going to guess Ty still has his head stuck up his ass."

With a grin, I nodded and replied, "I'd love to go with you. Do you have a tux?"

Dirk looked at me like I'd asked the stupidest question in the world. "Do I have a tux? You don't know me at all, Kaylee Holden."

Chapter Seventeen

Ty

"Kaylee has done an amazing job!" my mother said. Her eyes were dancing with happiness as my father smiled and looked around the ballroom of the Bitterroot River Inn.

Tanner slapped my back and laughed. "Your girl sure does know how to throw a party."

I shot him a dirty look and replied in a hushed voice, "She isn't my girl, so stop saying that."

Giving me a smirk, Tanner looked over to our parents and then back at me. "That's not what Brock said."

I rolled my eyes. "Brock doesn't know what he's talking about."

Our parents walked farther into the room as they went on and on about how beautiful it looked. It did look beautiful, and Kaylee *had* done an amazing job.

Tanner bumped my arm. "From what he told me, you two hooked up together, and you stayed at her place all night."

"Jesus, is my sex life really the topic of your conversations with Brock?"

"Not every conversation, but he did get me caught up on some stuff."

I glanced over my shoulder to give Brock a look that said he was getting his ass kicked as soon as this anniversary party was over. He caught my hard stare and frowned but then focused back on Morgan in his arms.

A pang of jealousy hit me in the chest as I watched him with his daughter. I quickly pushed it away.

"You want to tell me about it?" Tanner asked.

"No. Go find your date and leave me the hell alone."

Tanner laughed and stopped to wait for Lindsey Johnson. She was his go-to girl when he came into town and needed a date.

Lindsey walked in with Blayze and Lincoln, all of her attention on my nephew, who was turning out to be a lady's man just like his father and uncles.

"No date tonight?" Lincoln asked as she made her way up to me and stopped. She looked beautiful in the baby-blue gown she had on. It was sort of cute that Morgan's little dress matched Lincoln's. Another one of Kaylee's ideas, I was sure.

"Well, I had planned on asking Kaylee, but Brock informed me last night she had a date."

Lincoln raised her brow. "You were going to ask Kaylee?"

I smiled. "Why does that shock you?"

"Well, considering you had sex with her and then disappeared for three weeks, and then waited until the last night before the party to think about asking her . . . yeah, that would shock anyone."

"You never are one to mince words, are you, Lincoln?"

"Not when it comes to the people I love."

I nodded. "Duly noted. Is she coming with Channing?"

Lincoln gave me a little evil grin with a wink before turning on her heel and walking back over to Brock.

"Women," I mumbled as I made my way to the bar.

"What can I do for you, sir?" the kid behind the bar asked.

"Are you even old enough to be bartending?"

He laughed. "Yes, sir. I'm twenty-three."

I bristled. Since when did I become my father? "Give me anything in a bottle, beer-wise."

The young kid nodded, then handed me a bottle of a local craft beer. I took a drink as I scanned the room. Not many people were here yet, since the party didn't officially begin for another twenty minutes or so.

A flash of red caught my eye, and I damn near choked on my beer when I saw her.

Kaylee.

The dress she had on was off her shoulders and hugged her figure in all the right ways. It hugged the very figure I'd lost myself in just a few long weeks ago. When she walked, I noticed the slit that went damn near halfway up her thigh. I forced myself to swallow, feeling like I had a huge lump stuck in my throat.

"She's beautiful, isn't she?" the bartender said, clearly seeing whom I was looking at. "Whoever she's with is one lucky bastard."

I nodded, finished off my beer without looking at anyone else in the room but her, and then asked for another one.

Before I had a chance to take a drink, though, I heard a familiar voice.

"Better slow down, dude. The party hasn't even started."

Looking over my shoulder, I smiled when I saw Dirk. "Aww hell, does Brock know you're here?"

He laughed. "Yeah, I stopped by earlier today to visit with the little family. Morgan is a doll and looks just like Lincoln."

I smiled. "Yeah, she's a cute one. Blayze happy to see you?"

Dirk nodded. "Yeah, I saw him yesterday, when he was over at the house practicing on Dad's sheep for his big mutton-busting debut next month."

"Christ, Lincoln is going to pull her hair out with that boy," I said with a chuckle.

"Just like his daddy," Dirk said, then motioned to the bartender. "I'll have what he's having."

I took another look around the room, searching for Kaylee, but I couldn't find her.

Once Dirk got his beer, we made our way toward the table that had been set up for family.

"You come to town just for the party?"

He smiled. "That was one reason. I'm here on business too."

"Really?" I asked. "What sort of business?"

Dirk motioned for me to sit down at the table. No one was there currently. Brock and Lincoln had taken Blayze outside to the patio overlooking the small lake, and my folks were talking to the general manager of the hotel.

"PBR business," Dirk answered.

"Here? In Hamilton? Is someone wanting Brock to come back for something?" I asked with a sarcastic laugh.

"No, it's *you* I need to talk to."

My beer paused at my lips before I turned and looked at him. "Me?"

He grinned. "CBS wants you for a broadcasting position."

I drew in my brows. "You shitting me?"

"I am not shitting you." He took out a piece of paper and put it on the table, then slid it over to me. "This is what they're offering you for a three-year deal."

"Three years?" Even I could hear the surprise in my voice.

"Yep. Open it."

I did as he said and was dumbfounded as I stared at the six-figure number written down.

"That's per year."

For a moment, I stopped breathing and almost asked him for the contract to sign. Then a memory of Kaylee popped into my mind. Her under me, calling out my name as we both came at the same time.

Fuck. If this were any other time, I'd have signed it with no questions asked.

"Listen, I know it's a lot to take in, and I told the network you'd need a few days to think about it."

Turning, I stared at him in disbelief. "That's a lot of fucking money."

Dirk laughed. "Yeah, well, they want you on their team, and they're willing to pay you for it."

I glanced back down at the paper and was about to push it away when I saw Kaylee from the corner of my eye. I looked up to see her talking to Channing, and my heart felt like it was about to jump out of my body and break into a million pieces right there on the spot.

She fucking came with Channing.

Then, as if she could feel me staring at her, she turned and met my gaze. Her smile faded, but when she looked next to me and saw Dirk, it returned. She faced Channing and said something to him, then headed our way. It didn't surprise me that she'd want to come over and say hi to Dirk. The two of them had become good friends, and I knew she still kept in touch with him.

Dirk and I both stood when she approached. She went to Dirk and smiled. "Well, looks like I have the most handsome date in the room."

My mouth nearly dropped open. She sure as hell wasn't talking about me, which meant . . .

"Dirk is your date?" I asked, not even trying to hide the shock and anger in my voice.

Kaylee shot me a look that should have had me sitting my ass right back down in the chair. "No one else asked, so I was obviously available." She turned back to Dirk. "Shall we take a spin on the dance floor before everyone else shows up?"

Dirk smirked at me. If that asshole thought for one minute he was going to—

My thoughts stopped as I watched Kaylee take Dirk's hand and lead him to the dance floor. I sat back down and looked at the piece of paper on the table.

When I glanced back out to the dance floor and saw Kaylee laughing at something Dirk had said, I tried to ignore the burning feeling in my chest. Before I could even process things, Brock, Lincoln, and the kids had come over and sat down.

"You two want to go dance? I can hold Morgan for you, and Blayze can help." I winked at Blayze when he looked up at me.

"Yeah, I can help Uncle Ty if he don't know what to do when Morgan goes poo."

My eyes widened as Brock handed me his daughter. "Wait, no one said anything about her pooing."

Lincoln laughed. "She's already done that, in the truck on the way over. You're golden."

The two of them quickly headed out to the dance floor. When I looked down at my niece, I couldn't help but smile. I leaned down to whisper, "I don't think anyone can argue that you are the most beautiful girl in the room."

Blayze knelt on the chair next to me. "You really think so, Uncle Ty?"

I nodded. "I do. You don't think so?"

With a half shrug, he looked out at the dance floor. "My mama is pretty."

Smiling, I looked at Lincoln. "She's very pretty."

"And Aunt Kaylee is pretty too."

My gaze found Kaylee.

"I kind of have a crush on Aunt Kaylee. She's real pretty."

Looking back at my nephew, I couldn't help but let my smile grow bigger. "Can you keep a secret between me and you, buddy?"

Blayze looked at me and crossed his heart with his finger. "I promise I can, Uncle Ty."

In the last few months, Blayze had stopped pronouncing his *r*'s like *w*'s. It sort of made me a little sad that he was growing up so fast.

"I sorta have a crush on Kaylee too."

His eyes got big and round. "Really?"

"It's our secret, though, promise? That means no breaking out into a song and singing about it to anyone, especially to Kaylee."

Blayze rolled his eyes. "Uncle Ty, I'm almost in first grade, and I'll be six years old. I don't sing anymore."

Yep, I'd blinked and my nephew had grown up before my eyes.

Glancing back down to Morgan, I stilled when I saw those big blue eyes looking up at me. Then she smiled, and my heart melted, nearly leaving me breathless. "She smiled at me!"

Blayze leaned over and looked at his baby sister. "Nah, that's just her farting face."

◆ ◆ ◆

Kaylee stood in the middle of the dance floor with a microphone in her hand as she spoke a few words about my folks and their anniversary. She'd asked if me, Brock, or Tanner wanted to say anything, and we'd all declined. Speaking in front of a crowd didn't bother me, but speaking about my folks in front of a crowd—hell, I might start to get emotional, and I was not about to do that in front of friends and family. I knew that was why Brock and Tanner had said no as well.

Everyone laughed at something Kaylee had said, causing me to shake myself out of my own head. All eyes were on her, including Channing's. Dirk, on the other hand, was flirting with the girl at the next table, who didn't seem to mind that he was clearly there with another woman. Of course, Dirk and Kaylee were acting more like friends than an actual couple on a date, thank God.

"Stella and Ty Senior, would you do us the honor of starting off the next dance?" Kaylee asked. Everyone clapped, including me, as my parents walked onto the dance floor. I loved the way my father looked at my mother, like she was the most important thing in his world. Brock often gave Lincoln the same look. I couldn't help but wonder if a love like that would ever be blessed upon me.

My gaze drifted to the side of the dance floor, back to where I'd seen Kaylee. She was watching Mom and Dad, a smile on her face. She reached up and quickly wiped a tear away. Then her eyes shifted and locked with mine.

That night we'd spent together a few weeks before came right back. The feel of her under me, her arms and legs wrapped around me, drawing me in closer to her. I'd never experienced such a connection with another person like I had that night. I couldn't get deep enough inside her.

I could feel the corners of my mouth lift slightly into a smile. She gifted me with a small smile in return; then her attention was pulled from me when Channing asked her to dance. Anger quickly flooded in and replaced the warm feeling that had settled in my chest when she'd smiled.

Watching them made me feel sick to my stomach. His hand on her lower back, pulling her against his body.

"Who in the hell are you looking at, dude? If lasers were coming out of your eyes right now, they'd be dead."

I let out a gruff laugh and faced Dirk. "If only."

He laughed and shook his head. "Dude, go cut in."

A part of me wanted to. An even bigger part of me needed to know if my carelessness that night had had long-term consequences that I wasn't so sure I would be that upset with. I'd obviously not wanted to come right out and ask her if she was pregnant.

Then Channing leaned down and said something to Kaylee, causing her to laugh. It looked like Channing was about to kiss her when she pulled back from him.

I narrowed my eye and watched them carefully.

"I don't like him dancin' with her either, Uncle Ty. He's no good for her."

My gaze dropped to Blayze, and I laughed. "Where in the world did you ever hear that?"

Blayze kept his eyes on Kaylee and Channing. "I heard Grams telling Granddaddy that Channing wasn't nowhere near good enough for Kaylee."

I looked back out onto the dance floor and found my folks. They were smiling at each other. "Your grams is right about that one."

"I know! That's why I said it. But you look mad, and if you wants your secret to stay a secret, you best pretend a little better that her dancing with another boy doesn't make you angry, Uncle Ty."

"Being schooled by a five-year-old—ain't that some shit," Dirk said, slapping me on the back as he walked away laughing.

"Hey! I'm almost six, Uncle Dirk!"

I stood and straightened my tuxedo jacket. "I'm going to go ask a pretty girl to dance."

Blayze smiled. "I'm after you, Uncle Ty."

Glancing down, I winked at him. "You got it, buddy."

As I made my way closer to them, I watched Kaylee. The way she smiled at Channing. The way she looked at him. Was it different from the way she looked at me? Hell, my head was beginning to hurt. No woman had ever had me this fucking turned upside down before.

I tapped on Channing's shoulder. "Mind if I cut in?"

Channing's smile faded instantly, and he looked back at Kaylee. For the briefest of moments, I thought she was going to say she *did* mind. But she gave Channing a soft smile and took a step out of his arms.

I stepped into his vacated spot and looked at her. My heart sped up, and a nervous flutter hit the pit of my stomach. She really was the most beautiful woman in the room.

She stepped into my arms, and I pulled her close. Maybe a little too close, but I didn't give a shit. I missed the feel of her. The smell of her vanilla soap. The way she held her breath when I was near her.

"I've been meaning to call you or stop by to . . ." My voice trailed off.

Her brows lifted. "To what?"

Clearing my throat, I replied, "Talk. To talk."

"Oh, really? Seems to me you've been avoiding me, Ty." She looked away for a moment, then back up at me. "What did you want to talk about?"

After glancing around the room, I let out an exasperated sigh. "Maybe now isn't the time."

"Considering you're going out of your way to avoid me outside of this room, now seems like the perfect time."

"I'm not going out of my way."

Kaylee rolled her eyes and then looked away from me.

"It was irresponsible of me to have sex without a condom, and I wanted you to know if anything should come out of that . . ."

I cleared my throat again as she looked up at me. Her eyes were filled with something I couldn't read. For the first time since I'd met this woman, I had no clue what was going on in her head. "If you end up being—"

"I'm not. I've had my period since that night, so you're off the hook."

The instant pain in my chest shouldn't have been there. It should have been relief, I knew that, but that didn't mean anything. A sense of loss washed over me. "I wasn't going to ask to be let off of any hook, Kaylee."

Her mouth opened to say something, but then she closed it. We danced a few minutes in silence, and as the song was ending, she pulled back and looked up at me. "Dirk said he told you about the job offer with CBS."

I was positive I wore a shocked expression. "He told you about it?"

She nodded. "Yes. I think you should take it."

The pain in my chest grew tenfold. "You . . . you do?"

"Yes, it might be a good thing for you. Besides, you have nothing here holding you back."

My eyes searched her face, but it was completely void of any emotion. Nothing. "But I do. My family, and Blayze and Morgan. And who's going to make sure you don't set anything on fire?" I smiled, hoping it would also make her smile.

"I'm sure Channing could handle that just fine."

I took a step back. The feel of a knife being pushed into the middle of my heart nearly took my breath away. Kaylee stood there, not an ounce of regret on her face for the words she had just said.

So that was it. I had successfully pushed her away for good. The only thing I could do was nod, force another smile, then say, "Thanks for the dance, Kaylee. Enjoy the rest of your evening."

Before she could say anything else, I'd turned and headed off the dance floor. I pulled the paper Dirk had given me out of my pocket and dialed the number as I made my way toward the exit.

A male voice came on the line. "This is Sam James."

"Sam, it's Ty Shaw."

"Ty! Man, it's great to hear from you. I take it Dirk's spoken to you."

I didn't bother to look back into the ballroom. I wasn't sure if I could stand the sight of Kaylee in Channing's arms again. "He did."

"And?"

"I'm interested in talking."

"This is amazing news. How soon can you come to New York?"

"How soon can you have a private plane here?"

Sam laughed. "Pack a bag. You'll leave in the morning."

Chapter Eighteen

KAYLEE

The moment the words were out of my mouth, I wanted to tell him I was sorry. Instant regret pulsed through my body. The look of devastation on his face would haunt me the rest of my life, I was sure of it.

I couldn't move, though. The urge to tell him I hadn't meant it was so strong, but I was also so angry he had avoided me for weeks, then tried to tell me he would have been there if I had ended up being pregnant. All the emotions seemed to hit me at once, and I had no idea how to react or what to say. So I had purposely hurt him and then saw the pain in his eyes, and I hated myself for it. Then he simply walked away.

The moment I saw him pulling out his phone, I knew what he was doing. Nausea rolled through my stomach, and I almost went after him.

I waited for Ty to turn around, to give me one last look, but he didn't. He pushed the door open and walked out.

My hand instinctively went to my mouth in an attempt not to call out his name.

What if that had been Ty's attempt at telling me he wanted something more, and I had let my pride and anger push him away?

Oh God, what did I do?

"Kaylee, you shouldn't be standing on the dance floor all alone. Where did Ty go?"

The sound of Channing's voice only added to the guilt I was already feeling. I forced a smile before turning and facing him. "He got a phone call and needed to leave."

"Dance with me again?"

"I'm sorry, Channing. I need to check on the food and then hunt down Dirk, my date."

It looked like he winced, maybe at the reminder that I had actually come with another man and that he had come with a date of his own. The girl who'd been flirting with Dirk. What were the odds of that?

"Enjoy yourself, though!" I said, keeping my voice light and airy. The moment I spotted Dirk, I made a beeline for him.

He was at the table with Brock and Lincoln, holding Morgan. Even she was taken with him. Just like she had been with Ty. She was a smart girl and loved her uncles so. When I'd looked over earlier and saw Ty holding Morgan, I'd nearly fallen into a fit of tears.

I had no idea what in the world was going on with me; my emotions were all over the place. Case in point: the closer I got to the table, the angrier I got.

No. I knew exactly why my emotions were zipping along on the roller-coaster ride of emotion.

Ty. Shaw.

"Dirk, I need to talk to you."

Brock's phone beeped, and he looked down at it. Then his face turned white as a ghost. "Holy shit."

"What's wrong?" Lincoln and Dirk asked.

I, on the other hand, felt like there was a lump in my throat.

Brock looked over at Dirk. "Did you know about the job offer from CBS?"

Dirk nodded. "I was the one who presented it to him earlier this evening. Why?"

Brock looked back down at his phone, then scrubbed his hand over his face. "Ty just texted me he's leaving for New York City in the morning to meet with CBS about a possible commentary job on the Unleash the Beast Tour."

"What? Ty's leaving Hamilton? The ranch?" Lincoln's gaze snapped over to me.

"I can't believe it," Brock said, utter disbelief in his voice.

Dirk set his beer down. "Looks like he's ready for a change."

I shot a look in his direction, but he chose to ignore it.

"My dad's going to be fucking heartbroken. I mean, he'll be happy for Ty. Both Mom and Dad will, of course."

"Maybe this will be a good thing for him?" Lincoln offered.

Right at that moment, Tanner walked up. "Dude, did you get a text from Ty?"

Brock nodded his head. "Yeah, looks like he's going to entertain it this time."

"This time?" Lincoln asked, a confused expression on her face.

"Yeah, CBS approached him before about it, but Ty turned them down," Brock answered.

A million things raced through my mind. Would this mean Tanner would have to stay and help on the ranch? Surely not. They could hire someone like they had before, when Ty was on the PBR tour. How long would Ty be gone? Days? Weeks?

More importantly, how many women would be throwing themselves at him?

My hand went to my stomach, and I fought to hold down the urge to puke at that last thought.

Then I felt all eyes on me. I swallowed hard and met Dirk's gaze.

"Excuse me." I was barely able to get the words out without my voice cracking. I quickly turned and walked as fast as I could in my Louis Vuitton pumps.

The moment I walked out onto the patio, I dragged in a deep breath. Seconds later, I felt someone standing behind me.

"Want to talk about it?" Dirk asked.

I shook my head.

"Okay. Want me to hold you while you cry?"

I turned and walked into his outstretched arms. "It's all my fault, Dirk. He's leaving because of me."

"Shh, that's not true, Kaylee."

It *was* true. The look on his face when I'd mentioned Channing . . . I'd never be able to forget it.

I groaned into Dirk's tux as he gently swayed in a rocking motion side to side. His attempt to make things better.

"Brock and Tanner are going to hate me. Oh my God, Stella and Ty Senior will never forgive me!"

Dirk pulled back and looked down at me. "Kaylee, listen to me. Ty does what Ty wants to do. He always has, he always will. And as far as his family goes, they have always supported their sons in whatever they've wanted to do. Maybe this is a good thing for Ty."

I looked up at him, stunned into silence.

"Just hear me out on this. Ty's been fighting some serious demons the last few years, ever since the accident. He's missed that world—no one can argue that. After the accident, when he was told he would never get on a bull again, something inside him changed. We all saw it. Then the pain replaced the sadness, and he got lost in the pain-pill addiction. Something in him has changed again over this last year."

I looked down at the ground, only to have Dirk place his finger on my chin and lift my eyes to his. "*You* are what has changed him, and I know that scares him."

"Why?" I asked, my voice sounding wobbly. I hated sounding weak.

"You make him feel something he hasn't ever felt before. The old Ty would have had a beautiful woman on his arm tonight, then would have left early to most likely fuck her and walk away. Brock told me Ty hasn't been hooking up with anyone, not since you walked into his life."

"I don't know what to do, Dirk. I don't know if my heart can take another heartbreak. When I lost John, I lost a part of myself to a dark pit of sadness, regret, and blame, and I thought I'd never crawl out of it."

"But you did."

"With a lot of help from my therapist."

"Ty is stuck in his own personal hell. He's already lost the one thing that he thought made him who he was. Bull riding. Now imagine a part of him coming to life again, and you're the reason. He's probably scared shitless. And the Shaw brothers are not ones who like feeling scared."

I smiled and let a soft chuckle free. "How do you know he feels that way toward me?"

Dirk tossed his head back and laughed. "All you have to do is look at the poor bastard when you're anywhere near him. He can't keep his eyes off of you, Kaylee. And tonight he looked like he wanted to rip Channing's head off when you were dancing with him. Hell, I thought I was gonna get punched when he realized you were my date."

I closed my eyes and shook my head. "He said he doesn't want a relationship, but I know he feels the same thing I feel. I *know* he does."

A smile slowly grew over Dirk's face. "Then what are you going to do about it?"

With a deep breath, I stood up taller, then lifted my chin. "I'm going to let him go."

Dirk raised his brow. "Really? I kind of figured you were going to say you were going to go after him."

With a shake of my head, I said, "No. Ty needs to do this. If being away from bull riding is what's keeping him locked away, then maybe this is what he needs. I won't keep him from that."

"And you?"

"What about me?"

"Will you wait for him . . . or will you move on?"

I didn't answer him, and he looked over my head, out at the lake. He took in a breath and then slowly let it out before he focused back on me. "The circuit is filled with women throwing themselves at us. You know that, right?"

"Are you trying to tell me Ty is going to be sleeping around?"

He rubbed the back of his neck and shook his head. "I don't want you getting hurt, Kaylee. I care about you as a friend, and Ty is my friend also, but I remember the days when Ty would have women practically falling at his feet. If he thinks you've moved on, he's going to—"

I held up my hand. "I get what you're trying to say. I don't need to hear it out loud."

"Okay, but, sweetheart, you need to ready yourself if it does happen."

Chewing on the inside of my cheek, I turned and faced the lake. The mountains reflected off the water, and it was one of the most beautiful sights I'd ever seen. The peacefulness was almost too much to take in. I could have stayed out there for hours, just watching the ripples of water as the wind blew. The view was more serene than anything that was going on in my own head, after all.

I wrapped my arms around my body and fought off the chill that was making me tremble. Or maybe it was something else altogether different that had my body shaking. Whatever it was, I was going to leave it up to fate to figure out, because I suddenly felt too exhausted to even think about it.

Chapter Nineteen

Ty

I sat across the table as Sam waited for my answer.

"This weekend? In Billings?" I asked.

"Yes. You've been in front of the camera plenty of times, Ty. You know how it works. Give it a test run," Sam said.

Laughing, I scrubbed my hands over my face. "Okay, say it goes good, everyone is happy. Then what? The next invitational isn't until July."

"We'd like for you to go to Pueblo. Immerse yourself back into the world, go out on some PBR Majors, get back into the swing of things."

"You're asking me to just up and leave my family ranch. My family."

"Yes, we are, and if you weren't willing to do that, you wouldn't be sitting here right now."

He slid a piece of paper across the table with a figure on it. An even bigger figure than before. I glanced at it as Sam went on.

"Sign the contract, and this is yours."

"No contract, and money has never been my driving force—you know that, Sam. It was being the best at what I was doing at the time. If I didn't think I could do commentating, I wouldn't have come."

Sam smiled. "You Shaw boys always were cocky."

I returned his smile with a smirk. "We try."

"Fine, no contract. Let's call Billings a trial run. They'll introduce you as a guest commentator. If you like it, then you start up in August on the PBR tour. I still want you in Colorado. You need to get back into the world of PBR, Ty."

With a nod, I stood. "You're paying for a place there for me, then. That's all I'm asking for now. Once I figure out if this is something I want to do, I'll sign a contract."

"Of course. I think that sounds like a solid plan."

I reached my hand out, and Sam stood and shook it as I said, "Trial run, it is. I'll see you in Billings."

Sam stood, we shook hands, and I made my way out of the room. My heart was pounding. Was I really going to do this? Leave the ranch. Leave my family?

Leave Kaylee?

◆ ◆ ◆

My father stood to the side of the truck as I put my bags in the back.

"If Billings is a trial run, why do you need to go to Pueblo after?"

I could hear it in his voice. It wasn't disappointment; it was sadness. I knew my father liked having both me and Brock back on the ranch, so the knowledge that I was leaving for a few weeks had him rattled.

"It's just to get me back into the swing of things. It's been a while since I've been in that world, Dad. Nothing is permanent. I didn't sign any contracts. I need to see if this is something I want to get back into. I miss it."

He forced a smile.

"What about the education program you started?" my mother asked. "The breeding side of the ranch, Ty? You started that too."

I glanced over to Brock, who was standing off to the side. "Brock said he'd take over for me until I get back." I faced both of them. "I didn't sign a contract; I'm just testing the waters. Seeing if this is something I want to get back into."

My mother nodded, then winked. "Well, at least it's safer than your last gig."

I laughed and kissed her on the cheek. Turning to my father, I extended my hand.

"I'm proud of you, Ty. I want you to know that. Your mother and I will support you always, no matter what you do. If this is something you feel in your heart you want to pursue, we're behind you a hundred percent."

I pulled him in for a hug. "I appreciate that, Dad."

He gave me a firm slap on the back, and we stepped apart.

My mother cupped my face, turning it to the left and then to the right. "Don't be letting them put all sorts of makeup on that pretty face of yours."

"Yes, ma'am."

"And, Ty," she said, reaching for my arm to stop me from getting into the truck. "Don't get a girl pregnant."

My mouth fell open. "Excuse me?"

She rolled her eyes. "I'm not stupid. I know about the women you've . . . entertained . . . in the past. Don't be getting careless and letting them fall into your bed. It's time to start thinking about your future and not your penis."

Snapping my head to my father, I said, "Dad, seriously? Can you explain to her how wrong that all was?"

He laughed, and so did Brock.

"Son, someday when you do get married, you'll learn which battles to pick. This is not one of them I choose to gear up for."

I rolled my eyes. "Mom, you are not allowed to talk about my sex life or my . . . penis. *Ever again.*"

She lifted a brow. "Then don't give me a reason to, and we're all good, son."

With a sigh, I slid into the truck and shut the door. My folks stepped back as Brock leaned in.

"You sure about this?" he asked in a low voice.

"Of course I'm sure about it. This might not be bull riding, but at least I get to be around it. I need to see if this is something I'm meant to do."

His brows pulled in tight. "I meant, leaving without even saying goodbye to her."

"Who?" I asked, knowing damn well he meant Kaylee.

He shook his head. "She hasn't been herself since you went to New York."

I started the truck. "I'm sure she's fine. She's got Channing."

"Ty—" Brock started, but I cut him off.

"Take care of Mom and Dad, and don't fuck up the ranch. Mitchell Williams is interested in Might Fine. He's ready for the fourteen-pound dummy when he goes out for his next bucking session."

Brock nodded, but I knew the last thing he wanted to talk about was the bull I'd been training to buck. It had been my idea to get into bucking-bull breeding, and Brock and Tanner were on board with it. I couldn't help but feel guilty at the idea of leaving all that behind.

Brock finally smiled, then gave me a pat on the back. "I've got it covered here. Knock 'em dead, big brother."

◆ ◆ ◆

I should have been nervous, but I wasn't. My adrenaline was pumping as I let the sights and sounds of everything sink in. Dressed in jeans, boots, a button-down shirt, and a brand-new cowboy hat, I walked into the CBS control room.

Rich stood, reached his hand out, and then pulled me in for a bro hug. "Holy shit, Shaw. It's damn good to see you again, man."

Rich had been a professional bull rider before me and had retired not long after I'd won my world champion title.

"Rich, it's good to see you."

He shook his head and took a good look at me. "How in the hell did they talk you into this?"

"It's just a test run, that's all."

"Test run, my ass. Once you get back into this world, you're not going to want to leave. Unless . . ." He raised a brow. "You ever settle down, get married?"

"Nah."

"No girlfriend waiting at home for you?"

An image of Kaylee smiling popped into my head, but I quickly pushed it away. "No."

"Then this job is for you."

Laughing, I took a seat and looked at all the monitors. "What about you? I heard you got married and your wife has already popped out one kid."

"Yep, another on the way. I want to start taking some time off, hence them coming to you. We'll have three of us some weekends, two on the weeks I want to be home with my family."

"You fly back each week, right?"

"Yeah, but it's getting to me, all the traveling. Sometimes it's just easier going from city to city and not doing all the trips home."

I nodded.

"Bill heads home once a month. Of course, I'm pretty sure he and his wife are on the road to divorce, so he's not in a rush to *get* home."

"Oh, man, I'm sorry to hear that."

Rich laughed. "Dude, don't be. Bill has been . . . celebrating, if you will."

I nodded, understanding that he meant Bill had been sleeping around to celebrate his upcoming divorce. "How's Kim?"

"Doing good. She's also pregnant."

"No shit?"

He smiled. "Yeah, there's another reporter who's been shadowing her. Just do me a favor, pretty boy—keep your dick in your pants with this one. She's hot, and I'm pretty sure half the guys on the camera crew have tried to get into her pants since January. I'm thinking one or two have been successful. She's not as conservative as Kim, but Kim sees something in her."

I held up my hands. "Not a problem for me."

He let out a gruff laugh. "You say that now; wait until you see her. You think Kim is pretty—this girl is drop-dead beautiful . . . and *I'm* happily married."

"Just because you're married doesn't mean you don't notice a pretty woman," Bill said as he walked into the room and slapped me on the back, hard. "Fucking Ty Shaw. The buckle bunnies are going to lose their damn minds. Not to mention the Monster drink girls."

I rolled my eyes and shook Bill's hand.

"So, they're spinning me as a guest commentator?"

"That's the plan. Tell me you've kept up with all this. You know who's in first? How many points behind, all that good stuff?"

I shot Rich a look of disbelief. "Seriously, you're going to ask me if I'm prepared?"

"Hell yeah, I am. I need to know if your ass needs cue cards."

Bill and I both laughed. "Fuck you. I know the stats on pretty much all the riders and the bulls. What I didn't know, I read over last night to get up to speed, and it wasn't much."

"That's my man," Bill said, putting his headphones on. "You ready to become a star, my friend?"

I put on my own headphones and let Melissa, one of the camera-crew techs, put on my mic.

"I was born ready," I replied, giving Melissa a wink when she looked up and smiled at me. We'd met earlier, and I couldn't help but notice the fuck-me eyes she'd been tossing my way ever since.

"Ty, there's a party tonight for one of the camera guys who works down in the chutes. You should come—it'd be a good way to let everyone meet you," Melissa said, tucking my mic into place.

My gaze lifted quickly to Bill and Rich. They both nodded, indicating it was probably a good idea. "Sure, I'd love to go."

Her smile widened. "Great, I'll write down the information for you."

"You're on in five," a voice said in my earpiece.

"Or you could just send it to me in a text message," I replied, grabbing a pen and writing my number on a piece of paper and handing it to her.

"Great, will do."

When Melissa left, the three of us took our positions outside the control booth, with the arena and chutes behind us.

Rich bumped my arm and leaned in close to me and said, "And no fucking anyone on the crew, Shaw."

I grinned. "Killjoy." Rich didn't need to know I had no desire to fuck anyone.

Kim walked up to us, another woman following behind her.

"Rachel?" I said, stunned to see the one girl I had hooked up with multiple times standing in front of me.

"Ty? Oh my gosh, *you're* the guest commentator?" she asked with a smile as she quickly walked up and threw her arms around me. When she took a step back, she let her gaze sweep over my body. "You look amazing. How are you?"

"It figures the bastard would know her," Bill said to Rich.

I shot him a smirk, then put my attention back on Rachel. "I'm doing really good. How about you?"

She shrugged. "I'm good. Listen, let's catch up after, maybe grab a drink in the bar?"

"Yeah, maybe."

Her smile faltered some, and I felt like a dick. Rachel had always assumed we would be something more than what we were. To me, she was a fuck buddy. The one girl who hadn't been simply a one-night stand. She was good in bed, and I liked talking to her. It was never anything serious, although I knew she'd wanted it to be. She'd worked as an assistant to one of the CBS hot shots and flew in every week and followed him around like a fucking puppy.

She liked kinky sex, which I wasn't all that much into, but I'd found it a challenge when she dared me to have sex in the strangest places. She'd once asked me to fuck her on the back of a bull. The thought had crossed my mind, but somehow it had just seemed wrong. For the bull, not me.

"Okay, well, good luck!"

"Thanks."

Kim stepped up and gave me a quick hug. "Welcome back, Ty. Talk later."

You could for sure tell Kim was pregnant, but she didn't stick around long enough for me to say anything other than, "Sounds good, Kim."

After the two of them had walked away, I glanced at Bill and Rich. They both gave me that look that said they wanted to know how in the hell I knew Rachel.

"What?" I asked, a smirk on my face.

"You bastard, you've had sex with Rachel, haven't you?" Rich asked.

I laughed. "Yes, yes, I have. More than once."

"Bastard!" Bill hissed as the countdown started in our ears.

"It's showtime," Rich said as the three of us looked straight at the cameras.

I felt an excitement I hadn't felt in a long time. I fell right in line with my cocommentators, like this was a job I was made to do.

Chapter Twenty

Ty

The moment I stepped into my hotel room, I wanted to do a face plant on the bed. I was fucking exhausted. Trying to keep a smile on my face, thinking about everything we were talking about, and attempting to remember not to swear on live TV had worn me the hell out.

My phone buzzed, and I reached into my pocket for it. It was a text from my mother.

Mom: You looked so handsome. We all loved seeing you on TV. You for sure take after me. Sprinkle in some of your daddy's good looks, of course.

I smiled, typed out a reply of thanks, and then tossed my phone to the side, rolled over, and stared at the ceiling. An image of Kaylee popped into my mind, and I couldn't help but wonder if she had watched as well.

Sitting up, I reached for my phone again.

Me: We? Was there some sort of watch party?

The little dots started to bounce on the screen as my mother typed out her reply.

Mom: Everyone was here, except of course for Tanner. He's riding in Colorado Springs tonight, but he said he would try and catch the highlights.

I laughed.

Me: Brock and Lincoln there?

Mom: Yes, and Kaylee came with them.

And there it was. The answer I had been looking for.

Me: Thanks for all the support, Mom. Was Kaylee with Channing?

I stared at the blue arrow, trying to decide if I wanted to send that message or not. What the fuck did I care if Channing was with Kaylee? I didn't. I hit the delete button and stopped at *Mom* before hitting send.

Then my phone rang with a number I didn't recognize.

"Hello?"

"Ty, it's Rachel. I got your number from Melissa."

"Hey, what's going on?"

"Well, Melissa mentioned you coming to the party tonight. I thought maybe we could go together."

This had *bad idea* written all over it.

My phone went off with another text. When I pulled it back to see who had texted me, my heart immediately dropped to the floor.

Kaylee: Are you free to talk?

"Ty? Are you still there?"

Rachel's voice pulled me out of the fog I'd been pushed into with just a damn text message.

"Yeah, I'm still here. Sure, we can go together. I'll meet you down in the lobby. Sound good?"

"Sounds perfect. See you in a few."

I hit end and stared at the text. My hand started to shake as I went to reply, and that pissed me off. I dropped the phone onto the bed, opened my suitcase, and changed clothes. Really, all I did was take off the button-down shirt and replace it with a T-shirt.

I thought back to the last time I'd been with Rachel. Her hotel room, the night before my last ride. We'd fucked until around midnight; then I'd gotten dressed and left. Before I walked out the door, she'd told me she wanted something more, and I told her we'd talk about it after the invitation was over.

We never got the chance to talk about it, and honestly, I wasn't interested in anything with her other than casual sex. When she'd called me after the accident, I'd sent her calls to voice mail. It took four months of me ignoring her calls before she finally stopped calling.

It had been a dick move, but I hadn't wanted to talk to anyone who had anything to do with the PBR. Including the girl I fucked occasionally. We'd never been exclusive, and she knew that. Hell, she'd even dated a few guys while she was hooking up with me. And when she'd mentioned wanting something more, I'd known in my heart I hadn't wanted that with her. She was good in bed, a stress relief. A way to relax, and that was it. That was all I'd needed at the time.

Looking down at my phone, I took in a deep breath. Questioning what I needed in my life right *now*. I reached for it and pulled up Kaylee's text.

Me: Is it important? I'm about to go out.

The moment after I sent it, I regretted it. What a dick.

It took her a few minutes to reply, and when she did, it threw me, and it would fucking drive me crazy for the rest of the damn night.

Kaylee: It was, but it's been taken care of.

Damn it all to hell.

◆ ◆ ◆

Rachel informed me the party was being held at someone's house.

"I thought it was at the hotel. A birthday party or something. Wasn't it?"

She simply smiled, then gave me a sexy wink. "Maybe we can have some fun. Like old times."

I laughed. "I don't think so."

She gave me a fake pout, then looked down at her phone. We pulled up a few houses down, and I parked my truck behind a bunch of other cars. When we walked into the living room, Rachel grabbed my hand, trying to lace her fingers with mine. I pulled my hand away. There was no way I was going to give anyone the idea I was with her. As a matter of fact, my coming to the party with her was probably a bad idea. Not very many people knew we'd slept together, and I wanted to keep it that way.

We walked farther in, and there wasn't a single person there I recognized from today. Not one.

I looked down at the coffee table. A few lines of cocaine were laid out, one girl snorting as a guy looked on.

Fuck.

"Drugs?" I asked, looking at Rachel.

She shrugged. "I'm not into that scene—only a few are—but if you want a hit, go for it. They've got some pills usually too. If you want to experiment, I'm all for having some sex while high."

My heart raced in my chest as we walked into the kitchen. The familiar sight of people wasted and high on drugs made my skin crawl. A small bag of pills sat on the counter, instantly making my entire body break out into a sweat.

"Not interested, Rachel. Like I told you in the truck, I'm not going to have sex with you."

She pouted again, then laughed.

"This isn't the birthday party for the camera guy at CBS, is it?"

With a shake of her head, she replied, "Nope. I thought we could have more fun at this party. No one to see us, if you know what I mean."

I groaned and rubbed the back of my neck. "Rachel, I'm not into this scene, and I'm no longer into *you*."

She stared at me with a hurt expression, then smiled. "You say that now, Ty." Her eyes looked past me, and I glanced over my shoulder to see some guy looking directly at her.

Turning back to her, I asked, "Your latest fuck buddy?"

With a nod, she lifted up on her toes and put her mouth to my ear. "Want to watch us fuck?"

I jerked my head back in surprise. "What in the hell? No, I don't want to watch you fuck some guy. Listen, this isn't my scene. I'm leaving and heading back to the hotel. Do you want to come?"

"Yes, I'd love to come. If I remember right, you were good at that."

"I'm out of here."

She grabbed my arm. "Oh my gosh, Ty, get over yourself. Pop a pill and relax if you need to. I'll be back in fifteen minutes." She looked at the other guy and laughed. "Make it thirty."

Rachel walked toward the guy but went past him. He waited a good minute before he went up the same stairs Rachel had.

I scrubbed my hands down my face and took another look at the pills. Swallowing hard, I tried to ignore that it felt like the room was caving in on me. The air felt heavy, and I struggled to get my heartbeat under control. A sweat broke out on my neck, and I had to focus on my breathing.

Fucking hell. How had I gotten myself into this situation? I needed to get the hell out of there, and fast.

My phone vibrated in my pocket, and I pulled it out.

Kaylee.

I quickly turned and walked back through the living room, ignoring everyone as I rushed to the front door and down the steps of the porch. The cold spring air felt good as it rushed into my lungs.

Answering the phone, I said, "Kaylee, is everything okay?"

"What? Ty, this is Rich. Listen, don't go to that party with Rachel. It's not the same party Melissa invited you to. They're at the hotel, celebrating Bob Jenkins's birthday. Melissa told me Rachel was taking you somewhere else. Rumor has it she's wrapped up in a different crowd, if you know what I mean."

It took me a second to realize it wasn't Kaylee calling. I had no idea why I'd even thought it was her. "Yeah, I just saw it firsthand. I think CBS might want to consider finding someone else to take over for Kim while she's out."

"Fuck. Drugs?"

I started down the block to where I'd parked my truck. "That, among other shit."

"What kind of other shit?" Rich asked.

Sliding into the driver's seat of my truck, I felt a little bad about leaving Rachel behind, but clearly she was with the guy she was hooking up with now. "Let's just say she asked me to take part in a threesome."

"Dude! You turned it down?"

I rolled my eyes. "Very funny."

"No, seriously, that's all kinds of messed up."

"Yeah, it was. She was going to fuck some guy and wanted me to watch and, I'm sure, join in at some point."

Rich remained silent on the other end of the phone.

"Rich?"

"Yeah, I'm here. Just figuring out how to tell Kim she needs to find someone new."

"Listen, just keep my name out of it. Come up with some other reason why you don't think Rachel's the one."

"I will, just get your ass back to the hotel."

With a laugh, I replied, "I'm already on my way. I'm tired anyway— think I'll head up to my room."

"Hey, before you go, who's Kaylee? You almost sounded relieved when you thought it was her."

"She's no one. Her last text message to me must have been pulled up, and I'd seen that or something before my phone rang."

"Okay, if you say so. Good job tonight. Get some sleep. We've got two more nights to go."

By the time I got back to the hotel, I'd managed to get my breathing under control. I hadn't had a single urge to try any of the drugs that were at the party, but I also hadn't been prepared to get hit with all that shit. Then Kaylee's cryptic text message kept replaying in my head, driving me even more insane.

Once I got up to my room, I took a hot shower. After drying off, I wrapped the towel around my waist and sat on the edge of the bed.

I took my phone off the charger and hit Kaylee's name. It was late, almost midnight, but I needed to talk to her. The urge to hear her voice was something that both scared me and made me excited.

"Hello? This is Kaylee's phone."

The air in my lungs felt like it had frozen instantly at the sound of Channing's voice.

"Ty?"

I couldn't fucking talk. Not a word would form. Nothing.

"Ty?"

Finally, a rush of air hit me, causing me to take in a deep breath. "Hey, Channing. Sorry to call so late. I actually called the wrong number. Sorry."

"No worries, I think Kaylee—"

The room felt like it was spinning. Cutting him off, I said, "Listen, I've got to go. Take care."

I hit end and stared at my phone. Then I turned it off and sat on the bed for what felt like forever. When the room began to feel like it was moving in on me, I stood and quickly got dressed. I knew if I tried to go to sleep, I'd end up waking up sweating, with a racing heart. I wasn't really in the mood for that shit tonight. What I was in the mood for was to get shit-faced.

I made my way down the hall, waited for the elevator, and then stepped inside. Two women looked up, both smiling when they saw me.

"Evening, ladies," I said, hitting the button for the lobby and tipping my cowboy hat at them.

"You're Ty Shaw," one of them said.

With a grin, I nodded.

"Oh my God. I can't believe it. Ty Shaw!" the other one said, her blonde hair bouncy as she jumped a little and clapped. "I loved watching you ride."

Buckle bunnies. A year ago, I'd be punching the elevator button of the floor to my room and going back up, probably with both of them.

"Thank you," I said, giving her a wink. She practically melted on the spot.

"Where are you heading?" the blonde asked, then looked over at her friend. They were both pretty. One blonde. One brunette. Both dressed in jeans, boots, and shirts that showed off their impressive upper bodies.

"I'm heading to the bar, ladies. I need to get drunk."

They both giggled as they each wrapped an arm around mine.

"What a coincidence—we're headed there too."

I smiled. "Perfect."

Chapter Twenty-One

KAYLEE

"Thank you, Channing. I had no idea what to do. I tried calling Brock, Stella, and then Ty. I couldn't get any of them to answer the phone."

He laughed. "It's fine. I'm just glad I heard the call come over and was able to take it."

I smiled. "Me too. When I saw that cow with a calf coming out of her back end, I freaked. Probably not the best thing to do, calling 911."

Channing laughed again as he tossed his bag into the back of the truck he'd driven over from the fire station. "I was getting off shift, so it really wasn't a big deal. Plus, by the time I got here, you seemed to have things under control. I was impressed when I saw the towels, scissors, and iodine tincture."

I gave him a half-hearted laugh. "I googled what to do when a cow is giving birth. As far as the iodine tincture, that was pure luck. I saw it in the tack room. I was relieved to know Mama was going to handle it all just fine."

He grinned. "You did great, Kaylee. Thanks for letting me clean up in your house."

"Oh gosh, thank you for being here, in case it didn't go smoothly. I cannot believe I couldn't reach anyone. I guess they all turn off their phones before bed."

"Hey, before I forget, Ty called your phone a few minutes ago. I knew you'd been trying to reach him, and with it being so late, I figured you wanted to talk to him."

My stomach lurched. "You answered my phone?"

He frowned slightly. "Um, yeah. I'm sorry. I was going to bring the phone out here, but he cut me off, said he'd dialed the wrong number."

I was positive Channing could hear my heart now, pounding in my chest. What would Ty think of Channing answering my phone so late at night?

Shit. Shit. Shit.

I had never wanted to slap a man so hard in my entire life. What in the world would possess him to answer my phone?

Channing stared at me for a moment before he sighed. "Listen, I'm sorry if I did something wrong."

I forced a smile. "No, it's fine, just maybe next time don't be going and answering other people's phones."

He laughed like I was joking. There was something in his eyes, though, that told me Channing had known exactly what he was doing. He'd wanted Ty to know he was here.

"Thank you again, Channing, for coming over."

"Sure. I'll see you around? Maybe we can grab some coffee or something?"

"I'll see you around. Thanks again."

I purposely avoided answering his coffee question. Channing started the truck and took off. As he drove down the drive, another truck pulled in. Brock parked and got out. He looked over his shoulder at the retreating truck, then back at me.

"Hey, I take it you got my panicked message."

Brock laughed. "I did. Took everything I could do to convince Lincoln we didn't need to wake up the kids and all drive over here. That I could handle it."

I chuckled.

Brock looked back at the taillights in the distance. "Was that Channing?"

"It was. I freaked out when I couldn't reach any of y'all, and I called 911. Channing heard it come over the radio and called in that he was getting off of his shift and would come by. Of course, after I made the call, I calmed down and figured out what needed to be done. Channing was here, though, in case a problem occurred, which didn't happen. Mom and baby are fine—they're in the barn."

Brock followed me to the barn. I stood off to the side as he checked out the calf and praised the mama.

"How in the world did you get over here, Mama?" he asked, rubbing his hands over her gently.

"I looked the best I could with a flashlight to see if there was a hole in the fence anywhere. I couldn't find one."

"She isn't one of ours. Must be from the Wickers' ranch on the other side of you. I'll give them a call in the morning."

I nodded, then asked, "How do you know she's not one of yours?"

He pointed to the tag in her ear. "Not our tag."

I looked closer. "Well, hell, you mean those aren't just pretty little cow earrings?"

With a chuckle, he replied, "No. They're like identification. Tells us everything about the cow."

"I guess I should learn more about the cattle business."

Brock flashed me a smile and then a wink. "You should. My father would be in his glory."

Wrapping my arms around myself, I shivered. "Is it going to be warm enough out here for them?"

"Oh, yeah, they'll be fine. I'll stop by in the morning to check on them."

"Sounds good."

I walked next to Brock as we made our way to his truck. "Brock, may I ask you something?"

"Sure, Kaylee, you can ask me anything."

Chewing on my lip, I let out a deep breath. "Do you and your folks blame me for Ty leaving?"

His eyes widened in shock. "Blame you? Kaylee, why in the world would we blame you?"

One shoulder lifted in a shrug. "I don't know, because I'm pretty sure it was something I said to Ty that pushed him into making his decision."

"Ty's an adult; he makes his own choices."

I nodded, then looked up at him. "I love him, Brock."

A slow smile spread over his face. "I know you do, Kaylee."

"I don't know what to do. I know Ty is lost in a part of himself that he thinks he can't show to anyone. A vulnerable side of him that he tries desperately to hide. He thinks for some stupid reason he's not good enough for me. But I don't think it's just that; I think he's afraid I'll somehow hurt him, or maybe that he'll hurt me. I know he still struggles with the fear of being lost to drugs again. But that doesn't scare me, Brock. I would never leave him, or doubt his strength to fight for anything. What scares me is the idea of him not being in my life."

"And you want more than friendship with him?"

"Yes."

"Then, tell him."

I shook my head. "I don't want to push him away. He already told me he wasn't looking for a relationship, but . . ."

Brock raised a brow. "I think we both know he cares about you, Kaylee. Maybe what he really needs is to know he's worth the fight. That you won't give up on him, no matter what he says."

"He called tonight when I was in the barn with the mama cow and her calf. Channing took it upon himself to answer my phone."

"Oh, shit," Brock said.

"Yeah. Oh, shit. I hate saying this, but I think Channing did it on purpose. I don't want to think he would do that, but why on earth would he answer my phone?"

Brock rubbed his chin. "I have an idea . . . if you're willing to get on a plane for a quick ride."

"Depends. Am I going somewhere warm with a beach?"

He laughed. "No. Billings."

A feeling of hope and excitement built in my chest. "This better be a good plan, Brock."

"I'll sweeten the deal—it'll be a private plane."

"Jet. None of those propeller planes that will make me throw up the entire time."

"Deal. I'll pick you up first thing in the morning." Brock glanced at his watch. "You better get some sleep—sun's up at six a.m. Have a bag packed."

Brock pulled out his phone, hit a number, then looked at me. "The calf will be fine. Get some sleep, Kaylee."

"Okay."

A muffled voice came through on Brock's phone. "It's Brock. I need a favor."

He climbed into his truck and waved at me as I took a few steps back, then turned and headed into the house.

Once I'd tracked down my phone, I went to my call log. Ty had called thirty minutes ago. Maybe he was still up. I hit his number and quickly got to work getting a small bag and packing some clothes.

A part of me wasn't sure I could leave him a message. Maybe I should simply show up.

What if he was with someone, though?

I sat down on the edge of the bed. I quickly hung up after his message played and I heard the beep to leave one of my own.

He'd said he was going out. Who was he going out with? I'd look pretty stupid knocking on his hotel door tomorrow and finding some girl in his bed. Then again, by the time I got there, he would most likely be up.

"For the love of God, just call him back and leave a message, you pussy!" I said out loud.

I hit his number again, and this time I left a message.

"Hey, Ty. It's Kaylee. I had a bit of a problem earlier: a mama cow was standing in front of my house with a calf coming out of her back end. Not something a girl sees every day, I can tell ya that. I couldn't get ahold of anyone and ended up calling 911. If it's not a fire, it's a baby calf being born in my front yard. Anyhoo, Channing heard it, and . . . well, he came over to help out. That was the only reason he was here. I don't know why he answered my phone. I was down at the barn at the time. Anyway, I don't know why I'm telling you all of this on the phone either. I'm leaving in the morning to head out of town. I'll see you soon. Okay, bye."

I hit end and then stared at the phone. *Jesus, did I really just ramble all that off on his voice mail?*

With a roll of my eyes, I got back to packing a bag. I took a quick shower, brushed my teeth, and crawled into bed. I had hardly closed my eyes when my alarm went off at five thirty in the morning. I quickly got dressed, made some toast and a cup of coffee to go, and grabbed my bag, charger, and purse. As I was walking out onto the front porch, Brock was pulling up.

I took in a deep breath and slowly let it out.

"Lord, please don't let this be a huge mistake. Please."

Chapter Twenty-Two

TY

Bright lights caused me to squint. Tires sliding on the pavement pierced my ears before the sound of metal crunching caused me to scream out in pain.

Jerking up in bed, I dragged in a breath. Then another. My heart raced in my chest, and I could feel the sweat on my forehead. The room felt cold, so cold I swore I could see my breath as I panted to regain some semblance of normal breathing. I dropped back down onto the pillow and closed my eyes.

Fucking nightmares. When would they stop?

My phone rang on the nightstand, causing me to groan and reach for it.

"H-hello?" The word barely came out of my dry mouth. Clearing my throat, I tried again. "Hello."

"So, it's true: you were at the bar last night getting shit-faced."

I groaned and looked up at the ceiling. Thank God I'd shut the curtains last night and the sun wasn't shining in. "Rich, I'm not in the mood for your bullshit."

He laughed. "I also heard you were talking to two women."

My heart stopped, and I quickly looked around the bed. It was empty. I closed my eyes and let last night flood back into my memory.

I had gone to the bar with the two girls. We sat at a table, and I had a few beers, a couple of shots. The blonde managed to hook up with some guy; I had no clue who he was. The brunette stayed at the table. It was me and another bull rider, Mike Warner, by then, and Dirk showed up a little later.

Then I remembered the brunette reaching under the table and rubbing on my dick.

It took me not even two seconds to push her hand away. Why, I had no fucking clue. I needed to be screwed. I needed to have mindless sex with someone to get Kaylee out of my head.

Slowly, I sat up, then scrubbed my hand over my face.

"Yeah, I didn't hook up with either one of them. Pretty sure Dirk did, though."

Rich laughed again. "Listen, Bill and I are meeting for breakfast in the restaurant down here in the hotel. You want to join us?"

I didn't, but that was no way to start off what was possibly going to be a working relationship with these guys. "Sure. Give me a few minutes to get cleaned up, then I'll be down."

"Sounds good. See ya in a few," Rich said.

Once the call ended, I stood and made my way into the bathroom. After a quick shower, I brushed my teeth, then got dressed. I grabbed my wallet and phone and put my black cowboy hat on. I noticed I had a few voice-mail messages. One from my mother, one from Brock, and one from . . .

Kaylee.

My heart wobbled a second in my chest as I held my finger over her message, then hit my mother's first.

"Good morning, sweetheart. How are things in Billings? We miss you already. One of the neighboring ranches had a cow wander onto

Kaylee's place, and she started laboring in front of her house. The poor thing panicked and called 911. Anyway, give me a call."

I rolled my eyes but smiled. Only Kaylee would call 911 because a cow was in front of her house having a calf. At least it hadn't been a fire.

The next message was from Brock. "Give me a call, ASAP."

That made me take notice. I wanted to listen to Kaylee's message first, though.

I hit play, and her voice made my breath hitch and my chest tighten. Just that sweet sound made my entire body feel warm. Comforted. And that freaked me out.

She rattled on about the cow, its giving birth, the 911 call, and the reason why Channing was there. I couldn't help but smile again. Had she been worried what I was thinking when I'd called and that dick had answered? I didn't want to admit it in the light of day, but that asshole answering her phone had been what had caused me to go and get shit-faced.

Pulling up Brock's name, I hit call.

"Ty," he snapped.

"Brock."

He sighed. "Are you alone?"

Laughing, I asked, "What kind of question is that?" I opened the door to my room—only to find the brunette from last night getting ready to knock on my door.

I stopped in my tracks, and she smiled as she looked me over from head to toe, then licked her ruby-red lips.

"It's the kind that needs to be answered right away. Kaylee is probably walking into your hotel right now, coming to find you."

I froze. "Kaylee?"

"No, it's Mary," the brunette said.

A strange growling sound came across the phone. "Fucking hell, you asshole! You slept with someone last night?"

"What? No!" I said, then looked back at the girl.

"Yes, silly, that's my name," she said with a giggle.

I wanted to roll my eyes at her, but I wasn't that big of a jerk. "Brock, I'm walking out of my hotel room, and someone was just about to knock on the door—hold on."

"That better be the case."

I sighed. "Mary, did you need something? I'm running late for breakfast," I said, more into the phone than to her.

"Oh, well, I just left your friend Dirk's room, and I thought maybe you might like to—"

"No, thank you," I said as I pulled my door shut and walked around her and headed to the elevator. Dick move, but if Kaylee *was* here, the last thing I wanted was for her to see some woman standing outside my hotel room.

"Brock?" I said into the phone, not even bothering to look back at Mary, or whoever the hell she was.

"Yeah, damn Dirk. One of these days, he's going to meet a woman who'll knock him flat on his ass and make him stop all the manwhoring."

I chuckled. "I don't know—the guy likes his pussy."

The elevator doors happened to open just at that moment when I was talking about Dirk's proclivities, and two older women glared at me.

"Excuse me, ladies," I said, stepping into the elevator as Brock lost it, laughing. "I might lose my signal," I said to Brock, giving them both my best smile. My charm didn't work, though, and all I got were two scowls in return.

Oddly enough, I never lost my signal.

"So, do you want to tell me why Kaylee is here in Billings?"

"Not really."

I rubbed at the instant headache in my temples. "Brock."

"Listen, this is between the two of you, but something happened last night, and she was worried you were going to read into it wrong."

Even if I tried to hide it, I wouldn't have been able to contain the slight upward turn of my mouth. "Channing?"

"Yeah. Ty, listen, do me a favor: don't blow her off or act like you can't stand being around her. She took a flight in this morning to be there."

"A flight?"

"Just promise me you won't be a dick to her."

"Brock, I wouldn't do that to her. I mean, we have a sort of . . . messed-up relationship, or friendship, or whatever the hell it is. I know I've hurt her before, and I had some messed-up reason for justifying it, but I'm not going to hurt her. Ever again."

"Good, or I'd have to break your other leg in a few spots."

"Like that would ever happen," I scoffed. "I'm supposed to meet Rich and Bill for breakfast, and I'm running late. I'll keep an eye out for her."

"Ty?"

"Yeah?"

"She loves you. I just thought maybe you should know that before she gets there, and maybe it's wrong of me to tell you, but it's out there now."

I stopped walking, anxiety instantly filling my entire body. Swallowing hard, I forced myself to move, then forced the next question out as I approached the hotel restaurant.

"How . . . how do you know that?"

"She told me last night."

"What do you mean, she told you last night?"

"I'll talk to you later."

"Brock. Brock!"

The line went dead, and I let out a growl as I shoved my phone into my pocket. I was going to kick his ass for getting involved in my personal life. And why in the hell was Kaylee telling my brother she was in love with me? She couldn't be in love with me. Yes, what we shared that night was fucking amazing, but she didn't know the real me. She couldn't—because that was the part of me she wouldn't want to love.

"Ty, how did you sleep?" Bill asked. He stood and gave my hand a quick shake.

"Good, thanks."

The waitress walked up and smiled when I looked at her. "What can I get you?"

"A bloody mary, and just some scrambled eggs, whole wheat toast, and a bowl of fruit, please."

She nodded as she wrote it down, then asked Bill and Rich, "Anything else, gentlemen?"

They both answered no.

"Hair of the dog, huh?" Rich asked with a laugh.

I groaned. "I'm getting too old for this shit. How do these guys do it and then climb onto a bull?"

Bill laughed. "You should know—you used to be one of them."

"Yeah, well, I guess being twenty-three versus twenty-nine makes a big difference in endurance."

"Oh, most definitely. Just make sure you're ready for today. You did great yesterday, and the bosses loved it. That's all that matters."

"So, what are you guys going to do about Rachel?" I asked, thanking the waitress for my drink and taking a long swig.

"I spoke with Kim this morning; she's going to handle it."

With a nod, I took another drink.

"So . . . you and Rachel dated?" Rich asked.

I almost snorted. "Hell no. We fucked, a lot. But it wasn't anything exclusive."

"Never were one to mince your words," Bill said.

"Why should I? That's what we did. She was a regular on the circuit, pretty and very willing. I didn't care who she slept with, and she didn't care who I slept with. It was good for both of us. And now it's not."

They both nodded.

"Can we move on from my past sex life, please? Tell me what I should be expecting if I take this job."

Bill gave me a confused look as he turned to Rich, then back to me. "If? I thought it was pretty much a done deal."

The waitress set my food down in front of me, and I dug into it like I hadn't eaten in weeks. "No, I didn't sign a contract. I told them I wanted to see if this was something I wanted to get back into. It took me a long time to get used to the idea that the PBR wouldn't be a part of my life anymore, so coming back, and into something totally different, is something I need to think about. I'm not ready to make any long-term commitments."

Rich leaned back in his chair. I couldn't tell if he was pissed or honestly confused, like Bill seemed to be.

"Sam didn't say anything about this being a test run."

"'Trial run'—those were the words he used," I said, a smirk on my face.

"Ty, why wouldn't you want to do this? The pay is great, you get to travel, you're surrounded by friends you've known since you were, what . . . seventeen?"

"I didn't go pro until I was twenty."

Rich closed his eyes and took in a deep breath, then slowly let it out. Clearly he wasn't in the mood for fucking around this morning. "You're the guy we want. The guy we need."

I chewed my toast, swallowed, then took another drink of my bloody mary. "Why me?"

"Why you?" Bill asked, a befuddled expression on his face. "Have you looked in the mirror lately, Shaw?"

"I have. This morning. What do my looks have to do with this?"

Rich shook his head. "The PBR and CBS are trying to pull in more of an audience. Women are one of the fastest-growing populations of viewers. You put a pretty face in front of the camera, a guy who used to ride . . . *and* you have a tragic story to tell."

"Which I'm not telling. That's all in the past, and I'd like to leave it there."

This time, Rich and Bill exchanged a look that said they knew something I didn't. I put my fork down and wiped my mouth, dropping my napkin onto my plate. "What are they not telling me?"

"Sam wants to make your comeback more like a documentary. They want you in Colorado so they can keep an eye on you, film you as you get back into the world of PBR. They've already talked about interviewing some people who rode with you—some who rode after, some before. They were even planning on contacting Brock and your folks for interviews."

I was positive my lower jaw was on the table. "Are you fucking kidding me? They didn't say a goddamn word about this to me in New York."

"That's because it was in the contract. They were probably hoping you'd sign and not look at it."

Laughing, I looked at them both in disbelief. "I wouldn't read it? I may not be able to ride a bull again, but I didn't hit my head and go stupid. I would have had my lawyer look at it."

Bill spoke next. "Well, that's the plan. Listen, I don't give a rat's ass if you want the documentary done or not, but Rich and I both think you'll make a great addition to CBS Sports. You know this world like the back of your hand. You were a damn good rider—probably even better than your brother."

I grinned, then shook my head. "You better not let Brock hear you say that."

Rich smiled. "Ty, just think about it. You don't have anything holding you back there in Montana."

The air in the restaurant changed instantly—and I looked to the entrance. I didn't even have to see her to know she was here. I smiled at the sight of her. Blonde hair pulled up into a messy bun on the top of her head, strands hanging down in wavy curls. She had on jeans and a long-sleeved shirt and sneakers, and her bag was draped over her shoulder.

She looked tired as fuck. And she was the most beautiful woman in the world.

"Judging by the smile on your face, I'm going to guess my last statement wasn't entirely factual," Rich said.

I watched as the hostess walked Kaylee in and sat her down at a small table. She smiled and nodded her head as she took the menu from the waitress. I couldn't pull my eyes away from her.

"That's Kaylee, isn't it?" Rich asked.

Standing, I looked back at Rich and Bill. "You're wrong, Rich. I *thought* I didn't have anything holding me back, but that's not the case. If you'll excuse me, gentlemen."

I pulled some money out of my wallet and put it on the table.

Not giving them any time to reply, I headed over toward her table. The waitress was setting a cup of coffee down in front of Kaylee. She smiled, thanked her, then snapped her eyes in my direction. The moment her blue eyes met mine, we both smiled.

I hated that I had walked away from her that day on the dance floor. Hated that her words felt like someone was trying to kill me and hated that I knew deep in my heart she hadn't meant them, and I had been too stubborn to realize it at the time.

I stopped in front of her, watching her take a drink of her coffee. "Fancy meeting you here."

She shot me a sassy grin. "I know people who know people, and those people have connections."

I laughed. "I believe you do."

Digging her teeth into her lip, she looked nervous. "Ty, there's nothing going on between me and Channing. That day, at the anniversary party, I didn't mean what I said."

"Okay," I replied.

"Okay?"

"Yes, okay."

Kaylee glanced down at her coffee cup, then back up at me. "Do you want to sit down?"

I shook my head, reached for her bag, and tossed it over my shoulder.

The waitress walked back up. "Would you like a menu, sir?"

"I've already had breakfast, and the lady here will be ordering through room service."

Kaylee's brows pulled in tight. "Excuse me?"

I tossed a ten onto the table to cover her coffee, then reached for her hand. "Let's go."

Kaylee grabbed her purse and allowed me to guide her out of the restaurant. "Um, do you want to tell me where we're going, Ty?"

My head was telling me I needed to stop. This wasn't the right thing to do. Kaylee and I still hadn't talked about the last time we'd slept together. But my fucking heart didn't give two shits. The moment I saw her walk in, I knew I had to have her in my arms. In my bed. I needed to be buried inside of her.

"We're going to my room, Kaylee."

"Your . . . your . . . room?"

After hitting the button for the elevator, I stared straight at the metal doors, because if I looked at her, I would end up kissing her, and we wouldn't even make it back to my floor, much less my bed.

The doors opened, and I breathed out a sigh of relief when I saw the elevator was empty.

Kaylee walked in first. I hit the button for the eighteenth floor and waited until the doors closed, then turned and pushed her against the wall of the elevator. The sound of her gasp made my cock even harder than it already was, thanks to that smile of hers. For months I had walked around with blue balls because of this woman.

My mouth pressed against hers, and I expected her to push me away, but she didn't. Kaylee moaned softly, opening her mouth to me.

When I pressed into her body, I could instantly feel the heat. The chemistry, whatever the hell it was, that sparked between us.

I pulled back, leaving us both panting and needing more. So much more.

The doors opened, and I grabbed her hand, pulling her gently out of the elevator and down to my room. I silently said a prayer that Mary wouldn't still be hanging around. I unlocked the door, stepped to the side like the gentleman I was, and waited for Kaylee to decide if she was going to go in.

"I'm going to be honest with you, Kaylee. I don't feel much like talking right now."

Her beautiful mouth lifted slightly. "Exactly what do you feel like doing, then? Because I came a long way to get to the bottom of this."

I wanted to say that what I felt like doing was fucking her six ways from Sunday, but that wasn't what she deserved. She meant more to me than just a fuck. "I want to make love to you, then fuck you once or twice. Then we'll talk."

Her throat bobbed as she said, "I think I can do that," before she quickly walked past me and into the room. I closed my eyes and silently thanked God before following her into the room.

Chapter Twenty-Three

KAYLEE

The moment I felt his eyes on me, I couldn't ignore the pulsing in my lower stomach. I told myself we would talk; I would tell him how I felt about him. Then, if things progressed, maybe we would find ourselves back in bed together. I was really, really hoping for that last part to come about.

Then, the whole elevator thing, and what he said to me outside his hotel room. Yeah, talking could wait. My body needed this man like it needed its next hit of oxygen.

When I walked into his room, I crossed over to the curtains and pushed them open, allowing a stream of sunlight to fill the area. It had been my first instinct. Ty had a habit of living in darkness; I was about to change that. At least, I hoped I was.

The feel of the sun instantly hitting me helped to calm down my frantically beating heart. I wasn't sure if I was nervous, excited, or scared to death that Ty only wanted sex.

I turned and looked at the bed. It was clear only one side of the bed had been slept in, and the relief that flooded into my body was palpable. I was positive he noticed. When I lifted my gaze, I saw that he was watching my every move.

Then he smiled, and I lost any sort of willpower I actually believed I still had.

I wanted him more than anything. Yes, I'd told myself over and over on the way there that we would talk first. Before anything else. But those blue eyes looked at me almost in a pleading way. As if he needed to touch me to continue breathing. God, it felt amazing to have him look at me like that.

The memories of our night together came back, the sweet way he'd made love to me. It was back in an instant. Then his dimple appeared, and he stood there, dressed like the cowboy he was, in the black cowboy hat that made his blue eyes stand out, almost as if they were stars in a black sky.

I dropped my purse, causing him to drop my bag.

"Ty." The word barely above a whisper.

Ty crossed the short distance between us, cupped my face in his hands, and looked deep into my eyes. "I fucking missed you, Kaylee."

Smiling, I rose onto my toes, willing him to kiss me again like he had in the elevator only minutes ago. It didn't take him long to answer my silent plea. His mouth crashed to mine, just as needy and powerful as it was the very first time he'd kissed me. My hands went up to his hat, which I took off and tossed onto the bed.

Ty reached behind him and yanked his shirt over his head, breaking our kiss only long enough to get it off and toss it to the floor. He then went to my shirt, peeling it off my body and letting his gaze linger on me.

My body burned with desire. I had never wanted a man like I wanted Ty. Even after the night we'd spent together, I had stupidly thought it would be enough, but it was far from it. I craved him like a junkie craving their next fix. I couldn't help but wonder if Ty had felt the same for me, and if that need had scared him.

My hands went to his jeans, shaking as I fumbled with the button and zipper. Finally, Ty broke our kiss, stepped back, and started to take off the rest of his own clothes. I did the same, toeing off my sneakers and watching with hungry eyes as he took off his jeans, then his boxer briefs, gifting me with a vision of his cock.

Moaning, I was hoping I didn't have drool coming out of my mouth as I stared at it: hard, long, waiting to be inside me. "Good Lord, I forgot how big you are."

He smiled, taking over for me as he pulled my jeans down. He kissed along my hips, his finger barely sliding along the top of my white lace panties. I thanked God above I had made myself shower and shave last night.

With his eyes lifted and looking at me, he pulled my panties down, then blew warm air on me, causing me to draw in a quick breath. My body trembled with anticipation. Ty glanced up at me, then smiled before he gently pressed his face against me, inhaling a deep breath. An instant rush of desire pooled between my legs, and I instinctively put my hands in his hair.

Then he stood, and disappointment hit me like a brick dropping on my stomach.

Damn.

Ty winked. "I'll taste you, baby, don't worry. Right now, I need to see all of you. Touch you. Feel myself inside you." As he reached behind my back to unclasp my bra, he brought his mouth to my ear. "I don't have any condoms, Kaylee."

That knowledge made me happier than it should have. For two reasons. One, that meant he hadn't planned on hooking up with anyone. Two, I got to feel him bare inside me. Again.

"I don't care."

He drew back and looked me in the eyes. "The pill isn't a hundred percent, you know, and Brock already bitched me out once."

"Pull out if you want . . . but I need to feel you, all of you."

He gently kissed me, and it felt like the floor beneath me was swaying. This wasn't the kiss of a man who simply wanted a quick fuck.

Ty reached down, picked me up, and carried me over to the bed. He laid me down gently, then crawled over me, kissing my neck, my breasts, and down my stomach to the inside of my thigh. I was panting like a damn dog in heat. Lifting my hips shamelessly, begging for his mouth to be down there.

"You are so beautiful, Kaylee. So damn beautiful."

My eyes caught his while he settled between my legs. "I thought you wanted inside me," I said with a smirk.

"Change of plans."

Then he ran his tongue between my lips and flicked my clit, sending me nearly off the bed in the process. He grabbed my body and held me down while he licked and sucked until I was grabbing the pillow and crying out his name as my orgasm zipped through my body like a tornado.

I was still trying to come down from the high when I felt him over me. His fingers intertwined with mine as he pushed them into the bed on either side of my head. Expertly, he guided himself to my entrance and slowly worked his way in. Both of us moaning with each delicious movement.

"Ty," I gasped, wrapping my legs around him, attempting to pull him inside me faster, deeper.

He closed his eyes once he was fully seated, not moving as he lowered his forehead to mine. The weight of his body was a delicious punishment, and something I knew I was going to need for the rest of my life.

"Look at me," I said, causing him to adjust his body. Our eyes met. We were one, together in the most intimate way possible. Connected as lovers, but I knew in my heart of hearts it was so much more than that. "You were made for me."

He tried to shake his head, but I withdrew my hand from his and pressed my fingers to his lips.

"Listen to me, Ty. I love you."

He closed his eyes, and I placed my hand on the side of his face. "Ty."

When he opened his eyes again, he whispered my name, and it sounded like a prayer carried on a breeze. "Kaylee."

"You are everything to me. Every single flaw, imperfection, struggle, demon, painful memory . . . they're mine now also. The same goes for me. All of my doubts, struggles, fears—they're yours. Together, we make a beautiful puzzle with all our crazy pieces."

He stared at me, his eyes holding so much fear. I wasn't about to stop. He needed to hear this. He needed to know how I felt about him.

"I don't want the man you think I need. I want *you*, Ty Shaw. The only man I would lay my life down for. I'd go to the ends of the earth to show you how much I care for you. How much I love you. I want to be buried into the deepest, darkest part of your soul, and I want to bring you light. Heal your pain. Bring you the happiness you deserve and show you that you don't have to change for me. I want you as you are. And I won't change for *you*."

A tear slipped from his eye and slowly trailed down his cheek until it dripped onto my body.

I was stunned for a moment. To see this strong man show such emotion was almost too much for me.

"I've never felt this way with anyone else," I said.

He swallowed hard. "Not even—"

"Only you," I quickly confirmed.

His mouth pressed to mine as he moved slowly in and out of me. I could feel the love from him pouring into my body. If he couldn't say the words yet, it was okay, because I felt them with each movement. Each kiss he gave me. Each touch spoke a million words. I felt him getting bigger as his thrusts picked up speed. He was close, and God, so was I.

"Ty, I'm going to come again," I whispered, his mouth back on mine just as my orgasm was exploding and rushing through my body.

Then I felt him, felt his entire body tremble as he pulled his mouth away and met my gaze. "Me too, baby."

I wrapped my arms around him but let my legs fall to the side so he could pull out.

"It's always been you. It will always be you, Kaylee."

Those words slammed so hard against my chest that I let out a sob as he pulled out and used his hand. He came on my stomach, and as much as I wanted him inside me, it was hot as hell watching him put his seed all over my body.

When I glanced back up, his eyes were locked on me. I couldn't read what it was I saw exactly in those baby blues, but it didn't scare me. He had a different look in his eyes today. They told me everything I needed to know—and I knew in that moment I would fight for us, forever if I had to.

Then the look disappeared, and he smiled. A sexy-as-hell smile. "You need a shower, princess."

"But I rather like your cum on me."

He looked down at it, then back to me. "That *was* pretty hot, but I feel like a damn dog who just marked his territory."

I laughed. "You don't have to mark me. I'm all yours."

Ty's smile faded slightly, and then he leaned down and kissed me. "I want to do this with you, Kaylee, but I need to be honest. I'm scared shitless. Ever since the accident, there's a part of me that's . . . lost."

"Then I'll help you find your way."

"What if I take this job?"

"Then I'll be behind you a hundred percent. The nice thing about my job is I can travel and work from anywhere."

He smiled. "You'd do that?"

I nodded. "Yes. If this is what you truly want to do, yes."

"And if I wanted to just be a rancher?"

"Then I better start learning about the cattle business and birthing calves."

He laughed and slowly shook his head as his eyes searched my face. "I want to say the words . . . but . . ."

"Don't apologize for that. I want you to say them when you're not even thinking about it. When they just simply come out because you mean it."

Ty stood, then reached down and picked up his T-shirt and gently wiped off my stomach. "I didn't like pulling out of you when I came," he said as he helped me off the bed.

"Why not?"

He looked unsure of something.

"Do you want kids someday?" I asked, clearly taking him by surprise. He froze, so I went about what we were doing like it was no big deal. Making my way into the bathroom, I reached into the shower and turned it on. "It's just a question, Ty. That's all. I want kids. And little Ty Shaws would be sort of cool. Someday."

His throat bobbed as he swallowed and ran his hand through his hair. I took his hands in mine and walked us into the stand-up shower.

"Breathe, Ty. I'm not asking you to impregnate me today, or even next year. It's. Just. A. Question."

When we stepped under the hot water, I could see his body relax.

"Yes, I want kids. With you."

My stomach fluttered, and I couldn't help the smile that erupted on my face. He smiled in return, then kissed me, pushed me against the wall, and did what he'd said he was going to do. First make love, then fuck me. And fuck me he did. Thoroughly.

Chapter Twenty-Four

Ty

Bright lights made me look away as I attempted to block them out. The smell of burning rubber assaulted my senses. The sounds of metal crashing made me bolt up, my breaths coming short as I gasped for air. Again.

I instantly felt her touch, and my heart seemed to react. It slowed a bit, still pounding in my chest but not racing out of control. My lungs opened up, and air was able to get in. Her hands were on my chest, pushing me back down so that I lay on the bed. Then I felt her on top of me. She rubbed her warmth gently over me. It didn't take long for my dick to respond. My heart pounded, but for a different reason now.

"Shh, it's okay," she whispered, leaning down and kissing my chest.

The words were on the tip of my tongue. I wanted to tell her I loved her so fucking bad, but I couldn't. I had no idea why—or maybe I did, but I hadn't worked it out in my own head yet.

Kaylee reached between our bodies and guided herself over me, slowly sinking down until I was completely inside her.

"Kaylee," I said, my voice sounding like I hadn't had water in days. It was hoarse and wobbled ever so slightly.

"I'm right here, Ty."

She moved slowly at first, then dropped her head back as she sat up. When she moved faster, bounced harder, I reached up and felt her breasts. Every ounce of tension slipped away, and I allowed myself to get lost in her. It was the most euphoric feeling I'd ever experienced in my life. This woman had a way of making me feel safe. Needed. Loved. She was fucking amazing.

"Yes. Oh, God, yes," she cried out.

I couldn't take my eyes off her. She was more than beautiful. She was stunning. She was naked. And she wanted me. All of me. I wanted to give her that, more than anything.

But I needed to tell her the truth. She deserved to know about all the demons that lurked in my head.

"Ty, I'm going to come. Yes. Oh, yes."

"That's it, baby, come on my cock."

And that was all she needed. It hadn't taken me long to figure out that Kaylee got even more turned on by a little bit of dirty talk, which I was more than happy to provide.

Once her body had slowed to almost a stop, I flipped us over. I put my arms under her legs, grabbed on to her hips, and fucked her fast and hard. The sounds of our bodies slapping together ignited a feeling deep inside me I'd never experienced before.

Sex had always been just that. Sex. No matter who it was with, where it was at, it was only a way to release tension. Emotionally, it had always felt no different for me fucking a girl than it had from jacking off in the shower. Zero feelings. But with Kaylee, this wasn't just sex. No, this was so much more. *God*, it was so much more. I hadn't been able to put my finger on exactly what it was, but I had a damn good feeling why it was different. I simply needed to say it out loud. Bring it to life. Breathe life into the part of me that had yet to awaken.

"Harder!" she cried out, making my balls pull up.

Fuck. I didn't want to come yet. I needed her to come again.

I slipped my hand between us and played with her clit. Kaylee's eyes snapped open, and she looked at me.

"Goddamn it, Ty. You and your even numbers."

Smiling, I pressed my thumb on her clit, sending her over the edge before I joined her on the fall.

It was against my better judgment, and I told myself I was going to pull out again, but I couldn't. I needed to fill her. I needed to mark her in every way possible.

She was mine, and I wasn't ever letting her go. Ever.

◆ ◆ ◆

I stood over the bed and stared at her. Her blonde hair spilled across the pillow, and I swore she looked like a princess. I wanted nothing more than to crawl back into the bed and make love to her again.

Almost as if she could sense me looking at her, she opened her eyes.

"Hey," she softly said, her mouth turning up into a beautiful smile.

"Hey. I have to get over to the arena. I've arranged for a car to come get you in forty-five minutes. Is that enough time for you to get ready?"

Leaning up on her elbows, she tilted her head and let her eyes roam openly over my body, then scrunched her nose in the most adorable way. "Ready for what?"

"To come to the event this afternoon. I got CBS to give you a special backstage pass. You'll be up in the booth with me."

Her eyes widened with excitement. "Really?"

"Really," I said, leaning onto the bed and kissing her. "I've got to go. I'll see you in a bit."

"Okay. See you in a bit."

She looked like she was going to say something else, but instead, she dug her teeth into her lip.

"Tonight, we'll actually talk. Like for real."

With a nod and a smile, she replied, "Okay."

"See ya."

She lifted her hand and gave me a wave. "See ya."

It took every single ounce of willpower I had to step to the door, open it, and then walk out. As I headed toward the elevator, I couldn't wipe the smile off my face. It seemed like with Kaylee, we always did everything backward, but tonight . . . tonight we would talk. I wasn't sure how things would turn out, but I believed every word she'd said to me earlier. Every word.

When I hit the elevator button, a welcome sense of peace washed over me. I walked onto that elevator with the knowledge that everything was going to work out fine. For the first time in a long time, I was excited about my future. Our future.

Chapter Twenty-Five

KAYLEE

My body ached in the most delicious way. I stared at myself in the mirror as I ran my fingers along my kiss-swollen lips. Smiling, I closed my eyes and let the memory of earlier take hold.

Ty's mouth on mine, his body moving fast and hard. The way his eyes locked with mine when he came . . . it made my stomach jump simply thinking about it.

My phone rang, and I quickly headed back into the main room and grabbed it from my purse. It was Lincoln. "Hello?"

"Hey, so how did the talk go? I couldn't wait another minute. I was dying to hear from you, and since you're ignoring my text messages, I figured I would call."

I chewed nervously on my bottom lip as I sat on the edge of the bed and slipped on one cowboy boot, then the other.

"Your silence is not a good sign. I'm just saying. Y'all either fought, or you—oh, no. Kaylee."

"We're going to talk tonight, but we sort of talked."

"What does that mean?" Lincoln asked as Morgan made the most precious baby noises. There bloomed that silly desire to have one of those little monsters growing inside me.

"It means that I pretty much said what I wanted to say . . . while he was buried deep inside me."

"Ugh. First off, the visual wasn't needed, and two—Kaylee! You said you were going to talk to him *before* anything else."

I stood and walked back into the bathroom. After putting the phone on speaker, I quickly got to work pulling my hair up into a ponytail.

"Listen here, *Mom*, have you seen the man? I mean, you're married to his fine-ass brother. The moment he touched me, I decided talking could wait. I needed action instead."

A slight giggle came across the phone.

"Also, have you seen his body?"

"Kaylee!" she repeated in a stern voice, but I could detect a hint of humor there. I imagined a slight grin on her face.

"I had every intention of talking to him, but things just got . . . out of control."

"Did you use protection?"

That question, I didn't want to answer. "Sort of. He pulled out."

She gagged. "Oh God, another visual."

I, of course, neglected to tell her the whole truth on that one.

"Will you please buy some condoms? Y'all are playing with fire."

Pausing for a minute, I took in a deep breath. "I asked him if he wanted kids."

"What? Wow! Okay, so there *was* some talking mixed in with the hot sex."

"Yes, there was—I told you that already."

"And? What did he say?"

Smiling like a schoolgirl who's just gotten her first kiss, I replied, "He said yes, he wanted kids . . . with *me*. I also told him I loved him."

That was met with silence on the other end of the phone.

"Lincoln?"

"Hold on, I'm putting Morgan in her swing. I need to do a little happy dance, and I don't want to give her brain damage."

I walked out of the bathroom, checked the time, and realized I needed to be down in the lobby for my ride to the arena.

"Okay. Oh my God! Oh my God! You told him you loved him? Kaylee, holy shit!"

I laughed. "I know. He didn't freak. I mean, there was once or twice when I swore he was about to tell me, but he put the wall back up. I told him I wasn't going anywhere, and that I was going to fight for us."

"You go, girl! Oh my gosh, Kaylee. This is huge. Like, whoa."

"Right?"

I opened the door—and let out a gasp of surprise when a woman with long blonde hair also gasped, her hand poised to knock on the door.

"Oh, excuse me," she said, looking past me and into the room. "I was looking for Ty Shaw."

"Who is that?" Lincoln asked, still on speakerphone.

"Hold on, Lincoln." I quickly took her off and put the phone to my ear.

"He isn't here. Is there something I can help you with?" It was then I looked down and saw a little girl standing next to the blonde woman. Dark-blonde hair . . . and blue eyes that looked so familiar.

My gut instantly twisted, and I forced myself to swallow the lump in my throat.

"I saw him on TV; he was one of the commentators." She cleared her throat. "Are you his girlfriend?"

"Kaylee, what is going on? Who is she?"

I ignored Lincoln.

"Yes," I said, because I was 99 percent sure I could now call myself that.

"Oh. This is going to be a bit awkward. I've been trying to reach Ty for a number of months now." She looked down at the little girl.

"Kaylee? Please tell me what is happening."

"Is that your little girl?" I asked, giving the girl a smile. She looked up at me and grinned, her front tooth missing.

"Oh, no. No. No. I'm getting Brock. Don't hang up, Kaylee."

Tears pricked at the back of my eyes, and I looked at the woman.

"I'm married. I'm not looking for a relationship with him. I just want you to know that right up front. But . . . I'm a bit ashamed to say this, but I need to find out if Ty is her father. My baby is sick and needs a blood transfusion."

My heart broke, but for two very different reasons. I cleared my throat. "I'm so sorry."

She gave me a weak smile. "I'm not a close-enough match, and her daddy—her, um, stepdaddy—isn't a match either."

"Ty's the father?" I asked, my voice shaking.

"I'm pretty sure, but we used protection, so I know how that makes me sound. It was a one-night thing here in Billings after a PBR event a little over four years ago. I was at a wedding here in the hotel and met Ty at the bar, and one thing . . . um . . . well, you know."

"Yeah, I know."

"Kaylee," Lincoln whispered, her own heartache evident in her voice.

"Lincoln, I'm going to have to call you back. Let *me* take care of this . . . not Brock."

"O-okay. Call me. And Kaylee?"

"Yeah?"

"Take a deep breath. Okay?"

I nodded, even though she couldn't see me, then hit end. "I know where he is. Can you come with me?"

The woman nodded, then reached her hand out. "I'm Katy, Katy Olsen."

"Kaylee Holden."

It struck me as odd how similar our names were. Even the look of her. Blonde hair, shorter than mine. Her eyes were green, though, which made me look down to the little girl again, her brilliant blue eyes gazing back up at me. My chin wobbled, but only for a moment.

"The car should be waiting to take me to the arena."

"Will they let me in?" she asked as she and her daughter walked alongside me.

"Don't worry, I'll take care of it."

I pulled out my phone and sent Ty a text.

Me: Can you get another pass? For Katy Olsen.

He replied almost instantly.

Ty: LOL. Did you already meet a friend? Tell me she's not a fan or something, Kaylee.

Me: No, she's married.

Ty: Cool, I'll call and let them know.

A part of me felt horrible for not telling him, but I wanted to see if he'd even remember this girl's name.

As we rode down in the elevator, the little girl telling her mom how fast it moved, both of us smiled at her.

"I'm so sorry, Kaylee. I wouldn't have ever reached out if it hadn't been for Olivia needing medical treatment."

Bending down, I tapped her on her nose. "Olivia. What a beautiful name. Who is this?" I asked, pointing to the little bear she was clutching in her hands. She was just a little younger than Blayze. The thought that he might have a cousin he didn't even know made me feel sad.

"His name is Buzz."

With a smile, I gave Buzz a tap on the nose as well. "Hello there, Buzz. It's a pleasure to meet you."

The elevator opened, and I took in a deep breath and slowly let it out. I'd made Ty a promise, only a few hours ago, that whatever problems came our way, I was going to stick by his side. As heartbreaking as this problem was, and as much as I wanted to take off in a cab and just run, I held my head up and walked toward the doors.

Then I realized I hadn't responded to Katy. Before sliding into the black limo that was waiting for us, I took her hand in mine and gave it a squeeze. "I'm sorry. I just needed a moment."

She nodded.

"I love him, Katy, and I don't want to just spring this on him. So if he doesn't recognize you, will you at least wait until after the show? Then you can talk to him."

"Of course. Yes."

"Thank you, and I know you're only reaching out for Olivia, and I totally get that."

A look of relief washed over her face as she gave my hand a slight squeeze back. "Thank you, Kaylee. Thank you so much for helping me. I recently found out from googling him that he was born and raised in Hamilton. Then, when my husband saw him on TV, I told him, of course, about the one-night stand. He's the one who told me I needed to come to the hotel. Talk to Ty."

I swallowed hard and simply nodded before motioning for her to get in.

Olivia had fun in the limo and was sad that it was such a short ride. As we were guided up to the control booth where Ty was, Katy asked, "Is he going to be working for CBS now?"

"I'm not sure. I don't think he's made the decision yet."

"When I heard about the accident, I felt terrible. I don't know much about bull riding, and honestly I don't care to know. He was a good-looking guy who gave me some attention when I was in a bad place. I had just broken up with my boyfriend a few weeks before, so it was a wild and crazy thing to do. Not something I would normally *ever* do."

"Honestly, you don't need to explain, and I really don't want to know the details, if you don't mind."

Her cheeks turned red. "Of course. I'm sorry."

As we walked down a long hall, I asked, "She's not the old boyfriend's?"

"I . . . I don't think so. I'm not sure."

"You haven't had him tested?"

She glanced my way, a look of sadness on her face. "He died in a car accident about two months after I hooked up with Ty. I didn't even know I was pregnant yet. His family blamed me for the accident. Said he'd been distraught over our breakup. Once I found out I was pregnant, I didn't bother telling them. I assumed the baby was Ty's. But when Olivia got sick, I approached them to see about DNA testing. To see if someone in the family was a match. They're . . . well . . . the family is wealthy, and they accused me of trying to get money. They won't have anything to do with me or Olivia. I mentioned Ty possibly being the father, and you can imagine how that sounded to them. Knowing I'd slept with another man so soon after breaking up with their son."

I nodded. "I see. I'm sorry they won't help you."

She gave me a sad smile. "So am I."

As we walked up, Katy now carrying Olivia, I saw Ty. He looked my way and smiled when he saw me.

"Oh, my. If that isn't the look of a man in love, I don't know what is," Katy said in a hushed voice next to me.

His eyes moved to my right, and he frowned slightly but didn't seem to recognize Katy. He gave her a polite smile, glanced at the little girl, and then made his way over to me. He leaned down and kissed me. Not on the cheek or forehead, but on the lips, for everyone to see. "Hi."

It was one simple word, but I could hear it in his voice. Something was off. He turned to look at Katy.

"Ty, this is Katy Olsen and her daughter, Olivia."

The little girl looked at Ty, and he smiled bigger, but I saw it in his eyes.

He knew.

A sickness rushed to my stomach, and I almost felt the need to turn and find a trash can to get sick in.

"It's a pleasure," Ty said, narrowing his eyes slightly at her.

Katy simply nodded.

"Where should we be so that we'll be out of your way?" I asked.

Ty looked at me, a concerned expression crossing his face. "Would you mind if the three of us"—he looked back at Olivia—"the four of us, stepped across the hall to talk?"

I forced a smile. "It's nothing that can't wait until after the show."

Ty's gaze met mine, and I saw the wall going back up.

I took his hands in mine. "Ty, it can wait."

His eyes bounced from me to Katy, then back to me. "I'm not on the air tonight. I told them I wasn't interested in the job."

My eyes widened in shock. "But Ty, I thought you—"

"No," he said as he shook his head, stopping my words with a look of determination. "The only place I want to be is on the ranch, with you. Now, let's go across the hall."

A heaviness settled in the pit of my stomach. I knew I had gotten through to Ty earlier. He was willing to try a relationship with me, even though he had fears and doubts and the crazy notion he wasn't good enough for me. Now, he very well could have a child. I knew this was going to take us back a few steps. Suddenly, I wasn't sure if he was simply trying to appease me for the time being.

Placing his hand on the small of my back, Ty guided us to an empty room. Food was on a table, and it appeared people had been in earlier to eat.

Once Katy had walked into the room, Ty shut the door. Then an awkward-as-hell silence filled the air. I watched Ty as he took in the little girl, then looked at Katy.

"She's not mine."

I gasped. "Ty!"

He snapped his head to look at me. "She's not mine. I have never had sex without a condom." Facing Katy, he looked at her with an expression I couldn't read.

"I'm not here to ask you to be a part of her life, Ty. I need your help, and when I saw you on TV, I had to come. You were in Billings, and . . . I just need your help."

"Money?"

"Ty—" I started before Katy cut me off.

"She's sick. It's leukemia. I need to find out if you're her father. If you are, you might be able to donate stem cells."

Ty looked shocked. "Wait, back up a second. So, you believe I *am* her father?"

Katy looked at me, then back to Ty. "I don't know if you remember that night."

"You were in the wedding. I remember."

Okay, that hurt more than it should have. How many of his random hookups did he remember, or was it only certain women? I needed to stop thinking so hard about all of this.

"I only remember because you have the same name as my cousin."

Katy smiled. "That's right. You told me that."

Ty seemed like he was getting impatient.

After clearing her throat, Katy went on. "I'm not the type of woman to have random one-night stands. There are only two men who could possibly be her biological father. You, and my ex-boyfriend, who unfortunately died in a car accident shortly after you and I hooked up. His family is angry with me, for a few reasons, and they refuse to do DNA testing."

He folded his arms over his chest.

"Katy is married, Ty. She's only looking for a donor match. If you're Olivia's dad—"

"I'm not."

I sighed.

Katy went on. "If you *are* her father, your HLA could be a match."

"HLA?" Ty asked.

"Human leukocyte antigens."

"There haven't been any matches in your family?" I asked.

"Ideally, the doctors want to match at least eight to ten HLA markers. I'm only a five. No one else in my family is more, and Olivia doesn't have any siblings yet."

"How do we do this?" Ty asked. I could see it in his face: his heart was breaking for this child, who very well could have been his own flesh and blood.

Katy seemed to relax slightly. "We could do a DNA test first, to see if you're her father. That would only take two to three days. The HLA typing takes about a week or two."

Ty rubbed the back of his neck, then glanced over to me. I gave him a reassuring smile.

He looked back at Katy, then down to Olivia. "I'd like to know."

My stomach lurched, though I knew he'd want to know if he had a child.

Katy nodded. "Okay. I've already alerted Olivia's doctor that I've possibly found her biological father. Her father—or, um, her stepfather—has already done the HLA testing and isn't a close-enough match."

"Katy, would you mind if I spoke to Kaylee alone for a few minutes?" Ty suddenly said.

She smiled. "Of course not."

The moment she shut the door, Ty faced me. "I'm so fucking sorry. This is exactly why—"

I walked up to him and wrapped my arms around him, then lifted my hands and pulled his mouth to mine. I kissed him, and it only took him a moment to wrap his arms around me and deepen the kiss.

When he pulled back, he leaned his forehead against mine. "I thought I had problems before."

"This isn't a problem, Ty."

He closed his eyes. "Did you see her eyes, Kaylee?"

I swallowed hard. "Yes."

"How can you not see this as some sort of sign? The moment I let myself believe I can be happy, that there is a light at the end of this fucking dark tunnel, something turns it off again."

When I stepped back and away from him, I took his hands in mine. "Do the DNA test; let's find out if Olivia is yours. Then let's tackle the next issue . . . but this might not even *be* an issue, so let's worry about it when we have something to worry about."

He nodded.

"Ty, if you are her father, that wouldn't change how I feel about you."

He shook his head.

"Don't you dare say I deserve someone else, someone better. I don't *want* anyone else. I want you."

His eyes looked so incredibly sad, it nearly broke my heart in two. "If I'm not her father?"

"Then you need to decide if you want to still be tested as a match."

"Isn't this a little strange, Kaylee? There's a random woman I hooked up with four years ago, asking me to be tested to help save her kid who may or may not be mine."

"It's not the way I had imagined our relationship starting off, but I'm not afraid of a challenge."

Ty didn't smile at my attempt at humor.

"One step at a time. For what it's worth, Ty, even if you aren't her father, I think you should be tested. This little girl's life depends on it."

He nodded. When he walked to the door and told Katy to come back in, I felt my chest pull tight. Despite what I'd said, I honestly wasn't sure how I was going to handle it if Ty was a father. While Ty and Katy spoke about his going for the testing, I focused on keeping my breathing steady. This was not the time or the place to have a breakdown.

Olivia played with her teddy bear and kept looking up at Ty. While I couldn't shake the feeling that all of our worlds were about to be turned upside down.

Chapter Twenty-Six

*T*Y

After I'd informed Bill and Rich, and then Sam, of my decision not to take the job, the fucking rug had gotten pulled out from under me. The moment Kaylee had walked into that room and I saw Katy, I knew shit was about to get real.

It had taken me a minute or two to figure out who Katy was. The kid she was holding was my biggest wake-up call ever. Her blue eyes did look like mine; there was no doubt about it. And, much to Kaylee's credit, she never once faltered.

It was killing me, not being able to talk to her about all of this, especially with how amazing this morning had been and how we had left things open to talk. Trying to figure out what in the hell was going through her mind was driving me mad. She'd only asked earlier this morning about kids, and now there was a possibility I might have one.

I knew deep in my heart, though, that the little girl wasn't mine.

I didn't feel anything toward her. Nothing. If she had been mine, wouldn't I have felt some sort of connection? Something?

Katy was insistent that we head to her doctor's office and get the DNA test done as soon as possible. Since I wasn't going on air, I'd told her we could do it today. Kaylee stood by me the entire time, a smile on her face while she kept her thoughts pretty much to herself. She held my hand and gave me a reassuring nod when needed, but I saw it in her eyes. I also saw the way she looked at the little girl, whose only resemblance to me was her blue eyes. She was the spitting image of her mother. I had to admit I'd stared at her intensely, trying to see anything, and had come up with nothing each time.

Lincoln and Brock had been calling Kaylee nonstop. I finally sent him a text with the shortened version of what was going on and asked him to give me some space. For once in his life, he actually did what I asked of him.

There was a brief moment at the doctor's office when Kaylee had excused herself. She wasn't gone for very long, but I knew she was trying to keep her composure up. I hated that she was going through all of this. I hated that my past indiscretions were causing her pain.

Kaylee remained silent as we took an Uber from the hospital back to the hotel. CBS was nice enough to pay for another night for me in the hotel. I'd told them I would take care of it, not feeling right about it, but they had insisted. It could have been because I'd suggested doing one or two commentaries throughout the year, without any interviews into my personal life. I was shocked when they'd agreed that that was a good plan.

I was glad I'd done the trial run, though. It showed me that I wasn't missing out on anything. I'd once thought I'd belonged there, but I no longer felt that way. I knew where I belonged. In Hamilton, on my folks' ranch, trying to make a go of things with Kaylee.

When the door to the hotel room closed, I wanted nothing more than to grab Kaylee and get lost in her. But twice we'd done that. I wasn't going to hide from her anymore. She deserved more than that.

"Are you hungry? Would you rather get something to eat and then talk?" I asked.

She shook her head. "No. We can order room service or pizza."

I nodded and undid the cuffs of my shirt sleeves and rolled them up. Kaylee watched my every move.

As I sat on the bed, I looked over at her. She was leaning against the table. What in the hell was going through her mind?

"Before we talk about Olivia, I need to know what you're thinking, Ty. Your decision to not take the job threw me."

I laughed. "It shouldn't. The only reason I agreed to try it out is because I thought you were with Channing, and I needed to see if I truly did miss this world."

Kaylee tilted her head. "Okay. Then I want to know why you didn't think you were good enough for me. Let's start with that."

I sighed. A headache was already forming. Real talk wasn't something I ever liked to do. Especially after the accident. But those few weeks without Kaylee, and the thought of losing her to someone else, had made me wake up and realize I needed to talk about a lot of things, and not just about my feelings for her. I needed to tell her everything.

Before I had a chance to respond, Kaylee picked up the phone and hit a button. "I'd like to order room service."

After ordering pizza and a few drinks, Kaylee hung up the phone, kicked off her boots, and looked at me.

I motioned for her to sit on the bed, and she lifted a brow, a sexy smirk on her face.

"I'll keep my hands to myself, for now . . . I just want you near me. Please."

She climbed onto the bed, sitting with her legs tucked under her.

"Do you have a headache?" she asked, noticing me rubbing at my temples again.

"A slight one, but it's fine."

"Okay. Let's talk, Ty."

I nodded, took in a deep breath, and slowly let it out. "When I was on the Unleash the Beast Tour, the only thing on my mind was bulls, being number one, and the occasional hookup. I won't lie and say I was a good little boy who went to his room every night. I wasn't. I guess that much is obvious, considering what we're dealing with right now with Katy and Olivia."

She frowned and looked down at her fingernails. Okay, so that was more of a sore subject than she was letting on.

"I knew someday I would settle down, get married, and have a kid or two. It wasn't something I thought a whole lot about, because honestly, I never once met a woman who made me feel like I was in a hurry for it. There were moments I felt lonely. When we'd go home and I'd see Brock with Blayze was when it would really hit me. I remember some nights, I'd lie in bed and pray for God to send someone my way. Someone who'd make me feel something. I knew my folks wanted that for me as well. It was hard for Mom to have both me and Brock out on the road. Then when Beck died, she closed up a little. That might be where Brock and I got it from."

I shrugged. "Anyway, I was happy as long as I could climb onto the back of a bull. Then the accident happened, and I never felt lonelier. For so many years, women had flocked to me because I was a bull rider; companies wanted me to sell their stuff because I was good at what I did. I was something more than just some cowboy who worked on his daddy's cattle ranch. It was the only thing I thought I was good at—and I was damn good at it. I poured everything into bull riding and the sport. I lost a part of myself after the accident. A big part. I felt like I was useless."

She shook her head, but I kept talking.

"A feeling of dread, for lack of a better word, settled inside of me. Heavy on my chest. I was in a fog. Unsure of what my future was going to be, and honestly, I didn't really give two shits.

"Then things went from bad to worse. I was told I wouldn't be able to ride bulls ever again and that the healing process of my leg was going to be long and painful. So I pushed myself, hard. Did everything the physical therapist told me to do and then some. The surgeries sucked, the pain was bad, but I thought I'd be able to handle it. Hell, I'd had broken bones and climbed onto the back of a bull before and rode a full eight seconds, so a leg surgery was going to be nothing."

I paused, taking a minute to calm my heart, which had begun to race some at the memories.

"The pain wasn't worse than anything I'd ever experienced before. The difference was, I didn't have a purpose. I wasn't trying to be the best bull rider in the world. When I knew I was getting onto a bull, the pain sort of just went away. I dealt with it. I think it was because I didn't have time to think about it. But with the pain after the accident and the surgeries . . . all I had was time. Alone. I'd sit there for hours and feel the pain course through my leg. I couldn't figure out why this pain was so different from the other broken bones and injuries I'd had over the years, and believe me, I'd had a lot.

"One day, I popped a couple of the pain pills the doctor had given me, and they numbed the pain. Then I learned if I mixed the pills with beer, I felt even better. They numbed the pain not only in my leg but my chest and in my head as well. I got to escape for a little bit from the buzz. The more I took, the deeper into the darkness I felt myself slipping, but for a while, I felt safe there."

I looked directly into Kaylee's eyes. I knew what I was about to tell her could change everything. She had promised earlier today that nothing would make her leave. But once she heard my dirty little secret, I knew it would trigger her own demons . . . and I wasn't sure she truly loved me enough to go through that nightmare all over again.

Kaylee reached for my hand and held it. "Don't stop, Ty. Please, whatever you're thinking is going to spook me, please don't hold it back from me."

I swallowed hard, then blew out a long, deep breath. "Right before my parents finally figured out what was happening with the drug abuse, things got pretty bad. I was popping pills and drinking a lot. I had gotten good at hiding it, but the higher I got on the pills, the more I slipped up. I look back now and wonder if I hadn't been leaving my folks clues all along to figure it out."

I thought about that for a moment before I went on. This next confession was going to be one of the hardest things I'd ever done. I looked at Kaylee and watched her face as I spoke.

"I haven't ever told anyone about this, but I know I need to tell you. I need you to understand why I pushed you away."

"Okay." Her voice was soft but firm. As if she was mentally preparing herself.

"I found myself sitting in my truck one day, a pistol in my hand. I was going to end the pain once and for all. Make the nightmares stop, because no matter how hard I tried, I kept slipping more and more away from myself. To a place where I didn't give two shits about anyone or anything. I almost took my own life that day, Kaylee."

Tears slipped down her face, and I hated that my confession was causing them. I wanted to ask her what she was thinking. Was she scared? Did this make her want to leave? Would she truly stick by my side, knowing how broken I had been—still was, in a sense?

"I'm sorry if this brings back memories of John."

She wiped them away and shook her head. "It's not that, Ty. I mean, of course it makes me think of him, but I hurt for you. Knowing that you've carried that burden with you all this time. Does your therapist know?"

I shook my head, and she gasped.

"I, um . . . I never told her. I never told anyone. I was too ashamed that I had even entertained it."

"What made you not do it?" she asked.

I looked down at her hand in mine and smiled. "I don't know. It wasn't like I was afraid to do it, but for one brief moment . . . I saw a flicker of light. A feeling of hope sparked somewhere down in my chest. I got out of the truck, walked into the house, and put the gun back in the safe.

"About five minutes later, there was a knock on the door. It was my folks. They confronted me about the pills and alcohol. I can't even begin to tell you the relief I felt that the truth was out, finally. Then the guilt set in. If I had gone through with that, my parents would have been the ones to find me. I hated myself. Still do, thinking of how close I had come to them walking up and seeing me sitting in my truck with a fucking gun in my hand, or worse."

Kaylee wiped her tears away, then took in a deep breath. "Ty, I think you need to talk to your therapist about it."

With a nod, I smiled. "It feels fucking good to just say it out loud, if I'm being honest." She sniffled, and I reached up and wiped her tear-soaked cheeks. "I'm sorry."

"You don't have to say you're sorry, Ty. Not at all."

"I thought things were going really good for me after that—right before you and Lincoln showed up, that is. Then when you got out of that car, I was almost knocked back flat on my ass. You took my breath away, Kaylee."

Her cheeks turned a beautiful shade of pink. "I felt the same way, Ty. I hadn't felt anything for so long, and you sparked something in me as well that day. Even Lincoln noticed. I actually called dibs on you."

I squeezed her hand, and we both laughed.

"Funny, when I told Brock about the two of you showing up that day, I told him you were off limits."

She flashed me a huge grin.

"Of course, all I could think about was getting into your pants. Then the more I got to know you, the more something inside of me started to change. I got to the point where I needed to see you every day, and when I did see you, it drove me fucking mad because I couldn't do the things I wanted to do. Like kiss you. Or tell you how beautiful you looked."

She smiled again.

"Those feelings scared me, because the last thing I'd let myself need had nearly killed me. I told myself all I needed was one time with you. I'd fuck you and get you out of my system. Then that night, in the bar, when we kissed . . . I knew one time with you would never be enough. You made me want something I'd never wanted before. It was something I had lain in my bed and thought about but wasn't sure I would ever truly deserve."

"I knew I kissed well, but I didn't realize my kisses were *that* amazing."

I laughed, and she let out a half chuckle, half sob.

"The only way I know how to explain it to you is to say I got spooked. I wanted you so much, Kaylee, and it wasn't just for the sex. I wanted to kiss you every morning. Be the last person you saw each night before you went to sleep. I wanted to know what you looked like when you woke up, what you did when you were angry, sad, happy.

"For the first time in my life, I wanted someone so badly, and I knew I could have taken you to bed and tried to get a quick fix, but you were so different. Beyond beautiful. Kind, funny, and stubborn as hell. I was afraid if I took the hit, I'd have to keep coming back for more, and if you found out how broken I was, you would for sure leave. Take yourself out of that situation. Especially when I found out about John. I couldn't do that to you. I cared too much for you, and honestly, I wasn't sure I could handle it if things didn't work out between us. So I tried keeping you at arm's length. And, well, here we are."

"Ty," she said, moving closer to me. She was on her knees, her hands cupping my face. Our eyes met, and I nearly let my own tears flow.

"That day in the kitchen at Brock's house, when I was holding the pills and you walked in. I was so fucking ashamed that you knew what I had been thinking. Then when you kissed me and took the pills . . . I just couldn't do that to you, Kaylee. I wouldn't make you go through another relationship where you had to worry about someone. I couldn't let you get involved with a man who would constantly wage this inner battle with his demons."

"That wasn't your choice to make—it was mine, Ty."

I nodded. "I didn't know it then, but I think I fell in love with you the moment you smiled at me when you climbed out of Lincoln's car for the first time. Then, in Billings, I ended up sleeping with someone, thinking I could get over you that way, and hated myself for it. Hated that I had done that to you. I only added guilt on top of all the other feelings."

"We weren't together, Ty."

I pulled her hands from my face. "The entire time I was with her, I pretended she was you. I'm pretty sure I said your name a few times, and she didn't even care. That's all kinds of messed up. You deserve someone—"

She pressed her mouth to mine and pushed me down onto the bed.

"I want you. All of you. The good, the bad, the ugly, the fucked up. The confused. I want it all, because I think every single part of you is beautiful. And I won't ever stop fighting for us, and I expect you to do the same. Besides, I've never had so many orgasms in multiples of even numbers before, so if you think I'm letting you go, you're crazy."

Laughing, I flipped her over so I was on top. "What about this whole thing with Katy? I saw it in your eyes this morning when you asked me about kids. Is that something you still want with me?"

Her hand came up and gently stroked the side of my face. "Yes. Ty, nothing changes a single thing about how I feel about you, or the future I want with you. I think I love you even more, and I know I'll *keep* falling in love with you. This is only the beginning. Our beginning."

My eyes searched her face, and I'd started to talk when she pressed her fingers to my lips.

"Don't say it because you think I need to hear it. I see it in your eyes, and I feel it when you make love to me. And as far as Olivia is concerned, like I said, let's just worry about that when and if we need to."

This was the most amazing woman I'd ever met. She filled a void in me that I never thought could be filled. She made me feel whole. She made me feel alive. She made me want more.

So much more.

Chapter Twenty-Seven

KAYLEE

Ty's hand went to my jeans, and my stomach jumped with excitement.

Then someone knocked on the door and called out, "Room service."

With a groan, Ty dropped his head as I pushed him off me, and he rolled to the bed, a look of disappointment etched on his face.

"We need food for energy. Once we get naked, I don't plan on leaving this room until we have to. Plus, I'm starving!"

"I like the sound of not leaving the room," Ty said as I climbed off the bed and opened the door.

"Hi! Can you set it all on the table, please?" I asked. I reached into my purse and pulled out a tip.

Once the guy left, I felt Ty's eyes on me, watching every move I made, and I loved how it made my body catch fire. We had been through a plethora of emotions the last few hours. There was no doubt about that.

I opened both beers and handed Ty one and then grabbed the pizza box and sat on the bed again. Ty sat up, his face serious as he sipped the beer.

"It's your turn now. How are you handling this whole Katy and Olivia thing?"

I took a bite of pizza and shrugged. "Honestly, I don't know. I don't want to let it bother me, but I'd be lying if I said it didn't."

He nodded. "Fair enough."

It was true. I really didn't know how to feel. Letting the idea that Ty might already be a father bother me would be wasted energy. Especially if it turned out he *wasn't* her father.

"I think we need to see what happens with that. I don't want to stress about it and cause tension between us. Did I want to bolt when I realized what was going on? Yes. I had the urge to run, but I didn't because you mean so much to me, and I don't want to walk away from this, from us. It feels too right."

"It does."

I smiled and bit my lower lip. The knowledge that Ty felt the same as me made my chest feel warm, and a little bubble of want moved in my lower stomach.

"One thing we need to talk about is the fact that you and I seem to be flirting with danger."

"No condoms?" he asked with a wink.

"Yes. We're just getting started with our own relationship, and I won't lie to you: a few weeks ago, when I thought that maybe all I was going to get from you was one night, I hoped I would be pregnant. I was actually upset when my period started."

He stared at me, something flashing across his face. Then he looked away, almost as if he was embarrassed.

"Talk to me, Ty."

Looking back at me, he said the one thing I hadn't expected him to say. "Then I can admit to you that I hoped you were as well."

My eyes nearly popped out of my head. "Really?"

He shrugged. "If I couldn't give you a commitment, I wanted you to have a piece of me."

My mouth hung open, and I slowly shook my head.

He gave me another half shrug. "Yeah, Brock was ready to kick my ass when I admitted that little tidbit to him."

"You told Brock that?"

"Well, he wanted to know what in the hell I was thinking, so I told him."

I covered my mouth and let out a chuckle. "We are going about this completely backward, you know that?"

Laughing, he took a bite of pizza. "I like being inside you bare, but if you want me to wear a condom, I will."

I chewed nervously on my lip as I really thought about it. "I know the right response here is yes, I think you need to wear a condom. We're just sorting through our own issues, and it would be foolish to bring in another player."

"But?"

"But . . . I don't want you to. I'm on the pill. I say I stay on the pill, and we—"

"Keep having sex and working on us, and let fate decide our course?"

My heart raced slightly at his response. "So irresponsible."

He winked. "Who gives a fuck?"

"Apparently not us. Then let's address one more thing, since we're walking down this path. If Olivia turns out to be yours, do you want to be a part of her life?"

"I wouldn't mind, but I know she has a father, and from the sounds of it, they're close. I don't want to confuse her, but I would like to get to know her if she's my daughter."

"That's fair."

"What about you?"

"I would want her to be part of our world. It's not her fault this is happening to her. My heart actually breaks for the poor little thing."

"Yeah, mine does too."

"So, we'll deal with that when and if we need to?"

"Agreed."

We both took a bite of pizza.

"Look at us being all responsible and shit!" I said with a giggle.

"Brock and Lincoln would be so proud."

Dropping the crust of my pizza into the box, I stood and peeled my shirt off, then worked on my jeans. I was finished talking.

Ty just looked at me, a half-eaten slice of pizza in his hand, as his eyes glazed over a bit.

"Dinner's over. It's time for your dessert, Mr. Shaw."

"Your wish is my command, princess." Ty took the pizza box and put it on the floor, then quickly stripped out of his clothes. He pulled me back onto the bed and started to shower my body with kisses. It felt like heaven, his touch. His kisses. Every worry, fear, and shred of doubt I'd had about everything slipped away with this man's touch.

When he buried his face between my legs, I nearly came on the spot. It only took Ty slipping his fingers inside of me and pumping quickly for me to come so hard I felt dizzy.

Then his mouth was moving back up my body. Ty looked me in the eyes as he pushed inside me, slowly.

He dropped kisses on my neck, then moved across my jaw until he kissed me deeply. The taste of my own desire still on his tongue. He placed his mouth by my ear as he moved in and out of me in a slow but delicious pace. "If this is wrong, I don't think it would feel so right."

I wrapped my arms around him and slipped my fingers through his hair.

"It feels more than right," I whispered back as Ty continued to worship my body.

After a few minutes of making sweet love, he picked up the pace and was soon kissing me deeply, passionately. Then he came. And, for a brief moment, I thought he might pull out, but he didn't.

Afterward, he walked into the bathroom and turned on the shower. Then he took my hand and led me to the steamy, hot water, where he brought me to another orgasm up against the tiled shower wall. Being with this man was mind blowing—that was the only way to describe it.

I could get really used to this. Ty making love to me in the middle of the day.

Everything seemed to be too perfect. And I knew this more than anyone: when something seemed too good to be true, it usually was.

I picked up the little dress and smiled. "This one is cute."

Lincoln turned and looked at the pink-and-white dress in my hands. She smiled back. "It *is* cute. Are those matching bloomers?"

"Yep!" I said, holding the dress up so she could see it.

"Morgan would look adorable in that."

"She would," I said, glancing down at Morgan, sound asleep in her stroller. Brock had taken Blayze out fishing this morning, so that gave us a chance to do a little shopping. A new children's boutique had opened on Main Street, and Lincoln had been dying to go.

"After this, I need to stop in at the office and give Karen these drawings I worked on."

I nodded. Karen was Lincoln's boss at the design firm where she worked. "When are you planning on going back into the office?"

Lincoln looked sad for a moment. "The plan was after three months of maternity leave, I'd go back."

I reached for her hand. "You don't want to go back, do you?"

Her eyes filled with tears, but she didn't cry. "I love working, I do. But the thought of leaving Morgan makes me feel sick to my stomach."

"Have you thought about going back part time?"

"Karen really needs someone full time. She's been so understanding about the baby and all."

"Then work from home."

Lincoln looked at me for a few moments. "Work from home?"

"Yeah. When you need to meet with clients, make arrangements for Morgan. Maybe you could even hire a nanny. She could tend to Morgan, and you could work from home and be there with her at least the majority of the time."

She chewed on the nail of her thumb as she thought about it. "That would probably work. And there's a back room at the office that's empty. I could ask Karen if I could make it into a little nursery on days when she needed me to come into the office. I'm sure she'd be on board."

"If she wants you badly enough, she'll be on board with it."

Lincoln hugged me. "Thank you for suggesting that. I don't honestly know why I hadn't thought of it before."

"That's what best friends are for."

After Lincoln had bought more clothes than Morgan needed, and a few outfits for Blayze, we made our way down the street.

"I'm starving. You feel like eating?" Lincoln asked as I glanced down at my phone. Ty should have been hearing from Katy any day now. It had been three days since he'd given his DNA and they'd taken blood from him to test for a match for Olivia.

"I'll try to eat," I said.

Lincoln took my hand and gave it a squeeze. "Still no news?"

I shook my head. "I'm really trying not to let this bother me, but I'm scared, Lincoln. I'm scared she's his, and I don't know how I'm really going to feel about that."

Ty and I had gone to Brock's house when we got back from Billings and then filled Lincoln and Brock in on everything. How the two of us were now dating. Ty admitted to Brock about that day in his truck, after which Brock stood and hugged his brother. It was a touching moment.

Ty didn't want to tell his parents, though, and I wasn't going to push him. Neither was Brock. He had originally said he was only going to tell his therapist, so his telling Brock had been a surprise. A good surprise. Then he told them about Katy and Olivia. Brock didn't seem to be as surprised as Lincoln was. I guess, with Ty having slept around so much, it shouldn't have been a shock.

"Kaylee, stop beating yourself up about this. Everything is so new with you and Ty that simply being in a relationship, with all the baggage, is stressful. You've just had a huge wrench thrown in. Of course you're going to be worried."

"Did it bother you that Brock had Blayze?"

She shook her head. "I want to say no, but that was so completely different. I knew going in with Brock that he had a son. Still, knowing another woman gave him his first child did play around with my emotions. Not much, though, because Blayze was a part of Brock, and I loved him so much. You're going into this new relationship with Ty, and you were blindsided. I'm honestly impressed with how well you're handling it."

We walked into a little café on Main and found two empty seats. I wrapped my arms around myself, suddenly chilled to the bone.

"I don't know how well I'm handling it, truth be told. I refuse to let Ty see the worry, but a part of me is so sad that I may not possibly be the woman giving him his first child."

Lincoln looked at me with sympathy in her eyes and a knowing smile on her face. Then her face grew serious, and she'd started to ask me something when the waitress walked up.

"Afternoon. What can I get you to drink?"

"Water for me," I said.

"I'll have the same."

"Here are the menus; I'll go get your drinks."

I opened the menu and started looking, but I quickly peeked over it to see Lincoln looking at me.

"What?"

"You really do want a baby, don't you?"

"Of course I do. I mean, not right away—I think we need to be in a relationship for a bit before we mix in a kid. And it would be sort of nice for Ty to be able to tell me he loves me without it freaking him out." I let out a half-hearted laugh.

Lincoln took in a deep breath and let it out. "I am the last person to tell you to take it slow. I mean, look how fast I got knocked up."

Pointing to her, I nodded.

"But I do hope you don't rush things. I know the two of you have been wanting this for so long, and I'm so over the moon you both got your heads out of your asses, but slow is good, Kaylee."

I reached for her hand. "I know, Lincoln. I know."

The rest of lunch was much lighter in mood as we talked about the plans for the summer. Blayze had been begging Brock and Lincoln to go to Disney. The little dude was going to owe me big time, because during lunch, I successfully talked Lincoln into what a great idea it would be for all of us to go to Disney. Of course, both of us being from the South, we pretended like we didn't remember how freaking hot it was there. And humid.

"If we went at the end of July, Morgan would be almost five months old. She could sit in the pool, and it would be a little more fun."

Lincoln laughed. "She's fun now!"

We both turned and looked at her, still sleeping in the stroller.

"Not to be a killjoy, Lincoln, but look at her. She's all cute and everything, but she's sort of boring."

Lincoln's eyes widened in shock as she looked at me and then down to her sleeping baby. "Spend a day with her—she is far from boring."

"All she does is sleep!"

"Ha! You know nothing. She cries. Poops a lot, demands food, then cries again."

I looked at the peacefully sleeping baby. "Every time I see her, she's sleeping."

"Ugh! You have no idea!"

As if on cue, Morgan opened her eyes and let out a whale of a cry.

"Holy shit, it's like she's doing it simply to prove me wrong! She's her father's daughter. Shaw blood is for sure pumping in those veins."

Quickly scooping up her baby, Lincoln moved like an expert and was soon feeding the once-sleeping princess, who had quickly morphed into a little monster.

"Wow, she's going to town on your boob," I said.

"She needs her diaper changed as well."

I crinkled my nose. "And why are you looking at me?"

Before she had a chance to reply, my phone rang. I looked down to see it was Ty. I knew he was out in the fields today, plowing and planting hay.

"Hey, how's it going?"

"Hey."

I instantly heard it in his voice. I sat up taller and forced my breathing to keep steady. "Everything okay?" I asked, attempting to sound casual.

"Katy's here."

The shocked look on my face made Lincoln take notice.

"As in, there at the ranch?"

"Yes."

I swallowed hard. "I didn't know you'd told her where you lived."

"Um, yeah. It seemed like the right thing to do."

Nodding, I replied, "Sure, yes."

"Do you think you could come back to the ranch?"

"Of course. I'm on my way right now. Lincoln and I just finished up lunch, so I'll get there as soon as I can."

"Be careful, Kaylee."

"I will. Um . . . see you in a bit."

I had almost said "I love you," but for some reason, I stopped myself.

I hit end and stared at my phone until Lincoln's voice pulled me out of my daze.

"Do you want me to drive you home? Ty can bring you back to get your car."

Forcing a smile, I replied, "Nah, it's fine. Do you need help with Morgan?"

"Nope. We're fine. You go."

When I stood, it felt like the ground was rolling underneath me. I was more nervous than I realized. Leaning down, I kissed Morgan first and then hugged Lincoln.

"See ya later."

She smiled. "Call me. And if you need me there, please let me know."

With the practiced smile I had mastered after John's death, I tossed my purse over my shoulder. "I will. Love ya!"

And with that, I rushed out of the little café and to my car. I didn't even remember the drive back to the ranch. My mind was so unfocused; I honestly couldn't believe I made it there safely. I drove straight to the main house, since Ty had sent me a text saying he was with his parents and Katy.

I could only imagine what was racing through Stella's and Ty Senior's minds. They could possibly have another grandbaby. One who was sick.

By the time I pulled up, I had my shit together. No matter what happened, I would be there for Ty because I loved him. I had no idea if this would put our relationship into a tailspin or maybe make him pull away more. But if he thought for one moment I was struggling, he'd think it was his fault.

Then I reminded myself about our talk in the hotel room, and I knew we were going to be okay.

We had to be okay. We had to.

Ty was standing on the front porch when I pulled up and parked behind a black Dodge truck. I assumed it belonged to Katy.

I got out and smiled as I walked up the steps. Ty gave me a once-over and then pulled me into his arms. "Before we go in there, I need to tell you something."

My heart jumped to my throat. Oh, God. Katy had already told him.

"Okay," I said, my voice sounding so much weaker than I wanted it to.

"I love you."

I stared at him. Had I just heard him say what I thought he'd said?

"I love you, Kaylee. You are the woman I didn't know I was praying for until you showed up in my life. There is not a single doubt in my mind that from the moment I first met you, I knew you were unlike any woman I had ever met, or *would* ever meet. You're the woman who made me see that I was worth loving. You brought me out of the darkness and into a light so fucking bright with possibility that it makes me excited for the future. For *our* future. I want to marry you, have as many kids as you want, and spend every moment of my life showing you how much you mean to me. You are my everything."

Tears rolled down my cheeks as I attempted not to fall to the ground in a crying mess. Ty reached up and cupped my face. He brushed the endless tears away with his thumbs.

"I wanted you to know that before we found out."

"You don't know yet?" I asked, sniffling.

He shook his head. "I wanted to wait for you. Katy did as well."

"Oh, okay."

"No matter what, it's you and me, right?"

I saw the worry in his eyes. Placing my hands over his, which were still on my face, I smiled. "Forever and always, you and me, Ty."

Chapter Twenty-Eight

KAYLEE

Ty laced his fingers with mine as we walked into the house. It took me a few moments to get myself put back together after Ty's declaration of love. My heart still raced, but it was no longer from nerves. I knew that no matter what happened, it was going to be okay. We were going to be okay.

When we stepped into the living room, Katy looked up and smiled. Sitting next to her was a man our age. He stood.

"Kaylee, it's good to see you again," Katy said, extending her hand. I shook it and then faced the gentleman next to her. "This is my husband, Bryce."

"It's a pleasure," he said as I returned his smile.

"Nice to meet you."

He appeared to be holding back his emotions, not giving any hints as to what was going to happen.

We all sat, and I quickly peeked over to Ty Senior and Stella. They both looked equally nervous and excited.

"So, I think it's best if I just get right to the news," Katy said.

Ty squeezed my hand, and I placed my other one over his.

"That sounds good," Ty said, glancing over to his mother and father nervously. They simply gave him warm smiles that said no matter what, everything was going to be okay.

"The DNA came back, and you're not Olivia's father."

It was instant, the relief I felt coming off of Ty. I let out the breath I hadn't even realized I was holding. Even Stella and Ty Senior seemed to be a bit relieved.

Ty pulled his hand from me and scrubbed it over his face.

"Oh, thank you, God," Ty said, a breath expelling along with the words. Then he looked at Katy. "I'm sorry . . . I mean, I would have been—"

She held up her hand and smiled. "Ty, you don't need to explain your relief, believe me. I get it."

"Your ex?" he asked.

"Yes, I must have already been pregnant when we . . ." Her voice trailed off when she realized what she was about to say.

Ty changed the subject. "So, was I a match for her, though?"

Katy shook her head. "No. You weren't."

"Damn, Katy, Bryce—I'm so sorry," Ty said.

"What if we see if we're a match?" Stella asked. "I know Ty's father and I are more than willing to donate."

Katy looked her way and reached a hand out to Stella. "That is so sweet of you, but we actually found someone who's an almost-perfect match."

"That's wonderful!" Stella said.

"That's great news," Ty and I said at the same time. He laced his fingers with mine.

Katy grinned and wiped a tear away.

"Who's the match?" Ty asked.

When her eyes met mine, I instantly knew.

"Kaylee."

All eyes were now on me. "I am?"

Katy nodded. "Yes. You match nine out of ten. It's the best match we've had so far."

"I didn't even know you'd donated to be tested," Ty said, looking at me with so much love on his face that it nearly made me give in to my crazy emotions and break down into a sobbing mess. I didn't, though.

I took a moment to let everything sink in. Ty wasn't the father. And I was the match. Me.

When we'd been at the hospital, I'd told the nurse I wanted to be tested as well, to see if I would match. I had honestly not thought twice about it. Now I was in shock, both because Ty wasn't the father and because of the way Katy was looking at me. She was putting all her hope on me and my blood to help save her little girl.

I faced Ty. "Well, I didn't want to say anything with everything that was going on. It was just something that felt right to do."

Stella stood and walked over to me. She reached down and pulled me into her arms.

"You are an amazing woman, Kaylee Holden. I just love you and am so proud of you."

And *that* made the tears fall. My own mother had never spoken those words to me, so to hear them from Stella, a woman I loved and admired, meant the world to me.

When she pulled back, I wiped at my tears. Ty Senior was next in line to hug me, then Katy. Ty stood next to me, his arm wrapped around my waist.

"What do I need to do?" I asked.

"Can you come to Billings for about a week?" Katy asked. "You'll get a daily injection for the growth of white blood cells. Then, on the fifth day, they'll place a needle in both of your arms: one to remove the blood, the other to return it to your body. It goes through a machine that circulates the blood and collects the stem cells."

"Any side effects?" Ty asked.

This time it was Bryce who answered, his arm around Katy. "You might get a headache. They say there could be bone soreness, and the needles might cause discomfort."

I nodded. "That doesn't sound so bad."

"You'll do it?" Katy asked, trying not to let her voice sound too hopeful.

With a smile, I replied, "Of course I'll do it."

◆ ◆ ◆

Two months later: July

I rode up on the horse to find Ty standing there, without a shirt on, pouring water over his body.

"Lord, have mercy, that is all mine," I said as I fanned myself. Ty Shaw had a weird way of making me all hot and bothered. Literally.

Watching him, I couldn't help but count down until the day was over and he would be coming home. Ty and I split our time between both of our houses. I stayed a week at his place, then he would stay a week at mine. The sex was amazing and hadn't slowed down one bit. Ty and his weird rule of not liking odd numbers ensured I always got at least two orgasms, which I had no complaints about whatsoever.

He must have felt my eyes on him, because he turned and looked at me.

"Hey there, beautiful. What brings you out here?"

Today, Ty was working on putting up a fence in one of the pastures. It was about a hundred acres of land he was fencing off, and it was for some of the horses to graze on.

"I thought maybe we could have lunch."

Ty smiled. I was quickly learning what life was like dating a rancher. He worked early in the morning and sometimes worked right up until dark. There was also a reason he had a body like he did. Just watching him swing an ax one day had nearly made me have an orgasm. He was covered in dirt six days out of the week. Stella made the boys take Sundays off, and the hired ranch hands took over.

I also learned fast that I could not allow myself to fall in love with the cows. Or their calves. I learned that when I helped Ty deliver a calf one night. It was my second go-round, but this time, I got my hands dirty. I thought it would gross me out, but I plopped that calf onto my lap and cried tears of joy. She was my baby as much as she was her mama's. Unfortunately, her mama had all the milk, and the calf ignored me.

And when the cows I'd been naming started to disappear, I stopped asking where they went. It was too traumatizing. Stella had told me in knitting class that I needed to learn to keep my feelings for the animals inside. Ty was stressed out when I cried the first time after he'd told me my favorite cow had been slaughtered. I didn't eat red meat for two weeks.

"Lunch sounds amazing."

After sliding off the horse, I untied the basket I had brought and grabbed a blanket. I made my way to a large shade tree and laid out the blanket, then got out the sandwiches and fruit I'd made up for the two of us.

Ty leaned down and kissed me. "How are you feeling?"

I smiled. "Amazing."

He sat. "Good."

He'd gotten into the habit of asking that question after I'd given blood for Olivia's treatment. After donating my stem cells, I had a massive headache for days afterward, then ended up getting the flu. Neither were related. Having the flu in late spring, though, sucked. Between the headache and the flu, which wiped me out, Ty decided he needed to ask me every single day how I was feeling. I loved that he cared so deeply.

"I heard from Katy earlier. She said Olivia is feeling better as each day goes by."

Ty smiled. "I'm glad to hear that. You still don't think it's weird you've become friends with a woman I slept with?"

"No. Are you uncomfortable with it?"

He shrugged.

I reached for his hand. "Ty, if me being friends with Katy makes you uncomfortable, I can pull back some. I *have* fallen a little for Olivia, though, and since part of me was injected into her, I sort of care about her and would like to keep up with how she's doing."

"I know, and I want Olivia to get better—I do. I just feel like every time things seem to be going in the right direction, the floor drops out."

With a reassuring squeeze of his hand, I said, "Don't be sorry for feeling the way you do. I completely agree with you. I don't talk to Katy that often anyway, and honestly, when we do talk, it's about Olivia only. I understand her need to feel connected to me. I gave her something that is helping her child."

He nodded. "Change of subject—are you ready for the weekend?"

I smiled. "Yes! Still not going to tell me where we're going?"

"No."

When I gave him a sad pouty face, he laughed. "Not going to work. I'm still pissed at you and Lincoln for talking us all into Disney World."

"Yeah, that was sort of miserable last week, wasn't it?"

"Mom and Dad mentioned something about payback, so you and Lincoln might want to sleep with one eye open."

Laughing, I handed him the fruit. "They had fun, and you did too. Admit it!"

He smiled. "I did have fun. It was nice to see Blayze and Brock together like that. I'm glad he retired from bull riding."

"She won't ever admit it, but so is Lincoln. Now she's got Blayze hell bent on it, though."

"He's got it in his blood. Look how good he's gotten at mutton busting."

I groaned. "Good Lord, even that stresses me out, and I'm not his mother."

"It's a sheep!" Ty said.

"He could still get hurt."

He grinned. "You have to admit, he's pretty damn good."

I chewed on my lip, then giggled. "He *is* really good!"

For a moment, I wondered what it would be like to have a child with Ty. If we had a little boy, would he want him to bull ride? Or maybe do something else, like Tanner?

Things between me and Ty had been amazing. He was right: they almost seemed too good. Ty still went to his therapist once a month. He told her about his thoughts of suicide, which was a huge relief for me. He also seemed to be letting his guard down more and more, even talking about his addiction to his parents and telling them that it would always be a struggle, or at least he felt like it would be.

The one thing we hadn't ever brought up again was our future. I didn't want to split my time between two houses; it was getting exhausting.

With a deep breath, I asked him that very question.

"Ty, where do you see us at in the future? Like in a month? In six months? In five years?"

He froze, and for a moment I saw the walls going back up. I didn't say a word. I simply rubbed my thumb gently over his hand and waited. Because that was what I promised I would do. I'd be there for him and not give up on us.

That still didn't mean my heart didn't pound in my chest as I waited for his answers.

Chapter Twenty-Nine

Ty

It wasn't like I didn't see a future with Kaylee. Hell, I dreamed of our future together. Since we had started staying with each other, my nightmares had all but stopped. When she wasn't next to me in bed, I found myself staring up at the ceiling, unable to sleep. I needed her by me, and that still scared me.

I didn't want to think of Kaylee as some sort of crutch or addiction. She was, though, because I was fucking addicted to being inside her. Kissing her. Hearing her laugh. And even the occasional argument when she had to be stubborn about something.

Her question only threw me for a minute or two. I could see it on her face. She thought I was withdrawing, but it was just the opposite. I didn't want to ruin my plans. I knew I wasn't scared to be with her. Hell, I had bought a ring, and even though my head was telling me to slow down, my heart was telling me I needed to jump on the bull and get it locked down.

The feel of Kaylee's thumb gently sliding over my skin calmed every nerve ending in my body.

I looked directly into her eyes and answered her. "In a month, I see us decorating one of our houses for fall, because I hope by then we'll decide whose house we're going to be living in permanently."

Her body visibly relaxed. "Do you have a preference?"

Thinking about it, I answered her honestly. "Yes. I think we should live in your house."

That surprised her. "Mine?"

Taking a bite of my sandwich, I nodded. "Yeah."

Then her smile erupted over her face. "Ty, are you sure?"

"Does that make you happy? The idea of living in your house?"

"Yes, but only if you're positive."

"I'm positive. I want to see our kids raised in that house. I can't explain why. Maybe it's because that's where you and I first made love. I feel a stronger connection there."

Her eyes filled with tears. "Me too." She chewed on her lower lip, trying to contain her emotions.

"Six months. That's a new year, so I'm thinking I see us on the floor in front of our fireplace. We're both naked, and you have been thoroughly fucked and are content in my arms."

"I like that one . . . a lot."

I laughed.

"Five years. That's easy. Married . . . to you."

Her cheeks turned a beautiful pink.

"At least one baby, maybe two."

That's when she lost the battle and let the tears fall.

"Do you see the same thing, Kaylee?"

She nodded, then launched herself over our food, pushing me back. "Yes. I do. And right now, I need you to be inside me."

"You don't have to tell me twice."

We both worked quickly to rid ourselves of the clothes we had on. All I had to do was kick off my boots and drop my pants and boxers;

Kaylee pulled off her jeans, leaving her top on. When she crawled on me and slid down onto my cock, I let out a moan.

"No one will show up, right?" she asked, her breathing ragged as she slowly moved up and down on me while she looked around.

"No."

"Thank God."

I reached between our bodies, and it only took the pressure of my thumb on her clit to have her squeezing around me. When she dropped her head to my chest, I rolled us over and slowly made love to her. Something about being under that tree, in the middle of the ranch, buried inside the woman I loved more than life itself, moved me.

I had planned on asking Kaylee to marry me this weekend, at the cabin, but this moment felt too right.

I felt my buildup and saw it on her face too.

"Come with me, Kaylee."

And she did. She pulled my mouth to hers, and we moaned while we came at the same time.

I held my body off of her but didn't attempt to pull out. Being connected like this was the best feeling in the world.

Looking into her eyes, I took a few deep breaths and then smiled.

"Will you marry me, Kaylee?"

Her eyes went wide, her mouth gaping slightly. Then her gaze bounced all over my face and landed back on my eyes. When she lifted her hand to the side of my face, I leaned into it automatically.

"Yes. Yes, I'll marry you."

I leaned down and kissed the single tear that had slipped free. "You just made me the happiest man in the world."

We lay there for a few more minutes, me holding her while we listened to the sounds of nature. When a bird landed in the tree above us, we both looked up at it.

"Look how beautiful he is," Kaylee whispered.

Before I had a chance to respond, the little bastard let a poop bomb go. And it landed on me.

Right. On. My. Mouth.

I jumped up, screaming as I searched for something to wipe it off, while Kaylee stood there, half-naked, laughing her ass off.

"Okay, they say it's good luck for a bird to crap on you, but I think you earned bonus points for it landing on your mouth."

I shot her a look. "You think it's funny?" I said between swallows of water and my practically rubbing my lips off. When she nodded, I reached out and pulled her to me. She pushed against me, laughing and screaming for me not to kiss her while she attempted to get away.

"Pucker up, baby, you're getting some of this good luck too."

I couldn't keep my eyes off Kaylee. She was moving around my mother's kitchen like she'd been living here her entire life. Something happened to my heart each time she laughed or my mother looked at her with love in her eyes. I loved that they were close.

I hadn't given her the ring yet; I was saving it for the cabin this weekend. I'd already enlisted Lincoln's help with planning it all.

Blayze sat on the kitchen island, his eyes also glued to everything Kaylee was doing.

"Kaylee, have you decided if you're going to help Mrs. Kennedy with her daughter's wedding?" my mother asked.

"I have. I told her I couldn't commit to it. As much as I love planning events, it's just not my thing. I tried it and love doing it for fun, for family especially, but turning it into a business—I don't think so."

A part of me had wondered if it was my fault Kaylee had been doing fewer and fewer events. She had also been working a shit ton on her book editing. And, much to her credit, she was trying to learn as much as she could about the ranch. I loved that she was taking an interest in what I did, so in return, I asked her questions about her job. I was honestly interested in learning why she did what she did for a living.

She even read to me part of a book she was writing. She told me it was young adult, more for kids in late middle school or high school. It was good; *she* was good. Damn good. I'd asked if she was going to publish it, and as of then, she'd only had plans to write it. She'd figure out what she would do once it was finished. Whatever she decided, I'd be right by her side.

"Blayze, should you be on that counter?" Brock asked as he walked into the kitchen with Morgan in his arms. The moment she saw me, she let out a scream of excitement and reached for me.

"Come here, princess," I said, taking her from her father's arms. "Did you miss your favorite uncle?"

My father walked into the kitchen and gave my mother a quick kiss on the cheek.

"Dinner is almost ready. Why don't you start taking the food to the table?" Mama motioned to Kaylee, Brock, and Lincoln.

Blayze jumped off the counter and reached for Kaylee's hand. "Want some help, Aunt Kaylee?"

I'd already filled Kaylee in about Blayze having a crush on her a month or so back.

"Ty, would you mind grabbing a bottle out of the little cooler I brought?" Lincoln asked me. "It's in the living room."

"Sure."

With Morgan in my arms, I headed into the living room. A large picture window looked out over the front yard and the front pasture. I could see someone driving down the gravel driveway. I walked to the front door and opened it, Morgan gazing up at me with those big blue eyes of hers.

"I know, princess, you're hungry."

With a quick glance back to the drive, I saw it was Dirk's truck as he drew closer.

"Is that my little sweet pea?" Dirk said once he reached us, making goofy faces at Morgan and causing her to giggle. Then she held her little hands out for Dirk to take her, which he promptly did.

"Come on, dude, even my niece? You've got to capture *her* heart as well as the millions of other single women out there?"

Dirk laughed and kissed Morgan on the cheek. "This is the only girl I've given my heart to, so back off. You got your own girl." I smiled, and Dirk raised a brow. "I don't think in all the years I've known you, Ty, I've ever seen that smile on your face."

"Probably not."

"Holy shit. You're in love with her."

I nodded.

He stared at me for a moment, then laughed. "Dude, you've got it bad. I'm happy for you."

"Thanks. I actually asked her to marry me earlier today."

Dirk's eyes went wide. "No kidding. Did she say yes?"

"Of course she said yes, dickhead. It's me we're talking about here."

Laughing, he walked past me and shielded Morgan from my outstretched arms.

"Give her back to me."

"No, you get to see her all the time. I don't."

"She's my niece, dickhead."

"Mine too."

"Not by blood."

"So!"

"So!"

When the door opened and Kaylee stared at both of us, we stopped. "Do you two hear yourselves?"

"He started it," Dirk said, giving me a smirk.

"Whatever," I shot back.

I walked up to Kaylee and kissed her as Dirk made a gagging sound from behind me. "There are little eyes watching—they don't need to see that crap."

"You're just jealous, Dirk. But someday, someone is going to catch your eye, and you're going to fall in love," Kaylee said.

"Hard pass," Dirk replied, walking by the two of us and going into the house.

"Welcome home, Dirk!" Kaylee called after him. He simply raised a hand and gave a wave.

When she turned back to me, I saw the happiness in those baby-blue eyes of hers.

"Your mama asked me why I was in such a good mood. Am I normally not in a good mood?" Her brows were furrowed, and it was the cutest thing ever.

I chuckled. "Well, even I've noticed the smile that seems to be plastered on your face permanently."

"Lincoln asked me if I was pregnant because there's an 'air' about me." She raised her hands and put air quotes around the word.

Our hands laced together as we walked back into the house. "Want to tell them?" I asked.

She jumped and faced me. "Can we? Oh my gosh, Ty, it's killing me not to say something!"

I pulled her to me and leaned down, brushing my lips over hers. When we both needed some air, I barely moved away from her lips and whispered, "I haven't given you your ring yet."

Her eyes sparkled with excitement. "That's okay."

"I was planning on it this weekend."

"You have it?"

Laughing, I kissed her on the tip of her nose. "Yes, baby. I have it. You okay telling them without the ring?"

"Yes!"

"Then let's do it."

"Okay. I'll let you do it when you're ready, since it's your family and all."

"Fair enough," I said, giving her one more quick kiss.

The second we walked into the dining room, Kaylee let out a squeal of delight.

All eyes turned to us.

"We're getting married!" she cried out.

My mouth dropped open, and I stared at her. So much for me telling the family.

Lincoln and my mother both jumped out of their seats and rushed Kaylee. Lincoln hugged her first, and then my mama wrapped them both up in her arms.

Brock and my father both stood and made their way over to me. Brock shook my hand, then pulled me in for a quick hug. "Congratulations, I'm so happy for you both."

I slapped the side of Brock's arm. "Thanks, Brock."

Then it was my father's turn. He gave me a wide smile, shook my hand, and also did the quick hug. "You couldn't have picked a finer woman, son."

"No doubt about that, Dad."

Then my eyes landed on Dirk. He grinned, then said, "My chances are getting better and better. Just need to get the last Shaw brother hitched, then all the single women will be mine."

Morgan let out a little scream of excitement that caused all the women to look over at Dirk.

"Don't worry, sweet pea, you'll always be my number one girl," Dirk said as he tilted Morgan back and expertly gave her a bottle.

A collective chorus of sighs echoed in the room as my mother, Lincoln, and my new fiancée all stared at Dirk and Morgan.

Chapter Thirty

KAYLEE

Ty didn't drive far out of town before we were pulling up to a small cabin that was just a ways down from a larger house. I stepped out of the truck and looked at the Bitterroot Mountains and smiled. The blue sky seemed to give way to the mountain ridge. Random puffs of white clouds dotted the sky, giving it that familiar picturesque look I had come to love so much. It stole my breath, it was so beautiful.

"That's Blodgett Canyon. You should see it in the fall. It's beautiful."

I turned to face Ty. "This whole area is stunning, any time of year."

Ty's eyes looked out over the vast land before us as he smiled. "I do love Montana."

My heartbeat sped up slightly. It was crazy to me how much my life had changed in the last year. Simply because my best friend had decided she needed to move to another state and start fresh. I let out a contented sigh and faced Ty.

"Do you know the owners?"

He nodded. "Yes, I went to high school with Roy and his wife, Carol. They bought this fifty acres right out of college. Roy had the guesthouse built for his family on the East Coast who come out to visit. Sometimes they rent it out as well."

"It's beautiful. Not as beautiful as the ranch, but a close second."

Ty beamed with happiness, then kissed me on the forehead. "Come on, I want to introduce you to them."

"Okay," I said, letting Ty slip his hand in mine and lead me over to the large home that sat a few hundred yards away from the cabin. A row of trees separated both houses, giving each property a sense of privacy. The smell of gardenias wafted around me. The scent instantly made me take in a long, deep breath. This was a place to come to completely unwind and relax.

Two dogs, a black Lab and a boxer, came running toward us, their tails going a mile a minute. Ty stopped and reached down to pet them both. I followed his lead. The Lab jumped and spun around, he was so happy.

"Hey, Frog! Louise! Good dogs."

I laughed. "Did you just call him Frog?"

Ty nodded. "Yeah. When he was a puppy, he used to do this really weird bounce, like a frog. Hence, his name."

With a gentle rub on the Lab's belly, I gave him a little pout. "Poor baby, you've got a terrible name."

His tongue was hanging out the side of his mouth, and he didn't seem to have a care in the world. I couldn't help but laugh.

"Ty! Damn, man, it's good to see you!" A dark-haired guy stepped off the front porch with a strikingly attractive woman by his side. Her chestnut-brown hair was pulled up into a ponytail, and her hands were resting on a very pregnant stomach. They were a pretty couple, and if I had to guess, I'd go with football star and head cheerleader. They had that look to them.

"Kaylee, I've heard so much about you from Ty! It's a pleasure to finally meet you," Carol said as she made her way over. She gave me a friendly hug and then stepped back and gave me a once-over. "He said you were beautiful; he didn't say you were stunningly beautiful."

I felt my cheeks heat. "Thank you," I said. I wished I could tell her I'd heard a lot about her, but Ty had literally just mentioned Roy and Carol to me only moments ago.

It was Roy's turn. He reached out for my hand and shook it. "It's a pleasure to meet you, Kaylee. When Ty called me and asked about coming up here, I had to say I was shocked. It's about damn time he finally met a woman who could put up with his shit."

I smiled, and then my gaze drifted to meet Ty's. He winked at me, and I felt my stomach flutter at the idea that Ty had been talking about me to his friends. I looked back at Roy and said, "Thank you so much for letting us stay here. It's beautiful."

"Just wait," Carol said, giving me a saucy smile that said she knew something I didn't. Then she laced her arm around mine, and we started walking up the steps of their house. "We just got back to Montana. We've been in Europe for over a year. So Ty had to fill us in on everything. I was stunned to hear Brock got married and had a baby. To your best friend too! It's like something out of a romance book."

"I didn't mention it, but Kaylee is a book editor," Ty said from behind us.

Carol stopped walking and faced me. "What kind of books?"

"I do a few different genres, but mostly romance and historical romance."

"Oh my gosh, you and I just became best friends. We are going to talk nothing but books this weekend. I need a list of all your favorites."

I laughed. "Okay."

Ty came up and wrapped his arm around my waist, pulling me from Carol's hold. "Sorry to break the news to you, Carol, but she's mine all weekend."

Carol pouted, then rubbed her stomach. "Ty, I'm eight months pregnant. Are you really going to steal my new best friend?"

"Yes. Yes, I am, because she's *my* best friend."

My heart hammered in my chest at his words. Ty looked at me with so much love in his eyes that I nearly melted on the spot. It was hard to believe that I'd ever had any sort of happiness before this man, because his smile alone filled my heart with so much joy.

Roy let out a laugh and wrapped his arm around his wife. "Listen, the cabin is stocked with food. You should have everything you need for the weekend. Any problems, just give us a holler."

"Thanks, Roy," Ty said.

"I made a lasagna and put it in the refrigerator. You just have to heat it up. There's also some fresh french bread, right out of the oven this morning."

"Wow!" I said. "Homemade bread *and* lasagna. I may never want to leave." I gave Carol a smile that said thank you.

"If you guys want, tomorrow morning I can make my famous french toast. Just let me know when you wake up."

"Will do," Ty said, suddenly taking my hand and leading us back down the steps.

"Okay, well, I guess that's Ty's sign he's finished being sociable," Roy joked.

"Have fun, you two!" Carol called out.

I looked over my shoulder and said, "Thanks again!" I couldn't help but giggle. "Why the sudden departure?" I asked.

"I'm ready to kiss you. Touch you. Be inside you."

A chill ran down my spine in anticipation of all that.

"But first, we're going on a picnic."

And just like that, I felt like a little girl again, excited for my first real adventure with a boy. Of course, my first adventure with a boy was his asking to push me on the swings and my thinking I had just scored better than Christmas morning, because the boy who'd asked was also the cutest boy in school. He ended up being the biggest dick in school too. I had a feeling this time things would be much different.

After we grabbed our bags, we headed into the small cabin. It was perfect. The living and kitchen area were one big room. Large plank floors made it all warm and cozy. The furniture was leather, giving the space a slightly rustic feel. Large throw pillows lined the sofa, and I imagined myself curled up with a blanket and a book.

The back of the cabin had large sliding-glass doors that led to a small patio with chairs and a fire ring. The view of the mountains looked like a picture from this spot. When I walked up to the glass doors, I could see a small lake. I smiled as I gazed out at it. The mountains reflected on the water, making it look magical and romantic. Just when you thought you'd seen the prettiest view, Montana yelled, "Surprise, here's an even better view!"

Ty walked up and wrapped his arms around me, his chin resting on my head as he asked, "What's the smile for?"

"This lake makes me think of one Lincoln and I saw when we first drove up to Montana. We were only a few miles from Hamilton and had gotten out to stretch. I remember feeling so lost on that trip. I was sad that Lincoln was leaving me, and the thought of going back to Atlanta seemed all wrong. The entire drive up here was beautiful, but there was something about that lake and the way the mountains reflected off the water. I had a sense of peace come over me. I knew in that moment that Lincoln was doing what she had to do, and eventually, I'd find my way again."

"I'm glad your way included a stop with me."

Turning in his arms, I looked up at him. My finger ran lightly along his jawline as I stared into those sky-blue eyes. "It's not just a stop. I think you were my destination the entire time."

Ty's eyes softened as he leaned down and gently brushed his mouth over mine. "I love you."

I smiled against his lips. "I love you too."

After a deep kiss that left my knees wobbly, Ty drew back and looked out the doors, then back to me. "Come on—we're actually heading to that lake for lunch."

◆ ◆ ◆

We quickly placed our bags in the bedroom, and I couldn't help but stand in the middle of the room and spin in delight. The master bedroom was decorated like something straight out of a romance book, with white lacy fabric and roses placed all over the room. The scent hit me immediately, and I couldn't help but smile when Ty pulled a single rose out and ran it over my face while he looked at me like he wanted to strip me naked and make love to me. Somehow he managed not to, and we headed over to the lake in his truck with a large picnic basket that had clearly been prepared ahead of time.

I gasped when I stepped out of the truck. The lake was even more beautiful in person. It was the most vibrant color blue.

"The color . . . ," I whispered.

"I think it's from the reflection of the sky."

I nodded. "Are all lakes in Montana this beautiful?"

Ty laughed.

I looked up at the mountains and around at all the trees. Birds sang together in what almost seemed like a practiced harmony.

I froze when, off in the distance, I saw a moose at the edge of the lake on the other side.

"Ty! Oh my gosh! It's a moose!"

He grinned and laid out a quilt and then set the basket on it. "You haven't seen a moose yet?"

I shook my head, staring at the large, stunning animal as he wandered back into the thick forest. What an amazing treat that had been. "No, that was my first one."

"It's like he was here to greet you," Ty said.

I nodded and then turned to see him sitting on the quilt. The spread of food before us. "Wow!"

"I may owe Lincoln a pretty big thank-you. Actually, she's already called in the favor."

With a chuckle, I took the glass of wine he gave me and sat down, tossing a little piece of cheese into my mouth and nearly groaning at how good it tasted with the wine. "What's the favor?"

"She's booked a getaway this fall with Brock, and she said you and I are on kid duty."

"For a whole weekend? She's trusting me with both kids?"

He laughed. "Well, I'll be there too."

"I think that sounds fun. We'll spoil them and let Blayze stay up late and watch horror movies."

Ty's eyes widened in surprise. "You're kidding, right?"

I took a sip of wine and shrugged, trying not to break out into laughter.

Ty looked out over the lake for a few moments before his eyes met mine.

"When I was a little boy, my granddaddy used to take us four boys up to this lake that was way up in the mountains. It was called Hidden Pines Lake. I loved going there with him and would sit for hours and just fish with him and my brothers. Beck used to hate fishing, but he loved being with my granddaddy, like we all did. He would tell us stories about when he served in the marines. I really think that was where Beck got the desire to join the military. He wanted to be like Granddaddy. Tanner, he was the one who always caught the most fish, and all the bastard ever did was put earthworms on his hook. Used to piss me and Brock off.

"The final time we went up there, we all knew it would be the last. Granddaddy was getting older, and just trying to get the four of us to spend a weekend up in the mountains was like pulling teeth. Each of us was always going in a different direction." He looked off, the memory hitting him. "Brock and I had spent hours in the sporting-goods store in the fishing department, asking the guys who worked there about all the lures. We thought for sure we'd have Tanner that year. 'This will be our year,' we declared. We'd spent all the money we'd made that summer hauling hay and riding in the semi circuit buying those damn lures."

I smiled. "Did you catch any big fish with them?"

Ty shook his head and laughed. It was such a beautiful sound, hearing him laugh. I couldn't explain it, but it somehow made my soul feel happy.

"Not one. Tanner, on the other hand—his basket was full of fish. Even Beck caught a few. Granddaddy said Brock and I didn't know how to turn off our minds and just be in the moment. At the time, I had no idea what he meant. By then, Brock and I were both bull riding competitively, and I remember the four of us bitching to my dad about having to go that weekend. I'm glad we did, though, because it was the last time the four of us were all together . . ."

His voice drifted off, and I could hear the sadness in it. I placed my hand in his and gave it a soft squeeze.

"Granddaddy pulled me to the side. Actually, he pulled each of us to the side and spoke to us alone. None of us ever shared with each other what he said. I guess it was sort of special for each of us, having Granddaddy give us his words of wisdom. He'd never done it before, and I'm pretty sure he knew his days were limited.

"Anyway, he started with the youngest and finished with me. I remember thinking that he'd begun to lose his mind. Most of the stuff he said made sense, until he got to one thing. He looked out over the lake and said to me, 'You'll find the meaning of life at the lake. She'll show you the light.'"

My chin trembled, and goose bumps erupted over my skin.

Ty turned and caught my teary gaze. "Granddaddy saw something; I think he saw you. I don't know if I've found the meaning of life, but I know *you* are my life. You light up my world and make everything beautiful, Kaylee."

Covering my mouth with my hand, I tried harder not to cry.

Ty reached into his pocket and pulled out a small box. He opened it, and I lost the battle. Tears streamed down my face. I wiped at my cheeks in an attempt to control the water leaking from me like a freaking dam had broken.

It was then I noticed the diamond. I saw sparks of colors in it.

"When I came across this ring, I asked the jeweler why it looked like I could see colors in the diamond. He told me it was a new technology this designer uses that creates flashes of light from the diamond. How incredibly perfect is that?"

I tried to laugh, but it sounded more like a half sob, half laugh. Ty took the ring out of the box and reached for my left hand, then slid the ring on. I gazed down at it, in utter awe at the beauty.

"I want to spend the rest of my life showing you how much I love you, and I really don't think that's going to be enough time."

"Ty," I whispered, not able to say anything else. I'd never in my life felt this powerful a love from anyone.

"I know I already asked and the ring is already on your finger, but this was how I had originally planned it."

He stood, helping me to stand with him. Then, he got down on one knee, held my hand in his, and looked up at me. My knees felt weak when I saw the tears in his eyes.

"Yes!" I cried out.

Ty shook his head and looked down, and then back up at me. "Damn, woman. I haven't even said anything yet!"

My hand covered my mouth as I giggled. "I'm sorry, go on."

"Kaylee, will you do me the honor of becoming my wife?"

I dropped to my knees, cupped his face, and kissed him. I'd already said yes twice. Now I needed to feel as close to him as possible.

When we pulled slightly back, Ty rested his head against mine.

"Ty?"

"Yeah?"

"Can we get married at that lake? Where your granddaddy took you? Just you and me. I don't want a big wedding or anything. I just want to be your wife."

He wrapped his arms around me, holding me against his body. "That sounds perfect to me."

Chapter Thirty-One

Ty

I paced back and forth, not even able to think straight. It had been a month since that day next to the lake. The day I'd slipped a ring on Kaylee's finger. We'd decided to get married sooner rather than later, since winter would be setting in, and getting up to Hidden Pines Lake could be tricky.

Kaylee suddenly appeared in front of me. I took a few steps back and placed my hand over my chest.

"You look . . . beautiful."

She smiled, her cheeks turning the perfect shade of pink. Her eyes moved over my body, and she dug her teeth into her lip. "You look handsome. Yummy handsome."

I raised a brow. "Yummy handsome?"

"That's a compliment, trust me."

Smiling, I walked up to her, but she took a step back. "Don't touch me!"

"Why not?" I asked.

"Because right now, all I want you to do is take your little guy out and lift my dress and take me right here. The photographer will be really pissed if I ruin my dress and my makeup."

"My little guy? *Little?*"

She rolled her eyes. "Fine, your big guy. Anyway, it's hard enough looking at you dressed in a tux. If you touch me, I'll explode into a horny mess. So no touching."

"What if she needs us to touch for the photos?"

"That's different. We won't be alone."

I shot her a sexy grin. "So, that's the key. Being alone."

"Ty!" she warned, her hand coming up.

"Ty! Kaylee! Come on, Blayze is about to lose his mind!" Brock shouted from downstairs.

I groaned as she walked by, stopping to quickly kiss me. "Come on! I can't wait to see Blayze and Morgan."

Carefully making her way down the steps, Kaylee glanced back at me and smiled. It was the same smile she'd given me the first day we met. The day I knew I'd fallen instantly in love with her, even though I hadn't realized it then.

When we got down the steps, a few gasps sounded, and Lincoln burst into tears.

"You . . . you . . . look . . . so . . . beautifuuuuul!" Lincoln said, rushing over to Kaylee and hugging her.

"Oh, sure, *she* can hug you, but I can't."

Brock walked up to me, reached for my hand, and shook it. "Sorry about that. Lincoln's been a little emotional lately."

I laughed as I watched Lincoln wipe more tears away and Kaylee go on and on about Morgan's beautiful pink dress. "Dude, is she pregnant?" I asked jokingly.

When he didn't answer, I looked at him. He wore a smile so big it nearly lit up the entire first floor of the house.

"*What?*"

He leaned in closer. "Don't say anything—no one is supposed to know. I think Mama knows, though."

"Of course she does. She has some weird power to detect shit like that."

Brock nodded.

"Is Tanner here?" Kaylee asked, glancing around the room.

My father grunted, and my mother plastered on a smile that was clearly forced.

"He had a ride in Cheyenne last night that he said he couldn't miss."

I saw the look of disappointment on Kaylee's face, and I made a mental note to punch Tanner the next time I saw him for making my wife sad on her wedding day.

"Oh, okay. Well, should we head on out there?" Kaylee asked.

My father opened the door—and walking up the steps was Tanner. I couldn't ignore the way it made my chest tighten, knowing that he had probably driven all night to get here in time.

"Tanner!" Kaylee exclaimed at the same time Blayze did. They both raced to get to my younger brother, Blayze winning by a long shot, since Kaylee was dressed in a white gown and heels.

When she got to him, Kaylee kissed him on the cheek. "You look exhausted."

He smiled. "I stopped at the house and showered and changed first. Sorry I'm late."

When I walked up to him, he reached out his hand to me, but I pulled him in for a hug. "Thank you, Tanner. It means the world to me. To both of us."

He slapped my back and hugged me before we broke apart. "You know I wouldn't miss it."

Kaylee and I had decided we would have a small ceremony in the front yard of her—scratch that—our house. Last week, we hiked up to the lake with Pastor Thatcher and had our private ceremony. We didn't wear anything fancy. No one else was there. It was just the two of us, sharing our moment together, like we'd wanted to do. It was one of the most profound moments of my life, up at that lake, marrying the woman who had changed my entire world.

Pastor Thatcher was back today, standing with his Bible as Kaylee and I walked up to the arbor, decorated with roses. Our family stood behind us as we exchanged vows once again, in front of the people who meant the most to us.

It was Kaylee's idea to have another ceremony after the real one. It was simple and less stressful and was more for my folks than anything. They had understood our desire to get married up at the lake and were supportive, but when Kaylee told my mother we would have another ceremony, I saw the way Mama's eyes lit up with happiness.

I could hear Lincoln softly crying behind us, and at one point, I was pretty sure I heard my mama asking my father for a tissue.

"You may now kiss your bride . . . again!" Pastor Thatcher said.

"Uncle Ty?" Blayze said, stepping up and pulling on my jacket before I could kiss Kaylee.

Kaylee and I both looked down at him.

"What's up, buddy?"

"I just thought you should know. I don't feel mad toward ya anymore—you know, for taking our girl."

Kaylee's head snapped up, and she looked at me, her eyes wide with both shock and happiness. "Our girl?" she repeated.

"Anymore?" Brock asked.

Once Kaylee and I had started dating, I took Blayze out to dinner one night. Just us two guys. I explained to him that I loved Kaylee and that we would be dating. He was mad and told me he'd need some time to get over his broken heart. He also asked me to keep that a secret between us two . . . men. Which I had.

"I'll tell ya later," I said to Brock as I looked at Kaylee and winked. "What can I say? I'm sure we're not the only two men who have fallen for the same pretty girl."

"Amen to that," Dirk added.

Kaylee spun around, a small yelp slipping from her lips. "You came!"

Dirk walked up and shook my hand before kissing Kaylee on the cheek. "Of course I came. I got here just in time. You look beautiful, by the way."

"Thank you for coming, Dirk," Kaylee said, giving him a quick hug.

He took a step back and turned to walk over to where Brock was standing with Tanner.

When Kaylee faced me, she looked down at Blayze and gave him the sweetest smile. Blayze beamed up at her—then looked at me and smirked.

I rolled my eyes. Damn kid was exactly like his father.

Kaylee and I both chuckled.

"Can I kiss my wife now?" I asked as everyone laughed.

"Do it before Blayze does!" Tanner shouted.

My hands cupped her beautiful face, and our eyes met. I couldn't help the tears that had built in mine. "I love you, so much."

Her eyes sparkled, and I swore I could see the reflection of the mountains in those eyes of hers.

As a tear slipped free and made a trail down her cheek, she whispered, "I love you more."

◆ ◆ ◆

While we didn't want a reception, my mother overruled us, as did Lincoln. So after our second ceremony, we headed back to my folks' place. A large tent had been put up, with a makeshift dance floor. White edison lights hung down from the ceiling, and tables lined the perimeter of the tent.

Kaylee had done most of the planning, making sure things stayed simple. White roses with white lights decorated the tables. We went with a good old-fashioned barbeque catered by one of the restaurants in town.

I sat in a chair and watched as Kaylee danced with Blayze. I didn't think my heart could feel any fuller than it did in that moment.

"You got yourself a damn good woman, I hope you know that," Dirk said, sitting down and hitting the neck of his beer against mine.

"You better believe I know. Not sure what in the hell she sees in me, but I'm going with it."

He chuckled. "You're good for each other. You make her as happy as she makes you, dude."

I gave him a nod of thanks. "When are you going to settle down, Dirk? It's gotta be getting old?"

"Old? Hell no. I'm perfectly happy with my life."

"You don't ever wish for something like what Brock's got?"

We both turned and looked at my brother. The happiness practically shot off him like bolts of lightning. He was dancing with Morgan.

"He deserves all that happiness. I'm glad he found Lincoln," Dirk said, a smile on his face.

I nodded. "She's pregnant again, but no one is supposed to know."

Dirk took a sip of beer and shook his head. "Well, then, no one told your mama, 'cause she's been telling everyone who'll listen that Lincoln's got a bun in the oven."

"I'm not the least bit surprised by that."

Laughing, Dirk shook his head. "She's telling folks she's going to be having a new grandbaby soon. Someone asked if Kaylee was pregnant, and Stella said no. So, that only leaves Lincoln."

"Brock's not gonna be happy about that," I mumbled.

"He'll get over it. Now, if you'll excuse me, there's a pretty girl I've never seen before walking this way."

I followed Dirk's gaze. I'd never seen the blonde who was walking up to the tent either. She looked familiar, and when Kaylee let out a loud scream, I knew instantly this was kin.

"Timberlyn! Oh my gosh! Oh my gosh!"

Timberlyn was Kaylee's cousin, and she'd recently graduated from nursing school in Georgia. From what I'd gathered from Kaylee, Timberlyn had also had a tragic incident happen to her, but Kaylee hadn't told me what it was, and I hadn't asked. I was just happy that Kaylee at least had family here, since her parents couldn't be bothered to come to their daughter's wedding.

"Who's that?" Tanner asked, taking a drink from his beer. I looked at him and saw the light in his eyes. Aww damn, both he and Dirk had the same thing on their minds. This was going to be amusing as hell.

"I saw her first, dude," Dirk shot back.

"You're calling dibs on her?" Tanner asked.

I stood. "It's Kaylee's cousin. She's thinking of moving here after seeing all the pictures Kaylee's been sending her. She just graduated college."

Dirk smiled. "Well, I'd be more than happy to show her around town."

"Bullshit, I'll show her around town," Tanner said.

"Maybe you should leave that to me and Kaylee," I said with a slight smirk.

Dirk pointed to Tanner, then looked at me. "Exactly why I will never get married. Ever. You are an instant killjoy. A guy just wants to have a little fun with someone who's here to visit. I can't think of a better woman. In and out. Literally."

I sighed and rubbed the back of my neck. "One of these days, Dirk Littlewood. One of these days."

He shook his head. "Never. I'm pretty sure I'll be struck by lightning before I ever entertain the thought of settling down with one woman."

"Ditto," Tanner added, but for once in his life, he didn't sound confident . . . at all.

I smiled as I watched Tanner's gaze following Timberlyn across the room. There was something familiar about the way he watched her. I recognized that look, and for some reason, I looked out at Brock, still on the dance floor with Morgan.

He was watching Tanner as well. Then he looked at me and raised a brow. He'd noticed too.

I focused back on my baby brother and Dirk, both racing to reach Timberlyn first.

"This is most definitely going to be fun to watch."

Epilogue

Kaylee

Christmas

I wrapped the shawl tighter around my body to chase away the chill as I stared out the window. Snowflakes fell softly, covering the mountains and meadows with a fresh coat of white. The snow sparkled like a thousand diamonds.

Glancing down, I smiled when I saw my own diamond.

One more look out the window, and I sighed in contentment. It was beautiful and perfect for Christmas Day.

The sound of Ty walking around upstairs had my heartbeat picking up. I was both nervous and excited this morning. This was our first Christmas together. I turned and looked at our beautiful tree. It was simple, silver and blue the only two colors on the tree, along with the white twinkle lights.

I sat down on the sofa, grabbed my tea, and crossed my legs. As I took a sip, my handsome husband walked down the steps and into the living room. His dark-brown hair was a mess, most likely from my fingers in it earlier, after he'd woken me up to make love to me. His blue eyes landed on mine, and he smiled.

My insides melted. How was it that he could still make me feel like all this was new? The flutters in my stomach, the way my heart felt like it skipped a beat, the way my body got covered in goose bumps when he simply put his hand on my lower back as we walked into a room together. The man knew how to bring my body to life.

"Good morning and merry Christmas," Ty said, bending down and kissing me quickly.

"Morning. Merry Christmas to you."

"We need to be over at my folks' place around ten."

"Okay."

I watched him walk into the kitchen, my mouth watering at the sexy sight before me. I dabbed at the corners of my mouth, 'cause, you know, the man still made me drool.

Ty was dressed in cotton pajama pants that hung low on his hips. His broad chest and back were bare, and with every move he made, his muscles flexed. I licked my lips and tried to keep my libido in check. She seemed to have a mind of her own, though.

"I made blueberry muffins to bring, and a quiche."

"Damn, that sounds good now!"

I laughed as I replied, "Do not eat any of it, Ty Shaw. I made some banana bread you can have, though. Or I can make us some breakfast."

Last Christmas, I'd been invited over to the Shaws' annual Christmas breakfast. Of course, Ty and I weren't together then, and we spent much of the day taking jabs at each other and then playing with all of Blayze's games. Looking back, I had to giggle. It was so obvious how much we liked each other and were trying to fight it.

Closing my eyes, I let out a long, slow breath. My occasional nightmares had stopped many months ago, pretty much after I'd stayed in Ty's bed every night. Ty hadn't had a nightmare since we got married at the lake. It felt good knowing he was able to leave more and more of his past behind as we grew our lives together.

He walked into the living room and set his coffee on the table, then added more wood to the fire.

"Want to open presents now?" I asked, my voice a little bit too excited.

Ty grinned. "Who gets to open one first?"

"Me! I want to open one first."

"Okay, let me see which one."

He walked over to the tree and bent down, picking up presents and looking at them, only to put them down and pick up others.

"You're picking up the presents that are for *you*! Pick one out for me!" I said, tossing a throw pillow at him.

"Fine, fine. Here, open this one."

It was a small box. I crinkled my brows and stared at it. "It's so light."

"Don't judge, Kaylee. Big things come in little packages."

My gaze lifted to look at him. "I'm glad you think so."

"Open it already!" he said, taking his coffee and sitting down next to me on the sofa.

Once I'd removed the wrapping paper, I pulled the lid off and looked inside. It was a brochure.

I picked it up and looked at it, and then looked to Ty. "You got me a brochure for Hawaii?"

"Yep."

I snarled my lip. "If I had known you were going to be a cheap bastard, I'd have thought twice about marrying you."

He laughed. "What else is in there, Kaylee?"

I set the brochure to the side and stared at the piece of paper. My eyes filled with tears as I picked it up and looked at my own handwriting.

A year ago, we were playing some silly game at Stella and Ty Senior's house, and one of the tasks was to write down one location on your bucket list where you would like to visit. Mine was Kauai. I'd never gone, because the idea of that long a flight made me nervous, but I mentioned it that night. It was my dream place to visit, and Stella told me I should go.

I lifted my eyes and met Ty's gaze. "You kept this?"

He smiled sheepishly. "Yeah. Stupid, I know, but it was important to you, and I thought . . ."

Every nerve ending in my body tingled as I anticipated his response. "You thought what?"

Ty looked me in the eyes, and I felt my breath hitch. Just when I thought he couldn't possibly make me love him more, he looked at me like I was his everything.

"I thought back then that maybe I could take you there someday."

My heartbeat quickened, and I covered my mouth in an attempt to keep myself together. This man. This amazing, beautiful, selfless man loved me more than I could ever imagine.

"How could you ever think you weren't good enough for me? To do this, keep this, and . . . and . . . I love you, Ty. I love you so much."

I threw myself at him, wrapping my arms around him.

"Oh, princess, I love you too. More than you'll ever know."

He held me for a few minutes and then pulled back and kissed me gently on the lips. Then he grinned as he looked down at the brochure. "I hate to say it, but I'm pretty sure I've got you beat this year in the gift department."

With a raised brow, I said, "I didn't realize we were competing."

He tapped my nose with his finger. "You're cute, Kaylee. I may be madly in love with you, and you may be my wife, but I'm always going to be the guy who wants to kick your ass at Monopoly, and gift giving, and competing for our nieces' and nephews' affections."

"I see," I said, getting up and picking up a present. I handed it to him before I sat back down on the sofa. "Well, I'm a hundred percent positive my gift kicks your gift's ass. Don't get me wrong!" I said, holding up my hands. "Your gift is mind-blowingly amazing, and I cannot wait to go. But we should probably book it sooner rather than later."

He stared at me with a confused look on his face. "Okay, I'm fine with that. Maybe get away some this winter."

I nodded. Then motioned for him to open the gift. Ty looked like a little kid as he unwrapped the shirt box. Taking off the lid, he moved the tissue out of the way and stared at it. Then he looked at me, then back to the shirt.

It took everything I had in me not to laugh. His confused face was my second-favorite gift this Christmas.

Ty took the shirt out and held it up.

"The blue will bring out the blue in your eyes," I casually said of the light-blue T-shirt. "I thought maybe you could wear it to your folks' place."

"Ah, yeah, sure."

He stared at it again and then looked back at me. "What the fuck is a DILF?"

I'd had a special T-shirt made that said, CERTIFIED DILF. EST. 2020.

I lost the battle and laughed. "You really don't know what it means?" I asked, trying not to laugh too hard.

Ty chuckled and shook his head. "No idea."

"Have you heard of a MILF?"

He looked up in thought. "'Mom I'd like to fuck.' Right?"

I nodded, then looked at the shirt, then at him. He just stared at the shirt, so I decided it was time for gift number two.

I crawled on top of him, pressing my core against his already hardening dick. "*Dad* I'd like to fuck."

When it finally dawned on him, his eyes teared up. "Holy shit, Kaylee. Are you serious right now?"

I nodded and let a little sob slip free.

"You're pregnant?"

"Yes. I found out two weeks ago. I'm almost six weeks pregnant."

He cupped my face and kissed me senseless.

Ty's kisses were so different from any other man's kiss. Even John's. I couldn't help but wonder if it was because of how deeply he loved me, and how much I loved him. Whatever the reason, they were addictive. I could have sat on that sofa all day and simply kissed him.

He finally pulled his mouth from mine and looked at me. "I can't believe it. We just started trying."

"Well, we know from your brother Brock that the Shaw swimmers are strong."

He laughed. "Wow. This is unreal. It's crazy! I need to make love to you right now."

"I like the sound of that."

Ty held on to me as he stood. I wrapped my legs around him as he turned us and laid me on the sofa.

"The sofa?" I asked with a laugh.

"I want you . . . now."

"Okay," I whispered, my hands going to his sleep pants and pushing them down.

Ty yanked my silk Victoria's Secret Christmas pants off and groaned when he saw I didn't have any panties on. "I hope you can handle fast, because I don't think I can do any foreplay."

His eyes burned with desire, and I used my legs to pull him closer to me. Ty pushed into me, and it felt like I had been taken to heaven and back. We were lost to each other as he leaned down and kissed me. It wasn't rushed; it was slow, beautifully slow.

"Ty!" I gasped when I felt my orgasm building.

"Kaylee," he groaned, burying his face into my neck as we both came at the same time.

After our breathing had returned to normal, he slowly pulled out of me, then reached for his pants. He moved to the side and pulled me into his arms, kissing me on the forehead.

"You're pregnant. We're having a baby."

I nodded and shivered as his hand went to my stomach.

"Our baby is growing inside of you. That is crazy insane."

With a chuckle, I agreed. "Beautifully crazy."

He nodded. "I don't care if it's a boy or a girl. I just want them to be happy and healthy."

"What's the first thing you'll do if it's a boy?"

Ty looked up and thought about it. "Buy him a bull."

"Oh, good Lord," I whispered. "If it's a girl?"

He searched my face, then traced over my eyebrows, down my nose, and over my lips. "If it's a girl, she's bound to be beautiful like her mama, so I'm going to have to buy me a new shotgun."

"A shotgun?"

"Yeah, to keep all the little fuckers like me away from my daughter."

I playfully hit him on the chest. "Are you scared?"

Ty didn't even hesitate. "No. Not one bit. Are you?"

Chewing on my lip, I nodded. "A little. Full disclosure: I forgot to feed Blayze once. Like, for almost a full day. Totally slipped my mind."

He leaned back and laughed his ass off before looking back into my eyes. "Damn, this is going to be the best adventure I think I've ever been on," he said, looking down at my stomach with an expression of pure awe.

I placed my hand over his, which was still on my stomach, and took in a deep breath before slowly letting it out. "Better hold on tight to that rope, Ty Shaw. It's our turn to be parents."

He winked. "This is going to be fun."

ABOUT THE AUTHOR

Kelly Elliott is a *New York Times* and *USA Today* bestselling contemporary romance author. Since finishing her bestselling Wanted series, Kelly has continued to spread her wings while remaining true to her roots with stories of hot men, strong women, and beautiful surroundings. Her bestselling works include *Wanted*, *Broken*, *Without You*, and *Lost Love*. Elliott has been passionate about writing since she was fifteen. After years of filling journals with stories, she finally followed her dream and published her first novel, *Wanted*, in November 2012.

Elliott lives in central Texas with her husband, daughter, and two pups. When she's not writing, she enjoys reading and spending time with her family. She is down-to-earth and very in touch with her readers, both on social media and at signings. To learn more about Elliott and her books, you can find her through her website, www.kellyelliottauthor.com.

CONNECT WITH KELLY ONLINE

Kelly's Facebook Page

www.facebook.com/kellyelliottauthor

Kelly's Amazon Author Page

https://goo.gl/RGVXqv

Follow Kelly on Twitter

www.twitter.com/author_kelly

Follow Kelly on Instagram

www.instagram.com/authorkellyelliott

Follow Kelly on BookBub

www.bookbub.com/profile/kelly-elliott

Kelly's Pinterest Page

www.pinterest.com/authorkellyelliott

Kelly's Author Website

www.kellyelliottauthor.com